Akiri

The Scepter of Xarbaal

Brian D. Anderson
& Steven Savile

First Published Longfire Press, NOVEMBER 2016

Cover Illustration Gene Mollica Studios

Brian wishes to dedicate this book to his wonderful son, Jonathan and his loving wife Eleni.

Steve wishes to dedicate this book to the memories of the writers who made him fall in love with the genre, David Gemmell, David Eddings and Hugh Cook, and to his partner in crime, Brian, King of Skype...

Archaria
Gol'Naruth

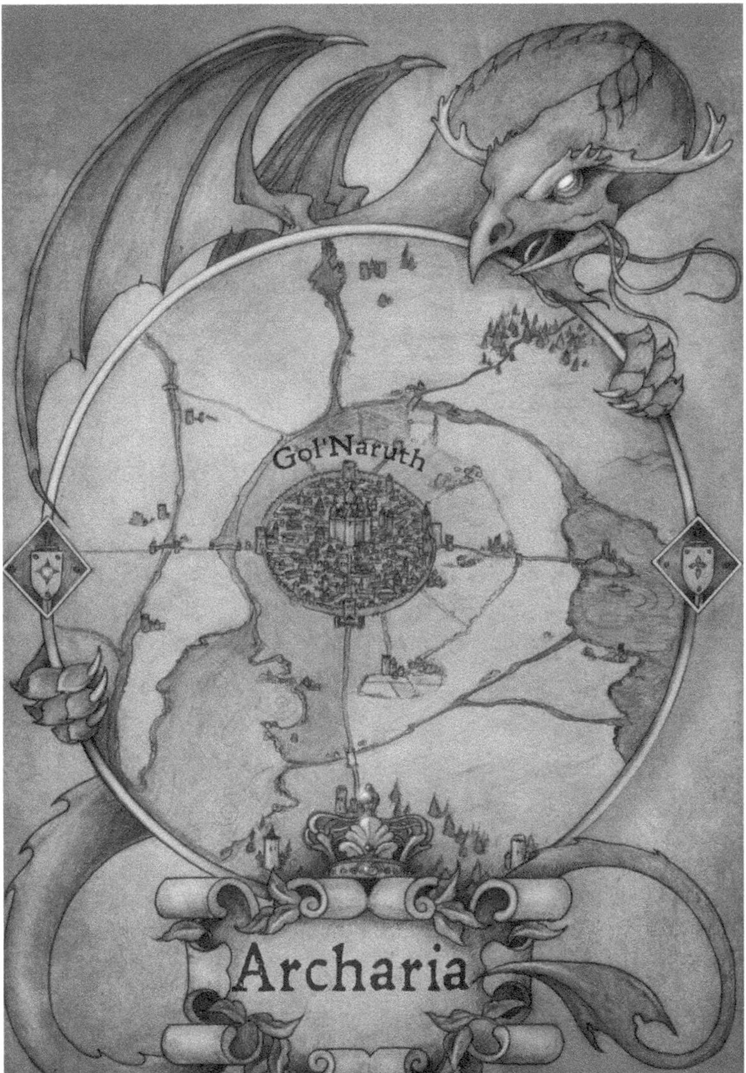
Gol'Naruth
Archaria

Prologue

Serhan closed his eyes and took a long cleansing breath. Drawing deep into his mind, he touched his center – his *merkesh*. He felt it rising within him, but after only a moment of bathing in its awesome power, he allowed the vibrations to subside. It was not time. Not yet. Soon, though; very soon. And when it arrived, all his many years of training and discipline would be tested to the full. As would his courage and resolve.

The steady thumping of Ragnir's huge wings fell into rhythm with the beating of his own heart. He ran a hand over her muscular shoulders. Her awesome power never failed to send a chill down his spine. Her flesh – hard as iron, yet still pleasing to the touch – rippled and tensed. She was ready. Ready for battle. Ready to kill. And ready to die if needs be. Without opening his eyes, he leaned forward and placed an ear against the base of her neck.

"Once more, my love," he whispered. "Then it will finally be over."

In response, Ragnir's rumbling growl resonated through his entire body. *Yes. Once more. I am ready,* the dragon told him, though not in words that anyone save Serhan could comprehend.

He sighed, allowing his mind to fully absorb the peace of the moment: his oneness with Ragnir; the breeze against his flesh while riding high above the ravages of the world where only the Tul'Zahar dared to climb; and finally, the incredible sense of freedom. Up here, he was truly his own master.

The distant clamor of steel and fire dragged him away from the perfection of the moment. He opened his eyes to see the glow of flames reflecting off Ragnir's deep blue scales, making her appear as if she was wrapped in a cloak of cloudless night sky. He cast his gaze downward. Such a spectacle had not been seen by human eyes in more than three hundred years. Vast oceans of warriors were pitted against one another. More than three hundred thousand of them was his guess. Five mighty nations had sent their best and bravest to do battle.

He tried to make out the individual armies, but after six straight days of fighting, it was impossible to distinguish one from another. By now, the alliance had merged into one massive force pressing forward against the power of King Zemel the Conqueror, ruler of Acharia.

Rings of fire erupted as the battle mages went about their deadly work. Serhan sneered contemptuously. *Battle mages. Bah!* Half-wit weaklings unfit for the Tul'Zahar, that's all they were. Even so, King Zemel had found a use for them where other kings had not. But of course, unlike Zemel, other kings were fearful of magic. King Zemel feared absolutely nothing. Not even the Tul'Zahar.

His desire to press Ragnir into a dive and dispatch these pathetic battle mages was strong. The thought of the terror they would know when faced with genuine power almost elicited a laugh. But Serhan knew it would have to wait. The task he was about to undertake was far more important. The battle mages would taste justice soon enough.

He placed the tip of his finger to the large gem set in the pommel of his sword and smiled. The sword had been forged for him, perfectly weighted and balanced for his hand. It had taken a month to fashion, tempered in the crucible of Tul'Zahar's greatest smiths, and given in exchange for the oath of loyalty he swore to the order. The jewel itself, though, that was a gift from his wife, given when she first discovered that she was carrying his child. Fondly remembering Leona's aspect, he allowed a small piece of his essence to leave him to create a faint impression of her within its facets.

Ragnir let out a booming huff and shook her head.

"I know, my love," Serhan said. "I must keep my focus. But this may be our final battle, and I would have her with me." He patted the dragon's neck. "After this, we'll find somewhere far away from the madness. Somewhere my son can grow up in safety without being surrounded by fields of blood." When Ragnir hissed and whined, he smiled and then added: "Yes. I'm sure there will be plenty of sheep and wild pigs to feast on, too."

Serhan shifted his eyes to gaze north. There, less than twenty miles away, loomed the ominous black spires of Gol'Naruth – King Zemel's stronghold. Should the vast forces of the five nations manage to advance that far, that would be the absolute limit of their achievement. They could lay siege for a hundred years and never so much as scratch a single stone of the city walls. These were protected by the magic of the Sulmarian Guild. Not even the mighty fires of the legendary elder dragons – were there any still alive to try – would be able to make the slightest blemish on them. Serhan smiled briefly. It was just as well for him that he would not need to test his strength against such an indestructible defense.

A blast of heat rose up from the battlefield. A small group of battle mages had joined together to form a protective wall of fire around themselves, but inch by inch they were being pressed back by the determination of an enraged foe. Serhan's keen eyesight could see that bowmen had already decimated the battle mages' shield bearers, leaving them exposed and vulnerable. Fire could roast a man and was a highly effective defense against advancing soldiers, but it was next to useless against arrows and bolts. Little by little the flames diminished as the archers continued to send forth their deadly attack. Serhan smiled. *Good riddance.*

Again he cast his eyes toward Gol'Naruth. The heat rising from the battlefield distorted the light, giving the fortress an even more forbidding appearance.

It was time.

Reaching to his belt, he withdrew a small silver horn, the rhylatite infused within making it glow in his hand. He raised it to his lips and blew three times.

The pure, clear call pierced the air in every direction, making all other sounds dull and distant by comparison. He chuckled softly. The king would have undoubtedly heard it too. He would know they were coming.

Three specks approached rapidly from the west. It took only a matter of seconds for him to recognize Drewin, Sadich, and Thradus. Astride their dragons, they drew their blades and held them high in salute. Serhan raised the horn aloft in reply.

Both Sadich's and Thradus's mounts were lean, their heads covered in razor sharp spikes, but Drewin's dragon was broad and powerful – just like Ragnir. Also like Ragnir, it had shed most of its spikes long ago.

They brought the dragons to a halt only a dozen yards away, coming into position in front of Serhan, their immense bodies rising and falling as they trod air to hold their position. The red flame crest was splashed magnificently across their polished black armor. Drewin – second only to Serhan himself in rank – boasted the red sash of the Tul'Zahar. Removing his helm, he shook loose his shoulder-length brown curls, dark eyes fixed on his commander.

Serhan noted the blood soaking Drewin's arm and spattered on his face. This had obviously been a hard-fought day. "Are you injured badly?" he asked.

He glanced down at his arm and spat. "Goddamn battle mages had me distracted for a moment. I took a crossbow bolt as a reward for my stupidity."

"Can you continue?"

Drewin threw his head back, laughing. "Are you joking? You think I'd miss my chance of glory over such a small matter?"

Serhan nodded approvingly. He was strong. Almost as strong as himself. In fact, were it not that he had taken the oath two years earlier than Drewin, his subordinate would now be the one leading the Tul'Zahar.

He shifted his attention to Sadich and Thradus. "And how are you two faring? Finding enough mischief?" The pair were brothers, inducted into the order only days apart. Still young, they were known for their practical jokes and spirited nature.

"Enough blood for everyone, for a change," Sadich replied with a sinister smirk.

"I think the steel in my blade has grown wearier than my sword arm," added Thradus.

Serhan frowned. "So you left your mounts and fought on foot?"

The pair looked to one another, then back to their commander. It was Thradus who spoke. "Only for a short time. We just couldn't stand seeing the soldiers have all the fun."

Serhan shook his head. "The soldiers are here to fight and die. The two of you have far more important duties. Too important to risk your lives over a bit of sport."

"I apologize," they replied in unison. But the smiles that lingered on their faces cast doubts on the strength of their sincerity.

Serhan grunted and turned to Drewin. "Have you seen the others?"

He shook his head. "I'm sure they'll be along shortly."

"They had better be." He looked to the battle far below. "Each moment's delay costs more lives."

As his eyes rose again, Serhan was just in time to catch the brothers exchanging what appeared to be a furtive glance. He also noticed their hands drifting ever closer to their blades. He furrowed his brow, wondering what was going on. Were they really acting suspiciously?

He dismissed such thoughts as nothing more than pre-battle nerves. Where were the others? He strained his eyes in every direction, but after more than five minutes there was still no sign of anyone else arriving. He blew his horn once again, but the skies around them remained stubbornly empty.

It was then that he noticed Drewin gradually positioning his dragon to the left – away from his commander's sword arm. The brothers had also moved and were now sitting slightly above him. His senses instantly sharpened and he allowed the magic dwelling within his *merkesh* to flow into his hands. Drewin immediately picked up on this.

"Is something wrong, Commander?" he asked, his own hand resting on the pommel of his sword.

"I don't know," Serhan replied darkly. "Is there?"

Drewin locked eyes with him for a long moment. Slowly, his mouth twisted into a smile and he gave a mirthless chuckle. "Always the perceptive one."

Serhan's jaw tightened. So his mind had not been playing tricks. Something was indeed seriously wrong. Treachery was in the air. "Where are the others?" he demanded.

"Dead," Drewin replied matter-of-factly. He pointed at his commander. "You are the last."

Serhan's eyes shot from Drewin to the brothers and back again. Ragnir, sensing her master's anxiety, was tensing uneasily beneath him.

"Why have you done this?"

His second-in-command raised an eyebrow. "You ask why? Surely you can't be serious. You have led us to ruin. You defied our king, stole his property, and have instigated a war that you must have known we could never win."

"King Zemel is a madman and you know it," he shot back. "The Scepter should never have been in his possession. It was not meant to be wielded by mortal man. I only did what I had to do."

Drewin nodded. "Yes. He is a madman. But a powerful one. Even without the Scepter, he would have destroyed us. At least now the Tul'Zahar will endure."

"And how exactly does killing your brothers do anything to save the Tul'Zahar?"

Drewin's face hardened and his eyes burned. "It is your fault they had to die. I tried to spare them. But such was their blind loyalty to you and to your folly that they would not see reason."

"Save your lies," Serhan spat at him. "You made a bargain with Zemel. And the price was the Tul'Zahar. You are without honor. The only thing that comforts me is knowing that in the end, Zemel will betray you, too."

"Enough of this talk," shouted Sadich. "I have listened to this self-righteous bastard for far too long. Let's just kill him and be done with it." The song of steel rang out as he drew his sword.

Drewin raised a hand in an attempt to stop the inexperienced youth, but it was too late. Serhan was already reacting. Thrusting his left hand out, a bolt of blue lightning sprang forth from his fingertips, striking Sadich squarely in the chest. With his right hand, he freed his own sword and leashed the bolt to the tip of the blade. Sadich's eyes shot wide. Before he could make any kind of defensive move, the lightning exploded, shredding his breastplate and throwing him completely from his mount. As he plummeted toward the distant ground, Thradus cried out his name. Both he and the riderless dragon then went into steep dives in pursuit his brother.

Serhan unleashed another bolt, this one aimed at Drewin. But his treacherous second-in-command would not be taken off guard so easily. He had already raised a defensive ward. Only a few tiny sparks made it through the shimmering disk of light – not nearly enough to cause any real injury.

Serhan urged Ragnir to dive hard left. As they dropped, he drew in more power, casting ward upon ward around both himself and his dragon. Blasts of fire and lightning at his back told him that Drewin was close behind. Faster and faster they swooped. The battlefield below was now coming up fast. With the wind roaring in his ears, he was forced to grip the saddle horn tightly to remain mounted.

When they were a mere fifty feet from the earth, Ragnir let out a thunderous roar and leveled off. With the enemy army directly below them, Serhan felt two more waves of magic attacking him from above, though this time they were not coming from Drewin's direction. He looked up and to his left. Sadich's dragon had apparently caught up with him in time because he was now back in its saddle, his face contorted with fury. Both he and Thradus were sending multiple spears of silver light raining down at Serhan. But it was an undisciplined, hit-or-miss assault fueled largely by their anger, and his wards were more than adequate to protect him from the few that did find their target. Those that missed, however, were causing chaos on the field below. Spear after spear of light shot past him to strike unsuspecting soldiers, ripping their bodies apart like wet parchment.

"Climb!" Serhan shouted.

Ragnir's wings pounded with unimaginable strength, lifting them well above the battlefield again in no time at all. But rapid as their ascent was, more attacks from the brothers continued to pepper him. Their dragons may not have been anywhere near as powerful as Ragnir, but they were far quicker and more agile. In mere moments they had managed to circle around to be positioned above and to his front, all the while continuing their seemingly useless assault against his wards.

They're trying to keep my attention, Serhan realized. His eyes desperately searched for Drewin, eventually spotting him only fifty or so feet above and to his back. As fast as he could, he sheathed his sword and began drawing in yet more power. Wards against magic were a simple thing for someone of his experience, and Drewin understood this as well as anyone. Serhan concentrated on shaping the more complicated wards that would counter physical attacks. One minute. That was as fast as he had ever created one. Would he be granted that long this time?

The ominous thudding of large wings approaching quickly spelled out the futility of such a hope. Ragnir let out a roar of agony as talons sank into her tail. Serhan drew his sword again and took a swipe at Drewin's mount. His blade found flesh, though only enough to cause a minor wound. Ragnir spun sharply, ripping her tail free from the other dragon's grip and almost throwing Serhan from the saddle in the process.

He knew he needed to get higher. But the brothers had ceased their magical attack and were concentrating on closing in. Growling with anger, Ragnir flew straight at them. Unwilling to face the enraged dragon head on, the pair split left and right, allowing Serhan to pass straight between them. For a moment he thought he might be able to get high enough to manage an escape, but then another cry of agony came from deep within Ragnir's throat. Twisting around, he saw that Drewin's dragon had one of his mount's rear legs clenched tightly in its maw. Held back by an almost equal weight, their ascent immediately slowed to virtually nothing. The two smaller dragons had been given the opportunity they needed. They dived in from either side to grab a wing each of Ragnir's firmly in their claws, twisting hard to inflict maximum injury.

Serhan rose from the saddle and prepared to charge at

Thradus, but it was too late. Their deadly work already done, all three attacking dragons simultaneously released Ragnir. Desperately she pounded the air, but her wings were now too badly damaged for any chance of flight. Clutching at the saddle horn as they dropped, Serhan braced himself for the moment they struck ground.

Ragnir's broken wings continued to beat furiously, at least slowing their descent sufficiently to save them from a truly devastating impact. Even so, when contact came, it was still hard enough to rattle every bone in Serhan's body. But there was no time to worry about that. Sharply aware that they were well behind King Zemel's lines and completely surrounded, he jumped clear of Ragnir and was ready in an instant, sword in hand. His eyes darted back and forth, seeking attackers. But the enemy soldiers nearby were already backing away. No one among them was fool enough to challenge a Tul'Zahar and his dragon, even when they were so obviously wounded.

Ragnir's tail was riddled with deep gashes and both wings hung limply, broken in the middle. Her back leg had been mangled beyond healing by Drewin's dragon. After blowing out a guttural breath, she limped forward to meet him.

"I'm sorry, my love," Serhan told her. He drew in what little power he had remaining and used it to ease the dragon's suffering. She lowered her massive head, pressing it into his chest while moaning softly.

It was a short respite. The ground shook as the three traitors landed a few yards to his back. Even though his wards were still in place, he knew there was no way for him to fight them all successfully. He spun to meet his enemy with rage-filled eyes.

"Don't be a fool," warned Drewin. "It's over."

"Face me, you coward," Serhan challenged. "Or has the king taken your courage as well as your honor?"

Drewin sneered. "To face one as accomplished in single combat as you is not an act of courage… Commander. It is rank stupidity. No. I think it would be much better if you just throw down your sword."

By now, Thradus and Sadich had urged their dragons to the left and right. Cruel little smiles appeared on their faces. He read it as eager anticipation. There was a certain kind of warrior who savored the killing to come. They belonged to that breed.

Serhan glanced down at the jewel that held the aspect of his beloved wife. "Very well, I will submit," he said. "But only on one condition."

"And what is that?" asked Drewin.

"Find a way to spare my family."

Drewin heaved a weary sigh. "I wish I could help you. I truly do. But King Zemel has plans for them. The boy in particular."

Serhan's grip on his sword tightened. He squeezed his eyes shut for a second. "I see."

There was nothing else left to debate. All he could do now was go down fighting and die with the honor expected of a Tul'Zahar commander.

The sinews of his powerful legs tensed. He could hear the dragons creeping in on either side of him. Drewin, on the other hand, maintained his position further back. Shrewd as always.

In a blur of speed, Serhan ran left, straight toward Sadich. Startled by this unexpected assault, the young dragon reared up, throwing its rider momentarily off balance. Before the creature could lower its head to offer a defense, Serhan dived low and rolled. Sadich twisted in the saddle and thrust his blade downwards, but Serhan easily avoided the strike. An instant later, he was back on his feet. With a grunt of satisfaction, he brought his sword hard down on the young man's shin. The razor sharp steel sliced effortlessly through armor, flesh, and then bone. Sadich instantly dropped his weapon, a wail of agony bursting from his mouth.

Serhan stepped in to finish the job, but just as he raised his sword, a mighty swipe from the dragon's talons struck him in the center of the back. It was like being hit with a battering ram. The sheer force sent him flying more than ten feet through the air. As he thudded back down onto the ground, violent spasms of pain gripped him, and he could feel blood already soaking his back. Only the superb craftsmanship of his armor had saved him from being ripped to shreds. Gasping for air but with sword still in hand, he somehow struggled onto his side.

Sadich had fallen from the saddle and was writhing on the ground, his lifeblood spilling over. The dragon, seeing its rider's distress, was standing over him defensively.

Serhan cast his eyes over to the right, wondering why no attack had come from that flank yet. It was quickly explained. His beloved Ragnir, though severely injured, had her jaws clamped tightly around the other young dragon's neck – a fatal grip from which it would never be able to struggle free. Thradus could see the inevitability of this and was scrambling to dismount, though not fast enough. With a sharp flick of her head, Ragnir flung the lifeless dragon contemptuously aside with Thradus still clinging atop it. She then turned her attention back to Serhan. With wings dragging and limping even more heavily than before, she started toward where he was lying.

Serhan opened his mouth to cry out a warning, but before he could utter a sound, Drewin's dragon leapt forward to seize Ragnir from the rear. First its talons sank into her back; then its jaws clamped down around her muscular neck. It was a similar deadly grip to the one Ragnir herself had used only moments before. And like the young dragon, there was no escape for her either. Had she not been in such a severely weakened condition, she might have stood a fighting chance. As it was, she had none at all.

Unable to bear the terrible sight, Serhan closed his eyes and let out an anguished scream.

He attempted to rise, but it felt as if his back had been shattered by the dragon's blow. Helpless, he could only lie there and desperately tried to shut out the sound of Ragnir's death cries. When they finally ceased, something inside – a final acknowledgement of her bravery perhaps? – compelled him to look over at her ravaged body. Blood glistened across her beautiful scales, shimmering in the glorious sunlight and for one precious moment seeming to be so *alive* still, despite the fact that her eyes stared lifelessly into oblivion.

"This is your own fault," said Drewin, sliding down from his saddle.

A short distance away, Thradus was knelt beside his dead dragon, frantically trying to use his healing magic to restore her life.

"Tend to your brother instead," ordered Drewin.

The young man straightened his back and wiped his face. His gaze then fell on the fallen and helpless figure of Serhan. Springing to his feet, he ran headlong at him, eyes blazing with vengeful intent. Drewin moved swiftly to block his path and wrap restraining arms around his body. Thradus struggled and twisted violently for several seconds in an attempt to wrench himself free, but Drewin was far stronger and held him easily.

"Sadich is dying," he shouted, forcing the youth to look at him directly. "Go help him. Serhan will suffer for what he has done. I promise you that."

Slowly Thradus calmed and was allowed to pull away. After casting one more hate-filled glare at Serhan, he hurried over to tend his brother.

Drewin loomed menacingly over Serhan. "Well fought, Commander," he said. "The others didn't last for more than a few seconds. But I knew not to underestimate you, even when outnumbered and taken by surprise. A pity Sadich and Thradus weren't as careful." He shrugged. "Oh, well. The inexperience of youth."

"Do what you came to do," Serhan growled, lifting his chin to meet the eyes of his one-time friend. "I don't care to hear your treacherous voice."

Drewin shook his head. "Defiant to the last. But you're right. There is no need to prolong this."

After muttering a few words, his hands began to glow with a faint blue aura. He reached down and touched Serhan lightly on the forehead. The effect was immediate.

Serhan saw a flash of brilliant white light… then utter blackness.

* * *

Consciousness returned once again. How many days he had been held, he could no longer tell. The stench of urine and feces mingled with the odor of burning coals. Sweat and blood blurred his vision, but he did not need sight to know where he was.

The slow groan of the iron door followed by a thud of

heavy boots told him that it must be time once again. Time for more pain.

"I must say I'm impressed. I never imagined anyone could hold out for so long."

It was Drewin speaking. Serhan never had any trouble in recognizing his treacherous voice. He wanted to reply, to curse him as a coward, but his throat was too dry and swollen.

"I thought you'd like to know that the allies are now in full retreat."

Serhan turned his head. He could make out only the misty outline of Drewin's body. A few seconds later, he felt a cup filled with water being lifted to his lips. Much as he wanted to spit the liquid back into the man's face, his thirst was too great. He couldn't help but gulp at it greedily. A cool rag then cleaned his face and eyes. Drewin smiled down at him and took a step back.

Seeing the traitor filled him with uncontrollable rage. He struggled violently against the chains securing his arms and legs to the rough wooden table, ignoring the pain caused by both the injuries suffered in battle and the days of relentless torture that had followed.

"Calm yourself, Commander," Drewin said. "I'm here to help you."

"Save your lies," he croaked.

Drewin put the cup against his lips once more, and again he drank. But this time he was able to hold back from swallowing the final mouthful and spat it back full in the face of his betrayer. It was only a very small victory, but it felt good nonetheless.

Drewin calmly dried himself, seemingly unmoved by the display of contempt. "I understand your anger," he said.

"And I believe you when you say that you don't know where the Scepter is hidden. Unfortunately, despite my assurances, the king does not. He still thinks you do."

"And if I did, do you think I would tell him?"

"No. I am certain that you would not. Regardless of how long they torture you, you will say no more than you choose. But I also believe you would be more helpful if you were properly motivated. Perhaps if your wife and child were to be set free?"

Serhan turned his head away. He could still see his wife's face. And their son, Baylin, only five years old. The image of his raven curls, green eyes, and innocent features was too much. He did his best to choke the tears back. "You'll kill them both anyway," he muttered. "No matter what I do or say."

"Oh no," Drewin retorted. "They *will* live. Even if you refuse his offer, the king will see to that. What you get to choose is the manner in which they live."

For the very first time, Serhan felt his resolve weakening. The hell King Zemel would put his family through was unimaginable. The door opened again.

"Look," said Drewin. "Your son is unharmed."

Serhan heard tiny footsteps entering the room. Slowly, he turned his head back. There stood Baylin. He was gazing up at him, his tiny face twisted in confusion.

Immeasurable sorrow washed over Serhan. It was harder than ever to keep his tears at bay. "Are you hurt, son?" he asked.

Baylin shook his head, but said nothing.

"And your mother?"

"She's… she's with the king," he replied, his voice uncertain and meek. "They told me she has to stay there until you do something for him." He took a small, nervous step forward. "Will you do it, father?"

Serhan looked into his child's eyes and forced a weak smile. "I need you to be brave for me. Can you do that?"

Baylin nodded.

"Then no matter what happens, just remember that I love you." He twisted his face to one side. It was impossible to contain the tears any longer. "Take him away and then do what you must."

Drewin sighed. "I'm afraid it's not that easy. I was sent to give you the king's offer. Should you refuse, I am to kill you… while your son watches."

Serhan clenched his fists and stifled his sobs. He would not die sniveling like a coward. "Then do it," he commanded. "Do it quickly."

After a lengthy pause, Drewin pulled a dagger free and placed the point directly over Serhan's heart. "I was to make you scream and wail first. But even *I* have limits."

Serhan looked up and nodded. "For that, at least, I thank you."

Drewin nodded in return. "Farewell, Commander."

He leaned in, and the blade sank deep. Serhan gasped just once, and then went rigid.

As the light of life faded, he could hear the whisper of his son's cries.

Chapter One

The chirping of crickets and the lonely calls of wolves blended in perfect harmony with the wind as it whistled through the pine needles high above the ground. From this lofty position, a lone shadow watched patiently. He had been there for two days, his eyes fixed resolutely on his target, never moving a muscle and never tiring. With only soft leather shoes and a thin pair of black cotton trousers to cover himself, the chill air bit sharply at his exposed flesh. But he did not shiver. Nor did the thought of a warm fire and a soft bed enter his mind. His focus was absolute, and his will could shatter steel. The mane of jet-black hair hanging down to his shoulders was tied into rows of tiny braids and bound together at the tip by a single onyx bead. A dagger fastened to his belt was his only weapon. This was to be a killing of a quick and quiet nature, and a sword would only weigh him down. In any case, should he find himself in unexpected need of such a weapon, he knew he could always claim one easily enough from the dead.

The small cabin just a hundred feet away to the north stood dark and unoccupied: a hiding place for rogues and bandits that was seldom used and – out of necessity – difficult to find unless you knew where to look. He had watched small animals enter through the broken windows, scavenging for whatever scraps might have been left behind. On one occasion a black bear had lumbered up to use the rough corner of the building to scratch its massive back. He had seen them all come and go. But they had not seen *him.* He had to ensure that no one did. Not until it was too late. That demanded a level of control few possessed; to be so utterly in command of your own body as to move soundlessly, lost to the naked eye. He was patient. He was fast. But most of all, he was deadly.

The jingle of steel and the hiss of voices reached his ears. They were still some distance away, but his hearing was unusually keen, as it was with all of those who belonged to the Dul'Buhar. This ability had been a gift from their king and was a secret they guarded jealously. Their physical prowess was legendary, as was their skill in combat. But no one knew the full extent of their powers, nor were they allowed to ask. Doing so meant death.

After several minutes, six torches appeared in the darkness to the east where the trees thinned and the ground became rocky and uneven. The assassin's eyes penetrated the night and looked closely upon the faces of the men. At once, he knew. The one he was waiting for had arrived.

Six men would be easy enough to dispatch. Particularly if they were the sort of sell-swords commonly found in the employ of merchants and lesser nobles. Though truth be told, he had almost been hoping for a greater challenge.

This particular noble – Lord Yelsing – must have earned himself some very special interest. General Kirlon had handed him this assignment personally, insisting that it warranted his immediate attention. It didn't matter in the slightest what the lord had done to merit a death sentence, but it was unusual for the Dul'Buhar to be sent on such a mundane mission. Normally, a small group of soldiers would have been considered more than sufficient to handle things of this nature.

As the target drew closer, he took note of the sell-swords' weary steps and sagging shoulders. It took them several attempts to force open the cabin door before they filed inside. Only a few minutes later, the windows glowed from lamplight.

He waited for another hour before descending from his perch, leaping with uncanny agility from branch to branch in complete silence, then dropping the final ten feet and landing lightly on the balls of his feet. Drawing his dagger, he crouched low and moved forward. The fool hadn't bothered to post a guard at the door. Not that it would have done him any good, even if he had.

While easing closer, he kept a close watch for any shadows moving in the windows. But all was still and quiet. He took a moment to reassess his approach and position. Something wasn't quite right. It was way *too* quiet. Men who had traveled to the point of fatigue would certainly fall asleep easily enough. But even when sleeping, they were by no means silent. Yet no hint of snores or groans reached his ears, nor any of the other sounds familiar to him from a life spent in a camp filled with warriors and soldiers.

With all senses on high alert, he crept cautiously onward. Upon reaching the cabin, he immediately ducked beneath the window and closed his eyes to further enhance his hearing. Still not a sound from the sleeping men reached him; only the scuttle of mice, the wind, and the music of the forest. His grip on the dagger tightened.

The unnatural silence was suddenly broken.

"There's no need to sneak about," called a voice from inside. "I know you're out there. Do come inside."

Springing upright, he backed away a few paces. Almost no one should have been able to hear his approach. Even one of his own would have had difficulty. But the fact was, whoever had called out *had* heard him… or at least knew he was coming.

"Are you going to stand out there all night?"

He took a few seconds to think. He had been betrayed. That much was without doubt. But by whom? And to what end? With no other course open to him, he walked to the door with determined strides and pushed it open.

Sitting at a table over to the left was his target – Lord Yelsing, elegantly dressed in a black satin robe stitched with interlacing patterns of gold and white. Beneath this he wore a finely tailored white shirt with polished silver buttons and matching pants. His black leather boots were clean and unmarked, for all the world looking as if they had never so much as touched the ground before. An elegant, gold-handled sword hung from his belt. He was slightly built, with close-set eyes, a hawk-like nose, and a prominently jutting chin. A mop of curly golden blond hair fell loosely to his shoulders.

"Finally, a face to put to the name," said Yelsing, wearing a friendly smile. "Akiri, I believe? Am I right? Please tell me I am. I will be quite disappointed if you are not."

Remaining on the threshold, the assassin scanned the rest of the room. To his right, a pile of ruined furniture had been shoved carelessly into the near corner, together with a heavily blackened iron stove that had toppled over and was clearly no longer of use to anyone. But it was what lay further back that captured his attention. His jaw tightened, and he realized that this situation was far beyond anything he had anticipated.

The bodies of all five guards were piled like firewood against the rear wall. From these, an untidy trail of blood droplets led directly to the table Yelsing sat at.

"Well, *are* you him or aren't you?" the lord pressed, though his tone remained cordial.

He nodded. "I am Akiri."

Letting out a sigh of relief, Yelsing resumed his seat. "That's good to hear. It really is. I was afraid you might not be and that I had failed on my first attempt. You see, this is all very new to me."

Akiri was rarely unsure of himself, but the relaxed and rather odd manner of this young noble gave him pause to think. The man appeared remarkably unconcerned about being face-to-face with a dagger-wielding assassin, though judging by the pile of bodies he had created, there was likely a very good reason for this. Until Akiri knew more, he decided that caution was his best approach.

"You clearly knew I was coming," he said. "But do you know *why* I am here?"

"Of course," Yelsing replied. "Or at least, I know why you *think* you are here. You believe you are here to kill me. But nothing could be further from the truth." He looked around and twisted his lips, as if tasting something bad. "A dingy place, I'm afraid. Ill-fitting for a night such as this. But what can one do?"

Akiri scrutinized him more closely. There was something unnatural about the man. Just as this thought was forming, the light from a lantern hanging from a beam overhead caught the man's eyes. In spite of their blue color, they were reflecting blood red. Almost at the same time, he realized that Yelsing was not breathing.

"Volkar," he hissed.

Yelsing chuckled with mild amusement. "How odd that you would know the proper name for what I am. With all those rippling muscles and such a grim demeanor, I wouldn't have guessed you to be the educated sort. Far more the slash-and-grunt type. But you're absolutely correct. I am a volkar. Though most people call me a *soul shredder.*"

Rapidly, everything that Akiri knew of the volkar passed through his mind. Once human, they had bound themselves to demon spirits in order to gain power and immortality. They survived on the souls of the living, consuming them at the precise moment of death. Volkar were strong, fast, and extremely deadly. Someone had gone to a great deal of trouble to bring this creature here.

"You should understand, Akiri, this is the first time I have killed for gold. I usually kill for survival." He flicked his wrist and cocked his head. "Though occasionally for sport as well, I must admit. So forgive me if I appear to be a trifle awkward."

"Who sent you?"

Yelsing held up his hand. "I will get to that, so please be patient. But don't worry. My instructions are very clear, and they most certainly include allowing you to know who sent me."

"Speak then, and let us be done with it." Akiri's eyes shot across to the pile of bodies. He would need to make it over to them before attempting anything else. If what he had learned from his studies was true, there were few ways he would be able to kill this creature. Without a sword, he would not stand a chance.

"Such a serious and sober fellow," Yelsing said, smirking.

"I would tell you to take more joy from life. But as *yours* is about to end…"

He waved a nonchalant hand before continuing. "In any event, I am first to explain what your death will be like. I have no personal experience with this, but I see the faces and hear the screams of my victims. Many of them beg for death within the first few seconds. I can only imagine the terrible agonies they must feel. So that is what will happen to you, I'm afraid. And when it does, I am then to ask you if you would care to plead for your life. But from one look at you I already know that you won't. Good man. Very brave."

Akiri was losing patience. But he needed to know more. He took a small step toward the bodies.

In an instant, Yelsing was on his feet with his blade drawn. His once friendly countenance was now dark and foreboding. "Not yet," he warned. "Or I will end this right now."

Akiri halted, his expression blank, but said nothing. Clearly wary of this, Yelsing remained standing, his eyes fixed on his intended victim. After a moment, he sighed.

"Of course, you are impatient to discover who sent me. Very well." He let the silence hang between them. Akiri studied him in those few seemingly endless seconds before Yelsing finally said, "I presume you are acquainted with General Kirlon Galliani. He was very keen for you to know that he is the instrument of your demise. Also that his brother can now rest in peace." He shook his head. "This man must hate you with a genuine passion. The effort it took just to find me must have cost him a fortune. On top of this, my price to come all the way from Malistad was considerable. I can't imagine there is much gold left in his coffers by now."

Akiri nodded. "So you expect me to bargain for my life by attempting to bribe you? Is that it?"

"In all honesty, I was unsure what might happen. I am no assassin, but some of my past victims have offered me gold in exchange for their lives."

"And did you ever spare any of them?"

Yelsing's eyes suddenly glowed violet. His lips parted to reveal teeth that were now a row of needle-like fangs. "My victims have no hope. And no amount of gold can save them."

"Then I shall save myself by using other means," Akiri told him.

His confident words acted as a goad to the volkar. The creature leapt forward with such incredible speed Akiri was only just able to step aside in time. Not that this gained him much of a breathing space. Despite the powerful force of his momentum, Yelsing was somehow able to pull up almost on the spot. He spun around, one arm extended, his hand curled into a vicious-looking claw. Ducking beneath it, Akiri made a rapid dive over to where the pile of bodies lay. In a single fluid motion, he pulled free one of the dead men's blades and swung back to face his adversary, slashing in a tightly controlled sweep. Steel found flesh and sliced a deep wound across Yelsing's chest.

Too low, Akiri thought.

Crimson fluid, far too thick to be human blood, oozed down the front of Yelsing's shirt. He dabbed at the wound, staring in disbelief. "I have not seen my own blood in a long time," he remarked, almost with a laugh. "A *very* long time." His eyes flashed from violet to red, and with a movement faster than any normal person could see, he freed his own blade.

Akiri's sight, however, was far beyond that of a normal person, and so was the speed of his reactions. After parrying the attack, he planted his foot into Yelsing's stomach and sent him crashing back into the far wall so violently that the ancient and half-rotten timbers shattered like delicate glass. Driven completely through to the outside, Yelsing landed hard in an untidy heap several feet away from the shack. Even so, he was on his feet again in an instant.

Akiri sought to press home any advantage he might have gained, swinging his sword in a flurry of strikes. But Yelsing had recovered from the surprise of being faced with such a worthy opponent and was skillfully blocking each of his moves. The action calmed as they circled each other warily, feigning attacks without either giving so much as an inch of ground. Then, almost as if at a given signal, both threw themselves into renewed assaults.

Akiri's face was stone and his movements sheer perfection – a result of both the power of his *order* and the many years of intense training. Yelsing, though skilled with a blade, was relying heavily on his preternatural speed and sheer strength. With each new strike, his blade came closer to its target.

The initial wound he had opened up would normally have been enough to ensure victory. Blood loss would soon weaken a human opponent; but Yelsing was not human, and the wound had already closed. Even so, signs of frustration were now clearly showing on his face. His next attack was wild, though it came at a speed that would have overcome most swordsmen. To Akiri, however, the strikes were haphazard and clumsy. Spinning left, he saw an opening and thrust six inches of steel between Yelsing's third and fourth ribs.

As he tried to yank his blade free, Yelsing lunged forward, spitting and snarling. In a sudden change of tactics, the volkar dropped his weapon and seized hold of Akiri's face, his steely fingers exerting unbelievably fierce pressure. Akiri reached for his foe's wrist, but he had barely lifted his hand when an intense pain, the like of which he had never imagined possible, ran like a raging river through his entire body. It was as if his blood had been turned to molten lead and his skin was being peeled away a layer at a time.

"You don't cry out," mused Yelsing. "You are indeed a prize. Had I known, I would have come for less gold."

Akiri dropped to his knees. No matter how much he tore at Yelsing's wrist and hand, the creature's hold was unbreakable. He could feel his strength – his very life – draining away. The pain was all-consuming.

"Yes," hissed Yelsing. "You *are* powerful. I can taste your soul's sweet nectar already. I am going to enjoy you."

Only the extreme discipline of Akiri's training kept him from losing consciousness. From the corner of his eye, he spotted Yelsing's discarded sword on the ground just a few feet away. This was his last hope. Letting out a feral scream to help muster every bit of his remaining strength, he heaved his body hard backward.

His movements had been slowed by the attack, but they were still sharp enough to catch Yelsing by surprise. Confident his victory was already complete, he could only gawk in utter astonishment as the opponent he imagined to be on the point of death suddenly pulled himself free and rolled over to snatch up the fallen sword.

Akiri saw the confusion fast fading from Yelsing's eyes. He had only a heartbeat of time in which to finish things.

"Die, abomination!" he shouted, swinging the blade at

Yelsing's exposed neck and slicing all the way through in one vicious but satisfyingly clean cut. The volkar's head rolled from his shoulders and landed on the earth with a dull thud. As though in a bizarre refusal to accept what had happened to it, his body remained stubbornly upright for several seconds before eventually crumbling to the ground.

Akiri watched grimly as the earth all around became soaked with thick crimson blood. He tossed the sword beside the body and backed away. Everything he had learned about the volkar told him that the beast was dead. Removal of the head or heart were two sure methods of killing such creatures, but there was only one way he would be totally satisfied that it would not somehow return to life.

Quickly, he gathered together some wood from the broken furnishings and splintered cabin wall to build a pyre, on top of which he placed the head and torso. After sprinkling the oil from the lanterns liberally, he lit the fire. In less than a minute, the flames turned bright green and began to hiss. Akiri watched without expression as the volkar was completely consumed.

Satisfied, he took a minute to search the cabin before making his way back through the trees to where he had stowed his equipment. After putting on a pair of leather pants and a shirt, he attached his sword to his belt and headed east. With his rapid pace eating up the miles between himself and the main army camp, one name echoed repeatedly in his head.

General Kirlon Galliani.

Chapter Two

Not wishing to announce his return, Akiri made a point of avoiding the camp's sentries – something he found disturbingly simple to achieve. It was an issue he resolved to deal with in short order.

He had deliberately timed his arrival for late in the evening, when the men would be fully occupied and far less likely to notice him. Flickering lights from a multitude of fires cast a soft glow over the countless rows of tents immediately ahead. The sound of music, the laughter of prostitutes, and the loud boasting of drunken men brought a heavy frown to his face. Battle was imminent, and in his mind, distractions like these were far from wise.

A sultry young woman approached from behind a nearby wagon. Bare breasted and face painted in the style of Hultria, she sauntered toward him wearing a seductive smile.

"Don't *you* look fierce," she said, her voice dripping with the promise of pleasure. "I bet I could put a smile on that sour face of yours."

Akiri shoved her aside without even bothering to look her in the eye. He heard her spit and curse, but paid it no attention. Even if he had been in the mood to bed a woman, she was not the type he would have chosen. He grudgingly accepted that they had their uses, but the idea of their presence in camp just before battle disturbed him. He knew that he could not expect most men to live without pleasurable company for long periods, but he was different – he was Akiri, leader of the Dul'Buhar. His seed was not spent without careful consideration. The women who shared his bed were of a certain quality, chosen specifically for him by the king.

The Dul'Buhar encampment – a mere dozen tents – was set to the west, well aside from the others. This was where the true virtue of the army resided. Here, the only sounds were of swords being sharpened, armor being repaired, and men in training. No one could slip into this area unnoticed. Not even Akiri.

A lone sentry – all that was needed to keep them secure – pressed a fist to his chest in salute. Akiri returned the gesture without pausing and strode straight toward the largest tent pitched in the very center. Inside stood a round table with a variety of maps and books laid out where they could be easily read. To the right lay a simple cot and three large trunks in which he kept his personal belongings, to the left a plain but well-constructed desk. Lamps hung from a hook in each corner, with another placed in the middle of the table.

Sitting down at the desk, he drew a sheet of blank parchment from a drawer and began writing. A man entered just as he finished. Although short in stature, the newcomer's broad shoulders and narrow waist gave him the illusion of height. His head was shaved clean, as was his face. The long blade at his side bore the black onyx of the Dul'Buhar on its hilt.

"Ah, Gradis," Akiri said. "I'm glad you're here."

The man saluted and approached the desk. "Did all go as planned?"

"No. As a matter of fact, it did not," Akiri replied, though without allowing any hint of the anger burning inside to show through. "I need you to gather three men and post them outside my tent. Instruct them that all those seeking to enter must first be disarmed. No exceptions. Should anyone attempt to force their way inside while still carrying weapons, do not kill them. Merely restrain them, then turn them away."

Gradis looked at him with confusion, but did not question the order. After saluting again, he hurried away to carry out his commander's wishes.

Akiri read carefully over what he had just written. Satisfied, he reached into the desk and removed a stamp bearing the king's crest. After thoroughly inking this, he pressed it to the bottom of the document, just below his signature. It was done. Justice would be served.

Pausing only to retrieve a small dagger from one of his chests and fastening it to his belt, he left the tent. As he stepped through the flap, he saw that the three men he had ordered Gradis to gather were already taking up position.

The scale of King Zemel's army was immense and the camp vast. At more than two hundred thousand men, it was a force designed to crush the enemy in one fell swoop. Nearly all of the tents accommodating the soldiers were identical in both shape and color, the only exceptions being those belonging to high-ranking officers. This similarity had caused many a man to become lost if he wandered too far away from his unit. But Akiri knew every inch of the ground. He knew *precisely* where to go, even though the walk to General Kirlon's tent took him quite some time.

Two guards were standing at the entrance, and on seeing Akiri's determined approach, they both noticeably stiffened.

"You cannot go in," said the soldier on the right. He sounded nervous – unsurprisingly so, given whom he was addressing. "The general is not receiving anyone right now."

"You will stand aside and allow me to pass," Akiri told him, retaining a calm and even tone. "I am the commander of the Dul'Buhar. General Kirlon cannot refuse me an audience. Should you choose to hinder me, you will pay for it with your lives. Am I understood?"

He had no desire to carry out his threat. He knew they were merely doing as they had been ordered, but he would not be stopped.

The guards glanced at one another and then back to Akiri. After a brief but tense moment of inner conflict that was reflected clearly in their expressions, they each took a single step away from the entrance. Akiri nodded approvingly and pushed open the flap.

Inside was far more lavish and comfortable than the sparse furnishings of his own tent. Several plush chairs surrounded an elegant mahogany dining table, while the bed at the far end was draped with netting and dressed in the finest silk sheets and wool blankets. A desk roughly the same size as his own, though infinitely more decorative, stood in the far right corner. Behind this sat General Kirlon, while two of his lieutenants were sitting in chairs facing him.

In his early fifties, the general was overweight by at least thirty pounds and far too out of shape to be of any use in a real fight. His round face and flat nose was accentuated by a scalp almost totally devoid of hair, giving his head a ball-like appearance. An unblemished complexion denoted a man well able to afford the luxuries needed to combat the ravages of wind, sun, and cold.

His narrow set brown eyes popped wide on seeing who had entered. "Commander Akiri," he said, quickly regaining his composure. "I was not expecting you."

"Of that I am certain," Akiri responded. "But now I think you should ask your men to leave."

Fear instantly struck the general's face. "I think it is *you* who should leave, Commander. You have no business here."

Akiri moved closer, forcing Kirlon to shrink back in his chair. "I think you will find I *do* have business with you." With ominous deliberation, he unfolded the parchment and placed it on the desk before taking a step back.

With trembling hands, Kirlon picked up the sheet and began to read. Ashen faced, he silently handed the document over to one of his lieutenants – who, after a thorough inspection, passed it on to the other. Without speaking, both men rose to their feet and drew their blades.

"You would sacrifice the lives of your men?" Akiri asked contemptuously. "The writ of execution is valid. You are a traitor and have attempted to assassinate a member of the Dul'Buhar. Your sentence is death. And I am here to carry it out."

The two lieutenants eyed Akiri nervously, but he made no move to draw his weapon.

In a sudden show of defiance, Kirlon leapt up from his chair, eyes ablaze. "You lie! You have no proof of this! Begone, or I will have you put in chains."

"As you well know, General, I have complete authority in these matters," Akiri responded calmly.

He turned his head to face each of the other men in turn. "And *you* know this too. My word is all the proof that is needed. You can either sheathe your swords and leave at once, or ignore what you know to be the king's law and try to stop me. I promise you that regardless of your choice, the outcome will still be the same."

Akiri saw the doubt in their eyes. Though he was absolutely correct in everything he had said, General Kirlon was a powerful man. Only the king boasted greater wealth and influence.

"Stand your ground," Kirlon ordered. "Or I will see you both beneath the executioner's axe by morning."

"And should you choose to stay here, I will save him the trouble," added Akiri. "The two of you are blameless, but this is your final warning. Go now."

The older of the two made a weak attempt to square his stance. "This matter should be brought before the king," he said.

Akiri shook his head. "A poor decision."

The dagger appeared in his hand before either of the lieutenants could blink. With deadly accuracy, he thrust the blade directly into the older man's heart. In one continuous blur of movement, he then seized hold of the second man's wrist, forcing his sword violently upwards. The look of absolute horror on his victim's face froze in place as his own sword was used to slice open his throat. Neither man had been able to so much as move a step before meeting their end. Together, and with almost military precision, both fell to their knees and then to the ground as the life drained from their bodies.

Kirlon could only stare in terror at the men he had been relying on to save him. His features collapsed. "Please. I'll give you anything. Anything you want. Gold… jewels… just name it."

Akiri regarded him coldly. What a pathetic specimen he

was. To think this sad excuse of a man commanded others. "You can offer me nothing I desire," he told him. "If you have prayers you wish to offer to your gods, you should say them now."

Kirlon's eyes darted around the tent, desperately seeking an escape route. None was available. He could possibly try to rip a way out through the canvas behind him, but it was obvious that Akiri would kill him long before he was able to accomplish this. His voice turned to a whine. "I can give you your freedom. Yes – that's it! You are a slave of the king, are you not? I can convince him to release you."

Akiri could not help but laugh at the suggestion. "You think cheap insults will save your life? I already have all the freedom a loyal servant of King Zemel could ever ask for."

"If you do this, the king will surely have you executed," the general sniveled. With legs that no longer seemed able to support his weight he staggered back, collapsing clumsily into his chair.

The bitter smell of urine filled the tent. Akiri sneered down at the now openly weeping man. What he was about to do was a service. Not only to the king, but to all those who had been forced to follow Kirlon's orders.

"My life is, and has always been, in my king's hands," he said. "He may take it if he so wishes."

The ringing of steel as Akiri drew his sword was like a melody heralding Kirlon's end. He lightly touched the general on the shoulder with the tip of the blade. "Look me in the eyes and face your final moments as a man. Meet your gods with honor. It will be swift and painless. You have my word."

After the briefest of pauses, Kirlon slowly raised his head and held his gaze. Though he continued to tremble, he was managing to sit up straight. Akiri gave him a respectful nod. At least in the end, the man had found a measure of courage. The steel passed through his heart and out again in the blink of an eye. Akiri had already turned away and was opening the exit flap when he heard the thud of Kirlon's head striking the desktop.

He paused to address the two guards outside. "Arrange for General Kirlon's body to be delivered to his family," he instructed them.

Shock and anger blazing across their faces, the pair rushed inside the tent while Akiri walked calmly on.

Back at the Dul'Buhar encampment, he carefully cleaned his equipment, then washed away the dirt and grime from his body. There were still a few hours to pass until dawn, so he would rest now. The coming day was sure to be eventful. The three men on duty outside his tent would see that none of Kirlon's captains attempted anything rash while he slept. Some would certainly take the general's death hard. Kirlon had surrounded himself with lackeys and sycophants, most of whom were only serving the king in order to ensure their position and gain favor with Kirlon and his family. Dealing with *them* might prove to be an altogether different matter; though it was one Akiri felt he was more than capable of handling.

He lay on his cot and closed his eyes, clearing his mind. Sleep always came easily to him. His discipline and confidence of his place in the world made it possible to leave behind all unwanted thoughts and emotions – the very kind that kept others awake at night and robbed them of their courage. But his courage never faltered. Nor did his conviction. He was Akiri. And that was enough.

The morning brought with it all that he expected. He had

barely opened his eyes when there was a commotion outside his tent as angry voices demanded entry, followed by loud shouts of protest as his men insisted that they must first be disarmed.

Akiri rose and quickly donned a pair of leather pants, heavy boots, and a loose fitting shirt. He had only just finished fastening a dagger to his belt when the tent flap was flung wide and three furious looking men stormed inside.

One he recognized immediately as Captain Freidris Galliani – a cousin to General Kirlon. The other two were strangers to him, though their demeanor and expensive clothing suggested strongly that they were either related to Kirlon, or at least nobles aligned with him.

He moved behind his desk and took a seat. "What do you want, Captain?"

"You know good and damn well what I want," he bellowed. "Your head on a pike. And I'll have it by the day's end."

"Is that right?" Akiri deliberately shifted his tone, his words taking on a dangerous quality. "So you have come here in order to make threats against me. I am sure a man in your position is well aware of how inadvisable it is to threaten the Dul'Buhar. Neither I, nor any in my order, serve under your command. And I have no time to suffer fools. So speak your business quickly and be gone."

"Speak my business?" Galliani repeated, his voice shrill with rage. "My business is to place you under arrest."

Akiri raised an eyebrow. "Under whose authority?"

"The king's, you dolt. You will surrender yourself to me now."

Akiri leaned back in his chair. "I assume you come bearing the king's seal."

The two men locked eyes. Galliani's face was bright crimson, with veins bulging prominently from his neck and forehead. He slammed his hands down on the desktop. "You murdered General Kirlon and two of his lieutenants. Are you fool enough to think you can escape unpunished?"

"General Kirlon was sentenced to death," Akiri said evenly, unmoved by the captain's display of temper. "He attempted to have a member of the Dul'Buhar assassinated. The writ was sealed and carried out. There is nothing more to say on the matter. As for the two lieutenants, they directly interfered with the execution of the writ. Their deaths were unfortunate, but unavoidable." He waved a dismissive hand. "If there is nothing else, you should leave now."

"So you refuse to surrender yourself?"

Akiri stood and leaned forward over his desk. Even when bent at the waist like this, his towering frame meant that he still met the man's stare eye to eye. "I surrender myself only to the king's authority. And as you have come without this, I will remain where I am. That you grieve the loss of your uncle is the only reason I am prepared to forgive your mistake in coming here in such a manner. But do not test my patience any further."

His aggressive posture was enough to force Galliani into taking a hurried step back. "This isn't over, dog," he snarled. He stormed out of the tent, closely followed by the other two men.

Gradis entered a few seconds after their departure, wearing a deeply concerned expression on his face. "Do you think he'll return?" he asked.

"Possibly," Akiri replied.

"It was wise to disarm them. Another death in that family at your hands could make things complicated."

Akiri frowned. “I care nothing for their politics. And so long as I am Dul’Buhar, I have nothing to fear from the House Galliani. Let them shout their fury at the sky. Kirlon’s execution was just. They can take the matter to the king if they so wish.”

“And I am sure they will,” Gradis said. “I know you well, Akiri. You refuse to acknowledge that there is more to life than what is simply right and wrong.”

Akiri allowed an uncharacteristically impish smile to touch his lips. “Yes, my friend, you know me far better than most. But I am not so blind to the ways of nobles that I do not see the danger I am in. The Gallianis will appeal to the king for retribution, but it is unlikely they will receive it. King Zemel is not a man who bends to the will of his court. They bend to *his*. And *he* is wise. He will see the right of my actions. This is not the first time I have been forced to deliver justice to a powerful noble. There is no difference here.”

Gradis shook his head. “I fear you are wrong. The House Galliani has blood ties to the king.”

“I am aware of this. But the king gives the Dul’Buhar authority in these matters for a good reason. You should trust in this.”

“I do; but men like Freidris Galliani are not to be underestimated. He may be a pompous ass, but he is not stupid. This is not over.”

“It is for now,” Akiri told him. “I have far more pressing duties to attend to at the moment. How do things stand in the field?”

Gradis nodded sharply. “Scouts have reported that there are fifty thousand men massed five days’ march to the south.”

"Are our commanders mobilizing?"

"Not yet. The news of General Kirlon's death has caused a delay. But I suspect it will be resolved soon enough."

Akiri crossed over to the table where a map of the region was spread out. After studying it for several minutes, a satisfied smile appeared.

"I know that look," said Gradis. "What do you see?"

Akiri knew him to be a fierce warrior and intelligent in most matters; in the field he could not hope to have a better man beside him. But Gradis was never able to grasp the entirety of a battle situation.

"Send word to General Laronso that I need to see him," he said.

Gradis saluted and hurried off.

General Laronso was one of the few men outside the Dul'Buhar that Akiri held in high regard. Though not a warrior himself, he had a keen intellect and a disciplined nature. The soldiers under his command were second only to the Dul'Buhar, and so far had never tasted defeat. He promoted men on the strength of their worth in battle or their intellect rather than on their wealth and position. At least half of his captains and lieutenants had no claim to noble blood at all.

Akiri spent a few more minutes examining the map before leaving the tent to join a few of his men in a small area they had set up as a practice yard. For the Dul'Buhar, constant training was a way of life. Combat, however, was only a part of their routine. One needed to be far more than just a skilled fighter to attain acceptance into such a select order. Members were also considered to be among the brightest scholars in the entire kingdom. Proof of this could be found in the fact that those who were too seriously injured in battle to return to duty were often given key positions in Zemel's court as advisors and teachers. For Akiri the thrill of combat was undeniably the aspect that he loved most of all. In a world where status and rank very often placed lesser men over far better ones, it was the only thing that was undeniably honest and fair.

The men greeted him with boisterous shouts and applause. They relished the chance to test themselves against their esteemed leader. To best him would be a great accomplishment – although thus far not a single one of them had ever managed to do so.

An older man overseeing the training gave Akiri a respectful nod. He was tall – as tall as Akiri himself – and bore the powerful shoulders normally seen on a blacksmith. Though not an official member of the Dul'Buhar, he was a legend among its soldiers. Even at his advanced age, few of them would be able to best him. He had been Akiri's first trainer, and after the Dul'Buhar was founded with Akiri as its commander, he had been asked to assist in keeping the men sharp and proficient. It was a role he had fulfilled superbly.

"Borlon," Akiri called, raising his hand in greeting.

The man eyed him critically for several seconds. "You are looking soft, Commander. It would seem you have been neglecting your training."

"Perhaps you would like to step inside the circle and see how soft I've become."

This suggestion was greeted with hoots of approval, but Akiri was not serious in his challenge. Both of them knew that these days he could beat his former trainer with relative ease.

Borlon spun around to glare at the men. "Back to it.

Quickly now, or you'll be telling people how you were pummeled by an old man."

Akiri snatched up a pair of leather gloves from a nearby table. "They are anxious to march, I think."

"Indeed they are," agreed Borlon. "Idleness is not good for a soldier. Though I hear you have been anything but idle yourself. Is it true? Did you really execute General Kirlon?"

Akiri nodded. "He hired a volkar to assassinate me. I was in the right."

"A volkar? He must have been in quite a state to have gone to so much trouble."

"He wanted vengeance for the death of his brother."

Borlon huffed a laugh. "You killed his brother too? Then the Gallianis will truly be out for blood."

Akiri tightened the wrist straps on his gloves and began to stretch his shoulders and legs. "A house of fools."

"Most assuredly, but *rich* fools. I hope you haven't bitten off more than you can chew."

"You sound like Gradis. I can handle the bloody Gallianis."

"I hope you're right. That head of yours would look terrible on a pike."

Akiri grinned. "You worry too much."

"And *you* don't worry enough."

Akiri spent the next hour in hand-to-hand combat with his men. As always, no one could come close to besting him. He found it invigorating, and could easily have continued well into the evening, but the sight of Freidris Galliani returning halted any further recreation. This time he was with two fully armored soldiers and carried a pair of iron shackles.

"This looks serious," remarked Borlon.

Freidris stalked toward him, his mouth twisted into a sinister smirk.

"What do you want now?" Akiri demanded. His men were already forming a protective barrier in front of him. He quickly waved them away.

"I have come to place you under arrest," Freidris announced. He swept a hand across the group of Dul'Buhar glaring at him. "And should any of you interfere, you will be summarily executed."

"I have already warned you, Captain," Akiri snapped. "Unless you have –"

Freidris pulled a parchment from his pocket and held it out. Akiri instantly recognized the royal seal of King Zemel across the top. Snatching the document away, he tore it open.

"As you can clearly see," stated Freidris, his smirk returning, "this is a warrant for your arrest. Signed and sealed by His Royal Highness."

Akiri re-read the warrant. It was indeed valid; and no matter how much the Galliani family desired revenge, they would never dare to forge such a document.

Freidris handed the shackles to the soldier on his right. Akiri's men instantly started forward.

"Stop!" Akiri commanded. "This warrant is legal. You will do nothing to dishonor the Dul'Buhar. Am I understood?"

The men snapped to attention. Though remaining obedient while Akiri allowed the soldier to apply the restraints, it was easy to see their muscles twitching repeatedly as they struggled to restrain themselves.

Freidris leaned in close to whisper in his prisoner's ear. "I will be the one who kills you. If it costs me everything I possess, it *will* be me."

Akiri did not react, even when one of the soldiers shoved him forward roughly.

Freidris led the way, taking obvious pleasure in the astonished looks they received as they wound their way through the camp. To see the mighty Akiri in chains… it was *almost* too much to be believed.

Throughout the humiliating march, Akiri showed no sign of fear or anxiety. Even when he was thrown inside a caged wagon, he retained faith that King Zemel would see the honor of his actions and allow him to return to duty.

And if not…

If not, in due time, death was a guest that all men must host.

Chapter Three

For three days, the wagon holding Akiri crawled steadily north. Throughout this time, Freidris refused him even the smallest morsel of food or water, offering instead only a spiteful diet of curses and threats. But if he was hoping to weaken and demoralize his prisoner, he was in for a big disappointment. Akiri had endured hardships that Freidris Galliani could scarcely imagine, and it would take far more than harsh words and a few days without food to break him. His mind was disciplined not to anger or allow any trace of fear to surface. For most of the time he simply sat in the center of the wagon with legs crossed and eyes closed, not uttering a sound.

It was mid-morning when they eventually arrived at a small country manor just off the road leading into the capital city of Gol'Naruth. Twenty armed men – mercenaries, from the look of them – were waiting near the front door. Akiri wondered if Freidris might be such a fool as to kill him here without a trial. That would be in complete defiance of the king's law and his own right as a Dul'Buhar.

The manor was modest for what it was, though still a palace to the eyes of a man like him: single story and of simple design, no doubt built from local timbers. Most likely it was used as a hunting lodge, as opposed to the minor lord's residence. To his right, Akiri could see a stable big enough to house perhaps a dozen horses, while to his left stood a smaller building that probably served as a guard shack.

As he neared he saw a tall woman, who looked to be in her midlife, emerge from the building. Even the distance couldn't hide the gray hairs and craggy lines of age around her eyes and mouth. She moved with the grace and poise of a true noblewoman. In her youth she must have been something to behold, he thought. Even now, after a life well-lived, she was remarkably attractive.

"Is this him?" she asked in a feminine yet commanding tone. "Is this Akiri?"

Freidris dismounted and bowed low. "Yes, mother. This is him."

She approached the cage, her eyes boring into him. "Do you know who I am?" she asked.

"Aside from being Freidris Galliani's mother – no, I do not," he replied coldly.

"I am Carlotta Galliani. Matriarch of the House Galliani. As I understand it, you have killed two of my kin. My sister is suffering badly because of you already. When she learns of Kirlon's death, I fear for what she might do."

She paused, but Akiri said nothing. "Have you no defense to offer?"

"My Lady," he said, giving her a respectful nod, "I am not answerable to you, or to your house. I am the commander of the Dul'Buhar. If I am to be charged with a crime, only the king can be my judge."

Carlotta sniffed contemptuously. "Dul'Buhar indeed! I have never understood why King Zemel allows you so much license. You *are* slaves, after all. Not like proper soldiers. You run around thinking you are untouchable." She moved in closer, a wicked smile on her face. "Well, my friend, you are not untouchable. Your time has come, and I will show you what power really is."

Akiri regarded her steadily. "If you intend to kill me, you should get on with it." His voice was flat and emotionless. "This cage holds me only because I allow it. As do these shackles."

She gave a mirthless laugh. "Do you take me for a fool? I am not about to risk the standing of House Galliani by murdering a Dul'Buhar dog. No. First you will be judged. And I promise you now that you *will* be convicted. Only *then* will you die. But of course, feel free to escape if you can. That would save me no small measure of trouble."

"I have no need to flee. I trust in the wisdom of my king."

"You do that," she mocked.

After a final lingering stare, she turned back to her son. "Feed him and give him proper clothing, Freidris. We wouldn't want King Zemel to think we are animals when he arrives, would we? After all, our prisoner does hold the rank of commander. Even if he is just a slave."

"Yes, mother." After casting Akiri a malevolent glare, he followed her inside the house.

The realization that the king was coming brought a brief smile to Akiri's face. All would be well soon, and then he'd be free to return to his men.

The four soldiers who had escorted Freidris were gathered in a tight group by the front of the manor, while the sell-swords wandered aimlessly. Such men were undisciplined. Beatable. Their courage lay in numbers, and they possessed no loyalty beyond the coin. Akiri wondered why the House Galliani even bothered employing such riff-raff. Surely they could count on better?

A short time later, a young servant girl brought him a loaf of bread, a hand-sized piece of dried meat, and a flask of water. She returned shortly afterwards carrying a brown cotton shirt, a pair of trousers, and leather boots. One of the soldiers ordered him to put his hands through the bars so that he could be unshackled.

"Get dressed," he ordered, once Akiri had been freed.

He was still stripped to the waist from the combat training with his men. Carlotta was indeed wise not to let the king see the most senior member of his prized Dul'Buhar half-naked and bound like a common thief; this would certainly be viewed as an insult and considerably reduce their chances of gaining the vengeance they sought. There was another good reason why he remained unshackled, even after having put on the clothes provided. It seemed Carlotta was doing her best to tempt him into making a bid for freedom. But he would not even consider such an action. Should they have attempted to murder him, that would have been different. He would have shown the Gallianis exactly why the Dul'Buhar were so feared. But even after doing that, he would still have sought out the king to explain himself. He would never run like a coward.

Carriages continued to arrive throughout the day. Several were escorted by spectacularly adorned guards and servants: a common practice when a family wanted to flaunt their wealth and status. Some were occupied by generals who had come from the camp, while others were nobles unknown to Akiri. By sunset, a total of ten carriages had arrived. Akiri smiled at the thought of so many haughty lords and ladies crammed into what to them must have felt like such a tiny place.

The king himself arrived astride a magnificent black steed just after sunset, his thick black locks bouncing across his broad shoulders in time with the horse's cantering gait. A thin gold circlet resting on his brow held the hair well back away from his face. He wore an elegant purple shirt with gold stitching and polished black buttons, together with matching pants. Though this attire was clearly fit for a king, it also looked to be comfortable and well suited for travel.

Ten royal guards surrounded the monarch, each carrying a silver-tipped spear and a longsword at his side. It was a small escort for a man so powerful, but King Zemel did not need protection. His command of magic meant that he could cast down anyone who might be so foolish as to accost him on the road. Stories of his ability had fallen into legend throughout Acharia.

After an hour had passed, King Zemel emerged from the house alone. He paused outside the door for a moment before approaching the cage. As he drew close, Akiri lay face down on the floor with arms outstretched.

"You have caused quite a stir, Commander," the king remarked in a surprisingly lighthearted tone.

Akiri rose to his knees, eyes downcast. "I apologize, Your Highness. It was not my intention."

"I know Kirlon was a fool, but did he deserve death?"

"His crime allowed for no other punishment, Your Highness," he said, then related the events that had led him to execute Kirlon.

"Yes, the volkar. I heard about that. After such a betrayal, I suppose you were only doing your duty." Zemel rubbed his chin. "It has been many years since I have seen you, Akiri."

"It has indeed, Your Highness."

"Your reputation has grown. And I hear your men are loyal only to you. Is this true?"

"No, Your Highness. Their loyalty lies with you. I have earned their respect, but it is *your* will they live to enforce."

"That is good to hear," he remarked thoughtfully. "And as for yourself… are you not afraid of what may become of you?"

"I trust in your wisdom, Your Highness. If you determine I am in the wrong, then my life is yours to take."

Zemel nodded. "That is the answer I expected." He turned to beckon over the guards. "Bring him," he ordered.

He set off back inside while the guards unlocked the cage. They escorted Akiri through the front door and into the main foyer. Trophies boasting of many successful hunts decorated the walls, along with the bows and slings used to kill the creatures. Doors along both sides led to the other rooms of the house, and a double door at the rear opened into a spacious dining hall. In the center of this room stood King Zemel, flanked on either side by the various nobles. Carlotta Galliani was standing immediately to the king's right, and her son to his left.

After approaching, Akiri bent down onto one knee and lowered his head.

"Stand up, Commander," ordered the king.

Akiri obeyed, but did not meet his monarch's eyes.

"You see, Your Highness?" mocked Freidris. "Such is his shame, he can't even bring himself to look at you."

"To look the king in the eye without permission is a challenge to his authority," Akiri retorted. "Being the noble you are, I would have assumed you'd know this."

"It is *My Lord*," snapped Carlotta. "You will address my

son as My Lord.... slave."

"As you wish, My Lady," replied Akiri, with no hint of deference.

"Look up, Commander," said the king. "I would have you look me in the eye."

Akiri raised his head. The king was wearing a heavy frown, a complete contrast to the smug smiles that both Carlotta and her son were displaying. As for the five generals present, there was barely concealed hostility in all of their looks. Akiri's reputation and authority had earned him several enemies amongst high-ranking officers, though none had the power or the courage to do anything but whisper curses and shoot him contemptuous glances.

For now, all the other nobles present wore impassive expressions. The nobility learned from an early age to hide their feelings so as not to reveal their intentions. It was all a part of the power game.

"Commander Akiri of the Dul'Buhar," King Zemel began ceremoniously. "You are accused of the murder of General Kirlon Galliani, Lieutenant Jutzi Marko, and Lieutenant Bernart Scotz. That they all died by your hand is not in dispute. What do you have to say for yourself?"

Akiri bowed. "Your Highness, I was simply carrying out a legal writ of execution. The two lieutenants attempted to interfere with this and were killed in the process."

"A writ you issued yourself," jumped in Carlotta. "Without trial or evidence. You murdered those men in cold blood. I demand justice."

"You demand nothing!" roared the king, the power of his voice causing the woman to cringe. "Be silent, or I will have you put in chains."

Carlotta lowered her head and took a hasty step back.

"Please forgive me, Your Highness."

Satisfied for the moment, King Zemel turned his attention back to Akiri. "Why was it necessary to execute him? What was his crime?"

Akiri repeated what he had told him outside, this time adding the events inside Kirlon's tent. "According to the laws Your Highness has written, I was well within my rights to execute General Kirlon," he concluded. "His treachery allowed for no other course of action."

Zemel gave him a lengthy stare before asking: "Tell me, Commander, why would General Kirlon want you dead?"

"He blamed me for the death of his brother, Your Highness."

A royal eyebrow rose. "Did you kill *him* as well?"

"No. He took his own life."

"After you stripped him of his honor," added Freidris, unable to hold his tongue.

The king shot him a warning glance, then gestured for Akiri to elaborate.

"He defied a direct order and led his men into a trap – one that any competent commander would have easily detected. Twenty of his men died as a result. When I learned of this, I took away his rank and had him sent to the supply lines where he could do no more harm."

Zemel nodded. "I see. And as a result of this disgrace, he took his own life."

"That is what I have been told, Your Highness. Whatever the case, General Kirlon blamed me for his death and sought vengeance by hiring a volkar to kill me. I heard this directly from the creature's lips. There was no doubt of his guilt."

Carlotta stepped forward timidly, not speaking until King Zemel nodded his permission. She then turned to Akiri.

"Are we supposed to simply take your word for this? You have no proof. Why should anyone here believe a word you say?"

"My Lady," he replied. "My word is all the proof I need. I am unable to bear false witness. No Dul'Buhar can."

She waved his promise away contemptuously. "So you say."

"So says King Zemel," he retorted. "We cannot lie from the moment we swear allegiance to the king and to the order." He paused, expecting to hear the king confirm this, but his monarch remained silent. "Our mandate gives us absolute authority in matters of military law. This alone should be enough… even for you, My Lady."

Carlotta glared at him hatefully. "Your mandate does not give you the right to commit murder."

"Enough!" declared the king. "Leave, all of you. I will speak with Commander Akiri alone. Then I will render my decision."

Carlotta opened her mouth to protest, but a sharp glance from Zemel kept her silent. Tight lipped, she joined the other nobles filing silently out of the room. Only one, a short thin man, remained behind. He wore an elegant silver satin robe bearing the crest of the House Kortain. His long silver hair was tied in a loose braid and fastened at the end with a blood red bead.

"Do you know this man?" asked King Zemel.

Akiri shook his head. "No, Your Highness."

"This is my most trusted advisor, Lord Jerimea Kortain. He is here to observe you."

Unsure how to reply, Akiri simply bowed and returned his attention to the king.

"What is the first thing you can remember?" Zemel asked.

Akiri thought for a moment. "Training with Borlon."

"And how old were you at the time?"

"Eleven, I think. Though I am unsure. I might have been a little older."

"Odd that you cannot remember anything of your life before that," mused the king, glancing across at Lord Kortain.

"Are you certain he cannot lie?" the old man asked.

"Absolutely. The spell that binds him to me will not allow it. No one is supposed to know this, though I suspect that bitch Carlotta somehow does. Remind me to have her killed before I return to Gol'Naruth."

Lord Kortain smiled. "I will indeed. And her son?"

Zemel rolled his eyes. "Oh, yes. Him too." He turned back to Akiri. "Is it true you are loyal to me?"

"Completely," Akiri replied.

Zemel paused for a long moment, rubbing his chin thoughtfully. "Humor me now. What if I told you that you had children? Would that change things for you? Would you want to be free to be with them?"

"No, Your Highness. I am more valuable to you where I am."

"I see. And if I were to told you that I intended to have your children killed?"

Akiri thought on this for only a second. "I would assume that you have just cause to do so. It would not be for me to question the matter."

Lord Kortain nodded approvingly. "It is exactly as you said. How much does he know about his past?"

"You heard him," answered Zemel. "Training with Borlon is his first memory."

"Ah," said the old man, raising a finger. "But what he is

able to remember and what lies deep within may be very different."

The king considered this, then nodded. "Akiri. What do you know of your family?"

"Nothing, Your Highness. It was forbidden for me to know. The Dul'Buhar is all the family I require."

"Very good. Even so, it might interest you to know that your father was the leader of the famed Tul'Zahar."

This time Akiri was unable to conceal his shock completely. He had learned of the Tul'Zahar during his early studies. They had betrayed King Zemel and waged war on him. It was because of their treachery that the rebellion they were still trying to put down had continued for so long.

"I sentenced your father to death for his crimes," Zemel continued. "And *his* blood runs through your veins. So I ask you again: Are you a loyal servant to your king?"

"I am, Your Highness," Akiri affirmed. "And should you wish me to pay for the wrongdoings of my father, I will gladly end my own life."

The king waved his hand. "No. Your father has already given any blood that was owed on that score. But you *do* carry his burden, Akiri. He stole something very precious to me and hid it away. I have searched for many years to recover this item, but to no avail. Now at last, I have discovered a way and want your help in retrieving it. Do this, and you will have paid your father's debt in full. You will also have provided a great service to me."

"I am at your command, Your Highness. Tell me what I must do."

The king smiled warmly and produced a small black stone from his pocket. "Do you know what this is?"

Akiri looked closely. "It appears to be an oath stone, very

much like the one I swore on when I was inducted into the Dul'Buhar. That was the first time we met."

"It more than just looks like the stone you swore upon, Akiri. It is the very one. Within this lies the source of your bond to me and the magic that gives you extraordinary strength and speed. As long as this is in my possession, you are in essence my slave. You cannot lie. Nor can you betray me. But it is also this very same stone that will prevent you from completing the task I am setting."

Akiri furled his brow. "I do not understand." He was already aware of the source of his power and of the oath stone's magical qualities.

"Do you not want to know what it is I seek?"

"I assume you will tell me when I need to know."

"Indeed." The king looked searchingly into his eyes. "I wonder… does it not seem odd that I was so close at hand? You executed General Kirlon only three days ago, and yet here I am."

"I did not give it thought, Your Highness."

"Of course not. You are trained not to question me. Why would you ever dream of such dissent? But now, I want you to consider the situation. I need to know if you can guess what has brought you here before me today."

Akiri closed his eyes and gave the matter careful thought. He stood absolutely still and silent for several minutes. Then, when he had what he considered to be a solution, he opened his eyes. The king was waiting patiently.

"You have it then?" Zemel asked.

"I cannot say for certain, Your Highness, but my instincts tell me that you knew of General Kirlon's plan to assassinate me in advance. Your lack of surprise at the events I related when we spoke outside suggests this to be true. As did your statement that you had already heard of the volkar's involvement. If you were indeed previously aware of these facts, then setting up this trial must have some hidden purpose. Regardless of the House Galliani's wealth, you would never allow them to question your law that states it was my duty to act as I did. Nor would you have provided them with a warrant for my arrest. Not without a reason I am unaware of. Finally, that yourself, together with sufficient nobles to form the proper number of witnesses, were all close at hand suggests that you timed this meeting precisely. You wanted them to see me accused so that they might spread the word throughout the court."

Zemel raised an eyebrow. "And why would I do all this?"

"Because you intend to find me guilty," Akiri replied.

"Yes, I do," the king admitted. He then smiled. "You are absolutely right of course. Right in every respect. I knew that fool Kirlon would attempt to have you killed. His overblown ego would not allow him anything else. And I knew that you would do your duty when he failed. But I promise you that there is a very good reason behind all this subterfuge." He nodded to Kortain.

The old man stepped forward and produced a scroll from within the folds of his robe. Unfurling the document, he held it up so that Akiri could see the drawing of a magnificent scepter heavily bejeweled with diamonds, rubies, and emeralds. The handle was etched with strange symbols, and the top crowned with an eagle's claw clutching a black egg that, assuming the drawing was to some kind of scale, must easily have been the size of a man's fist.

"Do you recognize this?" Kortain asked.

Akiri shook his head.

"It is the Scepter of Xarbaal."

"I have read about it, My Lord," Akiri said. "It was carried by the Syrizian god of death."

"What else do you know about it?" Kortain pressed.

"Very little. The legend says it was stolen by the King of Syriz a thousand years ago. It drove him so mad that in the end his own children killed him in his sleep and hid the Scepter away."

"It is more than a legend," corrected Kortain. He rolled up the scroll and placed it back inside his robe. "The Scepter of Xarbaal really does exist. Your father stole it from the king, and this is what you must now recover for him."

Akiri furrowed his brow.

"You object?" asked Zemel.

"No, Your Highness. It's just that the Scepter of Xarbaal is said to be dangerous. Too dangerous to be wielded by mortal man. I fear only for your safety."

"Legends are often exaggerated," the king said, dismissively. "I wielded this Scepter myself. With its power I attempted to bring peace to this troubled land, but your father was corrupted by my enemies. He stole it and hid it away from me. Because of his betrayal, we have been forced to endure a never-ending war. I want you to help me bring peace at last."

"Just tell me what I must do," Akiri said, bowing his head.

Zemel drew a breath. "I have recently discovered that your father passed the Scepter on to his brother, Tuvarius. Only *he* knows of its location. Unfortunately, he is being protected by King Lanmar of Galfaria. I need you to gain your uncle's trust and find out where the Scepter has been hidden. Once you discover that, you must retrieve it and bring it to me. On your return to Acharia, report to your

Dul'Buhar training garrison and await my summons."

"It will be done," said Akiri. "I will leave at once."

"I'm afraid it will not be so easy," Zemel told him. "Tuvarius is far from a fool. He will know very quickly if you still have any connection to me. Should that happen, then all this business of bringing you here will have been for nothing. The only way to succeed is if you are truly separated from my power… and from your own. This will leave you vulnerable of course, but it is the only way you will be able to get close enough to him."

"How will this separation be achieved?"

The king held up the oath stone. "I must release you from your bond. Once done, all the strength and power that you receive from this stone will vanish. You will become a normal man, possessing only the gifts with which you were born."

The idea of losing his bond with the king – and with the Dul'Buhar – was devastating; far more daunting than the prospect of merely losing his strength. While still considering the consequences, Akiri realized that he had been staring at the floor for an uncomfortably long time. He lifted his head to meet the king's eyes with firm resolve. "I will carry out your will, Your Highness. Regardless of the cost."

The king took a step forward and placed his hands on Akiri's massive shoulders. "You will be richly rewarded for your service. This I swear."

"I would ask only that once the Scepter is in your hands, I am allowed to once again take my oath and return to my duties with my men."

"Should you succeed, I will grant you far more than that, Akiri."

Zemel gave him a fond squeeze before backing away. “What comes next may be unsettling, and what follows, even worse, but I trust you can endure.”

Akiri steeled himself and nodded. “I will, Your Highness.”

Fully extending his arm, King Zemel held out the oath stone in his open palm. “Jarduun Malakar!” he shouted, his voice booming like thunder.

The oath stone rose and hovered just a few inches above the king’s hand. Akiri felt an odd warmth penetrating his flesh, saturating him to the very core. Zemel then pulled his hand sharply back, and in a puff of dust, the suspended stone vanished.

At once, the warmth became a searing heat. His body stiffened and his eyes were blinded. Mercifully, this lasted for only a matter of seconds. As his sight returned, the pain subsided. But a moment later he found that his legs could no longer support his own weight. He fell hard to his knees. Every muscle in his once powerful body had been completely drained of strength.

“This condition will last only for a day or two,” Zemel assured him. “Though your former powers will not return until you once again swear on the oath stone, you will still retain the strength of a normal man. And with your many other skills, that should be enough.”

Akiri wanted to respond, but instead fell over onto his side.

“Bring the fools back in,” the king told Kortain. “Let’s get this over with.”

As the line of nobles re-entered, Akiri could hear the shocked whispers at seeing him lying helpless on the floor. Carlotta and Freidris came to the fore. The smug grins on their faces filled him with anger. They would get what they deserve soon enough, he consoled himself, remembering what the king had in store for them before departing the manor. For now, though, they were savoring their imagined victory.

"I have found Commander Akiri guilty of murder," Zemel announced. "The penalty for this is death."

Freidris smiled viciously. Akiri could tell that he was already imagining himself dealing the fatal blow.

"But I have taken into account his loyal service," the king continued. "Therefore, I will be merciful. Commander Akiri is to be expelled from the Dul'Buhar and exiled from my kingdom."

A loud gasp flew from Carlotta's mouth. "But, Your Highness!" she cried out.

Her outburst drew a furious glare from the king, but she pressed on regardless. "A member of my family has been murdered, and yet his killer is allowed to live. How can this be?"

"You will hold your tongue," snapped Zemel. "Or I will have it cut out."

The threat was sufficient. Carlotta regained control and lowered her head.

The king continued. "As you wish to have retribution, Akiri will endure thirty lashes at the hands of Lord Freidris. This is the end of the matter. The sentence will be carried out in the morning."

Rough hands pulled Akiri to his feet and dragged him outside, then tossed him back into the cage. He could feel a little of his strength returning, but not enough to do more than roll over onto his back. As he did so, a voice sounded.

"Just because the king has given you mercy, don't think

you're going to escape justice." It was Lady Carlotta standing beside the cage. "And after Freidris has beaten the hide off you tomorrow, I'll see that you receive it. Count on that, dog."

Akiri managed a weak laugh, which from the hissing curse spat at him, only served to infuriate her further. He smiled, imagining the look of surprise and horror on her face when the king unleashed his wrath upon her and her whelp. Still, he knew he should not take her threat lightly. She had clearly set something in motion with the intention of ensuring his death.

He closed his eyes and allowed sleep to take him. There was nothing else to be done for now. He needed to recover his strength. Without that, even walking away into exile would be an insurmountable obstacle.

That night, his dreams were troubled. Strange, disfigured faces shouted out from the heart of a raging inferno.

Do not seek the Scepter. Flee, or you will die.

But even in a dream, he would not bow down to fear. He was Akiri. Flee? Never. He *would* find the Scepter, and then rejoin his brothers… and his king.

Chapter Four

The chill morning air urged Akiri to wake just before dawn. Only the servants and guards were already up and about, busily preparing for when their masters saw fit to rise. He was now able to sit upright and lean against the bars while contemplating the coming day. The prospect of the lashes did not bother him at all. His limbs were still weak, but his mind remained perfectly strong. He had trained all his life to endure pain that would shatter the will of most men. He would not wail. He would not give them the pleasure of a single sound.

It was well into the morning before the king emerged from the house. He didn't look at Akiri at all – though Akiri was certain this snub was merely to make everything look as convincing as possible.

In ones and twos, the nobles gradually gathered around the cage. The guards and servants spread out further back amongst the tents, all of them jostling for the best vantage points. Freidris was standing with his mother alongside the king, a coiled leather whip with a vicious steel tip in his hand. He grinned malevolently at Akiri, who simply smiled back and gave him an elaborate wink. It had the desired effect. Freidris' face turned crimson with rage, his knuckles turning white with the tightness of his grip.

King Zemel nodded to a soldier standing beside the cage, and the door opened on tired hinges. Akiri was dragged out, tied to the bars, and his shirt pulled from his back.

"Get this over with, Freidris," Zemel ordered. "I have no desire to be here for any longer than I need be."

"Of course, Your Highness," he replied.

Akiri quieted his mind. He knew what to expect; he had felt the lash of a whip like this before. It took a focused mind to get through the pain. And a strong will.

The snap of the first blow echoed from the surrounding trees. Waves of agony shot through him, but he remained silent, accepting the pain as a part of his self. A part of his reality. There was nothing he could do to avoid it, so instead he embraced it fully. Again the whip struck. But this time the sensation was dulled. It was as if his flesh had now become a suit of armor, protecting him from much of the stinging impact. Again and again Freidris let the whip fly, his loud grunts attesting to the effort he was putting behind each lash.

Akiri heard the whispers coming from both noble and commoner alike. "Why does he not cry out?" they were all asking.

He wanted to shout, *Because I am Akiri of the Dul'Buhar.* But he held his tongue.

When the final blow was struck, he could hear Freidris panting and wheezing behind him.

"Release him," the king ordered.

When the bonds were cut, he refused to collapse or even to slump low. Keeping on his feet with his head held high was essential to his pride. Quickly he put his shirt back on. He would not allow Freidris the pleasure of gazing upon the brutal damage he had inflicted an instant longer than was necessary.

After a few deep breaths, though he was still feeling pathetically weak, enough of his strength had returned for him to walk without the need of support. In reaction to this, the sell-swords he had seen when first arriving pushed their way through the crowd and surrounded him. He noticed a sinister grin on Carlotta's face. Whatever her plan, it was likely to involve one or more of these men.

"Move it," growled a large sell-sword with a broad scar across his right cheek. Grabbing Akiri's arm, he shoved him in the direction of the road. It came as a shock to realize how much more powerful than himself the man was. It was an unfamiliar sensation.

"He is to be taken to the border," said the king. "If anything happens to him along the way, I shall hold each one of you responsible. Have I made myself clear?"

"Very clear, Your Highness," said another man, presumably the leader. He was tall and lean, with wavy auburn hair and sharp features. His leather armor was in better condition than that worn by the others. "He will arrive unharmed. You have my word on that."

Akiri was shoved again, this time almost losing his footing as he stumbled. He could feel blood oozing freely from the many open wounds across his back. His legs felt unusually heavy, and his arms hung limply at his sides, but he moved forward with as much purpose as he could muster.

The walk to the eastern border would take at least three days. Once there, he would need to find a way of acquiring a weapon, clothing, and enough gold to sustain himself for the journey to Galfaria. But before any of that, he would need to survive whatever Lady Carlotta had in store for him.

It was on the first night after they had made camp that more differences to his past life became apparent. The sell-swords secured him to a tree, then set about drinking and fighting until late into the night. Though his vision was still keen, he could no longer penetrate the shadows in anything like the way he had done before. Nor could he pick out the sounds of small night creatures that had previously come to him so easily. The pace of the day's march had hit him hard too. Normally, even after a whipping, it would have presented no challenge at all. Now, the sheer fatigue had him dozing involuntarily.

The chill morning air woke him just before dawn. Though his legs were still sore, he felt stronger and far more capable of travel. The mercenaries awoke less than an hour later. After a meager breakfast of flatbread and a few mouthfuls of water, they were soon underway.

This stronger start did not last long. It was not even midday when the first waves of nausea began to wash over him. He tried to focus his mind and control the churning in his stomach, but it was soon apparent that he could not. Unable to stop himself, he dropped to his knees and began vomiting repeatedly. Beads of sweat formed on his brow, while a sharp pain inched its way spitefully through his skull.

"What the hell is wrong with you?" demanded the leader. Akiri had heard him referred to as Borna.

Akiri was incapable of responding. The nausea was overpowering, and within moments, he had emptied his stomach completely. Utterly helpless, he was unable to control the violent spasms running through his body.

"We can't let him die," one of the men said. "King Zemel will flay us alive."

He felt a rough hand lift his chin. "He's white as a ghost." His shirt was then lifted. "Look here, Borna. His wounds. They've already pussed up."

"So that's it," remarked the leader. "I bet that bitch of a whore Carlotta poisoned the poor bastard."

"We should kill him and bury him in the woods," a low grumbling voice suggested.

"If we do, King Zemel's sure to know," Borna shot back. "He's a demon, that one. Eyes everywhere."

"What then?"

Borna knelt down to examine Akiri for a few moments. He then looked up to the others. "There used to be a healer living not far from here. Mended my leg a few years back. She might know what to do if she's still around."

Although he was unable to speak, the word *poisoned* repeated itself over and over in Akiri's mind. The thought of dying in such a way infuriated him; it was death through trickery, the lowest form of deceit. It was now obvious that Freidris had poisoned the whip, though it had to have been with something slow acting, so as not to rouse the king's suspicions. He tried to go over in his mind the different poisons he had come across in his studies, but it soon became too much. His head was now swimming crazily, and he was unable to move his limbs even the smallest amount.

The last thing he felt before darkness closed in was his body being lifted by two pairs of hands.

* * *

The dim light of dawn filtered in through his half-closed eyes. Akiri lay on his back. He struggled to rise, but with his hands shackled behind his back and straps fixed tightly across his neck, waist, and legs, it was impossible. His head was resting on one side, allowing him to see that he was in the rear of a wagon.

"Good," said a soft feminine voice. "I was hoping you would wake before they arrived."

"Where am I?" he croaked. His mouth was dry and his tongue swollen. The wagon shifted as someone climbed up. "Why am I in chains?"

"There is an answer to both of those questions, my handsome friend," she replied.

From his blind side, a delicate hand touched his knee and moved with teasing slowness up his inner thigh.

"What do you want?" he demanded.

"I want you inside me," she said, giving a tiny laugh. "Look at you. You are a brute. Such muscles. So much strength in that body of yours. But sadly for me – for you too, I think – we don't have the time for fun. Your new home awaits, and your master will be arriving soon."

"My master?"

She clicked her tongue. "Now, don't be angry with me. After all, I did save your life. By the time those brutes arrived at my cabin, you were about to cross into the next world. They were quite relieved when I promised to see that you made it to the border."

Akiri struggled against the chains and straps, but it was useless. "Let me go at once, witch!" he growled.

"Is that how you thank me?" The wagon jostled once more as she jumped down.

"I'll thank you with cold steel if you don't release me," he promised.

This drew a wistful laugh. "Is that so? I suppose it is a risk I must take. A man like you will bring too high a price to ignore. And as I have kept my promise to that oaf Borna,

I see no reason why I shouldn't profit from this. You never know. As you are such a handsome specimen, you might end up the plaything of some lonely noblewoman."

Akiri realized there was nothing he could say to sway her. Escape was his only option.

Doing his best not to rattle the chains, he popped his right thumb out of joint. Even so, the shackles were fastened tight, and it would be several minutes before he could free his hand.

The sound of hoofbeats approaching urged him to work faster.

"Ah, here they are now," she said. "Don't worry. I'll make them promise to be gentle."

Akiri listened carefully while continuing to struggle. He counted the steps of four horses. Not much of a challenge had he still possessed his former strength. But as things were, he would need to use surprise and cunning.

"Hey, witch," called a male voice. "What treasure have you brought me?"

"I'm no witch, Killian," she replied, without any trace of anger. "The only magic I possess lies between my legs."

"So I have heard, Farlana," he replied, laughing. "My man Guerry is quite taken with you. Swears to the gods that you will be his one day."

"If Guerry's cock was as big as his stomach, I might. But sadly for him, I require a better equipped man."

The joke drew a round of raucous laughter from the men, and Akiri counted four distinct voices. One for each mount, which meant they did not know that the woman had brought a slave to sell. Either that, or they intended him to walk.

He readied himself as, one by one, he felt the straps being removed.

"A big one," remarked Killian. "Where did you find him?"

"What difference does it make? Do you want him or not?"

There was a long pause. "Ten gold."

"Have you lost your mind? A man like this is worth twice that."

"Then sell him to someone willing to pay it."

"Fifteen."

"I'll give you twelve," Killian told her. "And if you say no, I will get back on my horse and go."

Farlana grumbled unhappily. "Twelve it is then, you tree-climbing rat."

Akiri heard the jingling of coins. Soon after that, he was pulled by the ankles from the wagon and dumped on his back in soft grass. With both his hands still behind him, no one could know that they were now free. He regarded the source of the voices.

The woman was a little older than her voice suggested. Though she had managed to cling onto an aspect of her youthful beauty, the small cluster of fine lines around her eyes betrayed her. She wore a low cut blouse together with a tattered wool skirt. Strings of colorful beads woven into her flaxen hair completed the image. Akiri had heard of such women who lived in the wild, making a living peddling potions and salves. The dim-witted and uneducated usually thought them to be witches, but he knew they were simply knowledgeable in the ways of herbs and healing. The poor or desperate often sought them out to help their sick and infirm.

Killian was a surprise. If his narrow green eyes, sharp features, and slight build didn't give him away, the tiny points on the tips of his ears certainly did. A Sylfari: renowned archers and trackers from the western highlands. They had no nation to speak of, choosing instead to live nomadic lives in small groups. Unlike the Drogba, their cousins in the south, they were rarely aggressive. In fact, they were well known for being free with their hospitality and humor, and could often be a welcome sight for weary travelers.

Killian smiled down at him. "Does he have a name?"

"The sell-swords who brought him to me didn't say," Farlana replied. "But in his fevered ramblings he did mention the name Akiri."

Killian raised an eyebrow. "Truly?" He knelt down to inspect his purchase more closely. "That name is not unfamiliar. Surely you are not the Akiri I have heard of? A man such as he would never have come to such a pass."

Akiri could see the legs of the other men on the far side of the wagon. He would need for them to come closer before making his move.

"But I must say," Killian continued, "you do have that special look in your eyes. One that I am all too familiar with. Perhaps you *are* Akiri." He stood upright. "We shall see soon enough."

Two of the men walked toward him. Both were large, but from their movements, not especially agile. And neither was wearing any kind of armor, only a leather jerkin and wool trousers. The short blades they carried at their sides were still sheathed. Now was the time.

The moment they leaned down to grab him, Akiri sprang to life. His two fists shot up in vicious punches, landing simultaneously in each man's crotch. Both doubled over, crying out in pain.

Scrambling up, Akiri seized the hilt of the sword nearest to his right hand. As it slid free from its scabbard, he turned to see Killian and Farlana backing away. Though the woman was clearly afraid, the Sylfari appeared to be wryly amused, the bow and quiver of white fletched arrows he carried no doubt the reason for his smile. In response, Akiri hastily positioned himself to the right of the remaining man, who was already upon him with sword in hand, hoping this would make it much more difficult for Killian to get a clear shot at him – though so far he hadn't made any move at all to unsling his bow.

No longer possessing his once uncanny speed, Akiri still found the clumsy swings from his opponent were easy to block. With a flurry of strikes, he opened a deep gash on the man's left forearm, forcing him to retreat a few paces.

It was time to finish off Killian's two other helpers, but before he could turn, a powerful pair of arms wrapped themselves around his body from behind. It was the man whose sword he had taken. Grunting heavily, he lifted Akiri completely off his feet before slamming him hard onto the ground. Gasping from the impact, he rolled desperately to one side to avoid the swinging boot that quickly followed, but there was no time to scramble to his feet. As his foe moved in closer to aim a second kick, Akiri jerked the tip of his blade sharply upwards, piercing flesh near the top of the man's thigh. It was far from a killing strike, but the wound was more than enough to force a pained cry and have him backing away, temporarily out of the fight. The third man, still red-faced from his injured testicles and snarling furiously, had drawn his sword and was almost upon him.

A brief whistle was followed by an arrow suddenly embedding itself into the ground only a foot or so away from Akiri's head.

"That's quite enough," Killian called. He had already

notched another arrow and had it aimed directly at Akiri's heart. "I've seen all I wanted to see."

Knowing that he was trapped, Akiri froze. To underestimate the skill of the Sylfari would be a fatal mistake. The other three men gathered beside their leader, their hateful stares burning into him.

"Yes, I believe you might be *the* Akiri after all," remarked Killian, smiling broadly. "Retrieve my shackles, Durst."

The man Akiri had stabbed in the leg gave a surly nod and then limped over to the horses.

"My men are going to secure your hands," Killian continued. "You will not resist while they attend to this. If you do, I will place an arrow through your left… no… your right eye. Nod if you understand."

Akiri nodded.

Durst returned a moment later bearing a pair of silver manacles.

A faint smile appeared on Killian's face. "I assume that you are quite adept at freeing yourself from ordinary bindings. Fortunately, I keep a pair of Sylfari bracelets with me for just such occasions. Do feel free to test them."

Testing them was pointless, of course. The Dul'Buhar possessed several pairs which had proven to be inescapable.

Once Durst had secured him, he and the other injured man began treating their wounds while Farlana hurriedly took her leave. Clearly shaken by what had happened, she glanced back over her shoulder constantly as the wagon rolled away. Killian watched after her, shaking his head.

"She was quite stunning as a young girl," he remarked. "For a human, at least." He made a show of strapping the bow across his back. "Incidentally, if you have any thoughts of trying to escape…"

In a flash, the bow was once more in his hands and he had let fly an arrow. The missile buried itself into the front of the departing wagon, just beside where Farlana was sitting. The woman cried out in fright before urging the horse on even faster.

"Since when were the Sylfari involved in the slave trade?" asked Akiri, taking full note of the speed and skill displayed.

"As a rule we are not," he replied, his smile returning. "But I have been forced to find alternative ways to get by. It's hard to raise a family on a tracker's wage, and I'm not much of a tinker or smith. Slave trading is only a minor aspect of my endeavors, though. Most of the time I'm no more than an honest merchant."

Akiri sneered. "Is that what you are? Honest?"

"Of course," he insisted. "As honest as any other merchant, at least. But I find it profitable to occasionally delve into the darker side of the human world. You humans do so enjoy enslaving each other. *I* just take advantage of this. That's all."

"And do you admit to your own people this side of your business?" Akiri was well aware of how much the Sylfari detested slavery. In fact, though most unlikely to attack genuine travelers, they had been known to fill slave traders with arrows if they happened upon their caravans.

Killian's smile vanished in a split second before slowly returning. "They are not aware of my involvement, nor will they ever be. The fact you know a little of our ways tells me that you are not uneducated."

He glanced over at his men, who were still treating their wounds. "If you are really Akiri, I am faced with quite a dilemma. I could sell you to King Nehala. I'm sure he would love the chance to speak with you. But then kings are not to be trusted. He is just as likely to kill me and take you anyway. Then I'd be dead *and* out of pocket by twelve gold pieces.

"I could sell you to one of my clients. But even if you are not the renowned Akiri, it is very clear you are not the sort of man who can live as a slave. At the very least, I fear my reputation would be ruined should I loose you on some unsuspecting noble. You might even kill them. Then I would lose a customer, and my good name." He scratched his chin thoughtfully. "So what to do with you? It is a conundrum."

The men began mounting their horses.

"You could just set me free," Akiri suggested. "As you pointed out so rightly, I will never suffer slavery."

"But then where would that leave me? Even if I were willing to lose some gold, you have injured my men. I cannot allow that to go unanswered. They may be filthy brutes, but they are *my* filthy brutes. I'm afraid I must think of another way to profit from this." He gestured for Akiri to walk ahead of the horses. "And don't forget – I'll be riding right behind you."

The reminder was unnecessary. Akiri cleared his mind. Patience was his ally. He was Akiri, and he would not be defeated by a band of slavers led by a rogue Sylfari.

They walked until dusk. Occasionally one of Killian's men would ride close enough to let fly a spiteful boot, though this tactic came to an abrupt stop when Akiri ducked and planted his shoulder firmly into the horse's ribs. The animal reared and bucked, throwing its rider hard to the ground.

Sitting there nursing his bruises, the man looked up at Killian, clearly wishing him to mete out some kind of punishment to their prisoner.

The Sylfari simply laughed. "Leave him alone and you

won't get hurt," he warned. "The great Akiri is not to be trifled with. Even someone as stupid as you should know that."

The man rose and brushed himself off, grumbling curses as he hurried away to catch his horse.

Shortly after nightfall, Akiri caught sight of a campfire in a small clearing ahead. Four armed men came forward to greet them as they arrived. Further back, at the edge of the firelight, it was possible to see six wagons parked beside a narrow, eastbound road. All were filled with various goods, no doubt for trading.

Durst made a point of securing Akiri to a nearby tree with unnecessary tightness, and it was only after a short argument with Killian that he grudgingly fed him a few mouthfuls of the beef and potato stew that was cooking over the fire.

"I'll enjoy watching you bleed," he muttered, quietly enough for Killian not to hear.

That night, Akiri took careful stock of his surroundings and listened. The snatches of conversation he was able to overhear confirmed that he was in Rashkar, a kingdom to the east of Acharia. Wherever he was being taken, he was at least heading in the right direction. The road he could see would almost certainly lead to a larger and more frequently traveled highway that stretched east to west between the cities of Gothar and Lomhar.

Killian was sleeping on his side, facing him, a few yards away, his bow and quiver within easy reach. The rest of the men had taken up positions as close to comfortable as they could find, and were snoring and grunting.

He gently tested the chain holding him to the tree. Killian's eyes instantly popped open, his hand automatically moving toward his bow. With a sigh, Akiri relaxed his body and closed his eyes. An opportunity would present itself eventually. Killian was no fool, but his men were of decidedly limited intelligence. One of them would make a mistake before long; and when they did, he would be ready to take full advantage of it.

As the days passed, it became clear that they were not heading for any major city. Almost immediately after reaching the main road they left it again, turning north onto a small trail that led into a heavily forested area, a natural border dividing Acharia from Rashkar's lake region. Here, small fishing villages lined the banks of dozens of lakes, all of them fed by the Manitor River. Most of the inhabitants were simple fisherman and tradesmen, though the remote nature of some villages was also known to attract a good number of far less honest characters.

It was a week in, after catching sight of a bundle of yellow blooms in the back of a wagon, that Akiri realized exactly how far from the moral path of his people Killian had wandered. He recognized the plants immediately as being Frizzia, the seedpods of which were used to make *lovus*, a powerful and highly addictive narcotic that was illegal in most regions. He cast an accusing gaze at the Sylfari, who on this occasion could only avert his eyes in shame.

The next morning, a group of six horsemen appeared out of the woods. They advanced swiftly, and for a moment the situation was tense, prompting Killian's men to hurriedly arm themselves. Akiri's alertness increased as he watched for his opportunity. The fog of battle might easily hide his escape, but in short order Killian raised a hand in greeting and let out a high-pitched whistle, and his men sheathed their weapons.

The lead horse carried an ebony-skinned man wearing a white cloth vest and loose-fitting black trousers. A long curved blade hung from his broad leather belt, and a row of throwing knives was attached to a strap slung across his muscular chest. He slid nimbly from the saddle to grip Killian fondly by the shoulders. His five companions remained on their mounts a few yards away from the wagons.

After a brief discussion, Killian brought the newcomer to the rear wagon where Akiri was standing. "What do you think?" he asked. "Will he do?"

The man took a step forward, but Killian caught his arm. "Not too close, my friend. This one will rip your throat out if given the chance."

The man smiled. "Is that right? And you're willing to part with him?"

Killian spread his hands. "That all depends on how reasonable you are willing to be."

"Twenty gold."

Killian sniffed. "Have you been at the lovus pipe? This is the mighty Akiri we are talking about."

The man cocked his head. "Who?"

"Don't play stupid with me. Twenty-five… plus three percent of the take."

"I think it is you who has been at the lovus pipe, my pointy-eared friend." He scrutinized Akiri closely. "Twenty… and two percent of the take."

"You are a greedy bastard. You know that, don't you?"

"Take it or leave it."

Killian heaved a sigh. "Very well. We have a bargain."

The man gripped him by the forearm. "Have him there an hour before nightfall."

Without another word, he returned to his horse and rode off with his men.

Killian watched him go, and then turned to Akiri. "It would seem Fortune has smiled on me. Though not on you, I'm afraid." Without waiting for a response, he strode away and sprang up into the saddle. "Let's get moving, lads. Our guest has an appointment he cannot miss."

His words brought shouts of approval, as well as sinister smiles from the two men Akiri had injured. He could already guess at what Killian had in store for him. If he was right, it might well be his chance to escape. The fire of anger burned in his stomach when he looked at the Sylfari, but he had to push this aside. Anger could easily cloud a man's judgment.

They continued for several more hours before pulling up at a gated trail, where four rough looking armed guards were standing watch. After a terse exchange, the wagons were allowed through. Here the forest thinned, and Akiri could smell a stream or small river nearby, which he caught a glimpse of when they came to a rickety wooden bridge spanning a ten-foot-wide creek. Again, there were men standing guard, but unlike those at the gate, these took a special interest in Akiri, whispering to one another and smiling wolfishly.

The whistle of flutes combined with loud shouts told him that their destination was fast approaching. Soon the trees gave way to sparse patches of trampled grass and red clay. The stench of unwashed bodies, urine, and strong spirits rose up to assault his sense of smell. Several dilapidated wooden shacks were scattered about, along with a stable and an abandoned trading post. A smugglers' camp, Akiri reasoned, given its placement and state of disrepair. That or a dying settlement.

Ahead lay another group of shacks as well as a tavern, but what caught his eye was a tall, round structure with an open roof just beyond the last building. Akiri recognized it for what it was: an amphitheater, though a pale shadow of the kind found in cities throughout the world that rang with cheers and groans at the echoes of chariot races and lethal bouts. There, typically free men fought. Slaves did not make good fighters; they died too quickly. There was no entertainment in that.

This place was very different. Here, there would be no rules at all. Here, a man might be pitted against savage beasts, and terrified slaves would be slaughtered by heavily armed champions purely for the delight of the fanatical crowd. This was the kind of place where the demons of the world came to enjoy their sport.

Akiri was pushed into an individual holding cage beside the arena. Several other unfortunate men were also awaiting their fates in similar cages – though all but himself appeared half-starved and already on the verge of collapse. They were fodder, nothing more. Obviously, he was to be the main attraction of the evening.

Killian left four men to watch his cage while he vanished into the crowd, and Akiri's thoughts turned to escape. He needed to be free of the Sylfari shackles, and that should come about soon enough. Almost certainly, they would be removed before he was made to fight, if only to prolong the entertainment. He looked over at the other men, certain that none would pose any kind of challenge even in his reduced state. He would try to end their lives quickly and cleanly. No sense in causing a condemned man to suffer needlessly.

Dozens of people stopped by to view the latest combatants, with all of them taking a special interest in Akiri.

By nightfall, the place was abuzz with activity. The numerous blazing torches served to highlight even further the sheer squalor of the smugglers' haven. While whores and thieves plied their trades on the inebriated and unwary, small groups of ragged children darted about the debris-strewn ground, begging with sorrowful expressions for coins and food. Mostly they were ignored, or occasionally sent on their way with a sharp blow to the head. Akiri could feel only disgust that people would choose to live such callous and pointless lives.

From inside the arena, the impatient shouts of the rapidly swelling crowd began to drown out all other sounds. Killian returned, a scowl carved deeply into his face. He regarded Akiri with what might have been the slightest hint of pity. "You'll be going in last," he said, raising his voice to overcome the roar.

"And should I survive?"

He sighed. "You won't. You are without hope."

Akiri watched as he stalked away. The Sylfari's reaction was significant. Clearly, whatever he would be facing, it would not be the pathetic men imprisoned beside him. This was confirmed less than an hour later when, one by one, they were taken from their cages and led into the arena. Akiri could hear feral snarls and screeches, quickly followed by the screams of dying men and hideous shouts of approval from the crowd. A beast. He could not recognize the sounds it was making, but he was certain that this creature was what he would soon be forced to battle.

In less than two hours, only Akiri remained. He calmed his breathing and slowed his heart rate. Three men approached with crossbows, while a fourth unlocked the cage and pointed to a small archway.

"We've been warned you might try something," he said, eyeing Akiri warily. "These lads are here to see that you don't."

The crossbowmen were wisely standing too far back to be rushed. With little choice, he entered the archway as instructed. An iron gate slammed shut behind him, and he found himself in a short, narrow passage. Straight ahead, a wooden door remained closed. Akiri could hear someone announcing the next fight, promising the baying mob that this would be the most exciting spectacle they had ever witnessed.

"I'll have my shackles, if you don't mind."

He turned to see Killian standing on the other side of the gate. "What am I to fight?" he asked.

"Does it matter? But do you really wish to fight with them on? I could always remove them from your corpse instead, if you wish."

Akiri presented his hands through the bars. With nimble fingers, Killian removed the shackles and sighed. "I'm sorry about this. I had hoped you'd have at least a fighting chance to live. But it was not meant to be, I'm afraid. Farewell."

A moment later the wooden door was pulled open, allowing light from the arena to flood through. Cautiously, Akiri approached, pausing on the threshold. The fifty-foot-diameter sand-covered floor was soaked with large patches of fresh blood and littered with chunks of mangled flesh. The spectator seats climbed all the way to the very top of the building, every one occupied by a chanting customer eager to witness more carnage. With bloodlust-contorted expressions, their shouts and whistles grew to almost ear-shattering proportions as Akiri stepped further in. The door closed behind him with an ominous boom.

Directly across from him lay an identical door. On a small platform three rows of seats up stood a tall man in colorful robes holding a long wooden staff. He smiled at Akiri with a mouthful of half-rotted teeth.

A semi-hush developed as he swept the staff over his head ceremoniously. "Ladies and gentlemen," he announced. "I give you the mighty – the brave – the legendary – Akiri!"

The crowd erupted once more, the furious cheers shaking the very fabric of the arena. Ignoring this, Akiri's eyes searched for an escape route. The wall surrounding the arena floor was ten feet high, with armed guards spaced evenly all around the top. It was hard to imagine any hope of being able to scale this barrier before being hacked to bits.

He was still looking for a possible escape route when the door opposite began to creak open. A low growl emanated from the darkness beyond. A moment later, a pair of reptilian eyes glowed bright yellow. Akiri crouched, ready for whatever might come forth; but when it appeared, he quickly realized that this was a creature he could not have prepared himself for.

Its crimson scales shimmered in the torchlight as it crept out onto the sands. Akiri was momentarily stunned. A dragon. Although a juvenile, standing no higher than a large dog, its dagger-like talons and razor-sharp teeth more than made up for its size. To prevent it from flight, its wings had been tied to its body by a leather harness wrapped around its torso. Not that this was going to restrict it in any other way. Muscles rippled with each step it took.

Dragons this young could not breathe fire, Akiri knew this much, but it would not need fire to rip him apart. Even with his former strength and speed to aid him, defeating this creature would have been a monumental task. But now he didn't stand any chance at all. At best, all he could do was delay things for a short time.

Akiri noticed a chain fastened to the beast's neck that led back into the holding area. As he circled left, the dragon matched his movements precisely. He had no idea how intelligent these creatures might be. None had been seen in Acharia since the uprising, and in other lands they were remorselessly hunted. Some folk had even claimed they were now extinct, but this one was very much alive and moving with clear intent.

He waited until he was close enough and had a clear sight of the chain before diving low to make a grab at it. The dragon reacted instantly, but Akiri was able to raise the chain with both hands just in time. The dragon's jaws clamped down on it, its teeth biting on the metal that had been shoved inside its mouth much like the bit on a horse. The force of its body pushed Akiri back to the wall; its snout was only inches from his face, easily close enough for the stench of flesh on its breath to fill his nostrils. The dragon shook its head wildly and swiped a claw at Akiri's head and chest. He twisted away and kicked with all his strength. For an instant, he thought he had pulled himself clear. He had saved himself from being shredded to pieces, but it was not a total evasion. His trailing shoulder was caught. The contact was little more than a brush but was still sufficient to open a row of painful cuts. Blood seeped rather than gushed.

The dragon backed away, angrily spitting the chain from its mouth. Akiri scrambled to his feet, preparing for its next attack, but he didn't have to wait very long. With an ear-splitting screech, the creature leapt for his throat. Akiri sidestepped, but with an incredible display of agility, the dragon twisted in mid-air and brought its long tail swooping down to strike him squarely on his already injured shoulder. He fell hard on the sands, knowing immediately that the shoulder was dislocated.

Ignoring the dull throbbing pain, he grabbed his useless arm and shoved upward to pop the joint back into place as the clack of talons told him there was no time to get back on his feet. All he could do was thrust out his arms, planting his hands around the creature's neck just as it reached him. The smooth scales were almost impossible to grip, but Akiri squeezed with all he had, at the same time pushing at the ground with his feet in order to keep scrambling back just beyond the dragon's vicious bite.

There was only ever going to be one eventual winner. The creature's strength was tremendous. In less than a minute, Akiri found himself unable to hold the beast back any longer. His arms were on the point of collapse. He was beaten, but he would not die sniveling. Just as the dragon opened its jaws to deliver what would most certainly have been a fatal bite, he looked it fully in the eye.

It was as if he had been struck by a bolt of lightning. His limbs instantly became numb and his head began spinning. Several seconds passed before he realized that he was now lying flat on his back, eyes staring vacantly up at the night sky. As he regained his senses, the noise of the crowd, all but forgotten during the heat of combat, filtered back in. Gasps of disbelief and vile curses were descending like a vast, vulgar cloud. Scrambling to his knees, he urgently scanned the arena and found the dragon. Incredibly, it had backed away and was crouched close to the door where Akiri had entered.

He realized that somehow the power was returning to his muscles. Not a normal man's power, but the same incredible power he had been gifted through the magic of the oath stone. And there was more. He could sense the dragon's thoughts. Not in human words, but in emotion and intent. He felt its distress. Whatever had just happened, the beast was frightened and confused.

For a moment, all eyes were upon the cowed creature, the promise of human sacrifice seemingly forgotten. This was the chance he had been waiting for. The ten-foot-high wall was no longer an obstacle. In little more than a single breath, he was over it and had disarmed the nearest guard. Before the man had any proper grasp on what was happening, Akiri rammed the blade through his gullet and kicked his body into the crowd.

The other guards started rushing toward him, shoving people aside as they advanced. Akiri grinned viciously. With all of his strength returned, he could slaughter this lot like sheep. Only a pained cry from the dragon diverted his attention. The chain attached to its neck was being pulled tight, dragging it back into the holding area. As if driven by some protective instinct, he leapt back down onto the arena floor and swung the sword hard down on the chain. As the metal links parted, the blade shattered, leaving him with only a few inches of steel on the hilt with which to fight. Still unable to understand what was happening, the dragon backed away fearfully.

"It's all right," Akiri told it in a firm yet reassuring tone. "I'm going to help you."

Two guards jumped down, swords drawn. Akiri turned to face them, and in a movement far too rapid to follow, thrust what remained of his weapon sharply across the first man's chest. Without armor to penetrate, the jagged end of the blade sliced deep.

The second man, startled by Akiri's newfound speed and agility, drew back. Akiri sniffed contemptuously. *Coward.* As the first man crumpled to his knees, blood gushing down his stomach, Akiri relieved him of his sword and, in a series of blinding strikes, cut the remaining guard to ribbons before he was able to so much as raise the tip of his blade. The rest of the men atop the wall wisely decided to stay where they were.

Akiri turned back to the dragon and held out his palm. "Stay calm, my friend. I want to cut the harness from you. Then you will be free to fly again."

The dragon seemed to accept what he was saying and lowered its head. Akiri carefully slipped the blade beneath the harness and sliced through the main strap. For a short time, the creature remained motionless. Then it looked up, once again meeting Akiri's eyes. Waves of appreciation washed through him like a torrent. The dragon then spread its wings. They shivered at first, blood coursing through them as they unfurled, beating at the air to work out the pains from having been tied down for so long.

Akiri could not help but smile as it craned its neck and let out an elated cry. Its wings began pounding furiously, stirring up great clouds of sand and dust. Within seconds, it had risen above the level of the surrounding wall and had turned its gaze on those in the seats.

Their terrified screams quickly reached a crescendo. Only minutes before, they had been baying to see the blood of others; now they were desperately trampling over one another in a blind panic to preserve their own. After completing a slow full circuit of the auditorium, the dragon let out a mighty roar that spoke more clearly than anything of the contempt it felt for them. With a great thrust of its wings, it then rose straight up through the open roof and into the night sky.

Back down on the arena floor, more armed men poured in through an entrance in the stands, these carrying bows. Akiri sprang forward and once again scaled the wall. Only two men barred his way, but both quickly fell back when he approached. He had an almost uncontrollable urge to chase them down and exact revenge for their part in the capture and confinement of the dragon. Only his iron discipline forced him to push these feelings aside.

Outside, people were either running aimlessly or standing rock-still and gazing skyward with fearful expressions as the call of the dragon drifted down from the darkness above. People cringed and cried out in fear, but the sound was a beautiful melody to Akiri's ears. It was the sound of joy. The sound of freedom.

He scanned the chaos until spotting one of Killian's men. Like most of the others, the man was occupied solely in looking upwards for the dragon and paying no heed to his surroundings. Akiri simply walked up behind him, grabbing his collar with one hand and pressing the sword to his throat with the other.

"Where is Killian?" he demanded in his ear.

The man froze for a moment before answering. "He…he's over there." He pointed to a nearby row of buildings.

"Thank you," Akiri said. With a swift tug, he ran the blade across the man's neck. Before his body even hit the ground, Akiri had already removed the dagger from his victim's belt and was heading toward the direction indicated.

Pushing his way through the still frantic crowd, he rounded the side of the first building and immediately spotted Killian readying his horse. The same three men were already mounted nearby. The wagons, now empty of goods and horseless, were obviously being left behind.

"Quickly, lads," Killian ordered. "I want to be well away from here by dawn."

Akiri crouched low. Killian's men would be easy enough to deal with. But the Sylfari still had his bow strapped to his back. If he wasn't careful, that could still pose a very real threat.

"How do you think that bloody dragon got loose?" asked one of the men.

Killian didn't bother to respond. A rough voice calling his name from the corner of the next building a moment later captured his attention. Into view stormed the dark-skinned man they had encountered earlier that day. His eyes were blazing, and his hand was resting firmly on the hilt of his sword.

Killian looked up and smiled. "Ah, Jerral. I hear you've had a spot of trouble."

Three more of Jerral's gang appeared and took up position just behind him. "That slave you sold me has killed three of my men, and cost me my dragon," he growled.

Killian shrugged. "I *did* warn you to be careful. You knew who you were dealing with. Or did you think I was lying when I told you who he was?"

Jerral continued to glare, his muscles flexing and his jaw tight. "You knew damn well what you were doing, you bastard. Unloading your problems on me. *That's* what. Now I'm out a whole heap of fucking gold because of you. The dragon alone was worth at least a thousand."

"I'm sorry to hear this," Killian replied. "But why is it my fault? It was your arena. Your dragon. And your responsibility."

His three men on horseback eyed the trio accompanying Jerral. The hostility between the two groups virtually crackled. Finally, Killian held up his hand.

"Look, my friend," he said. "I genuinely feel bad for your troubles. And to show you the extent of my goodwill…" He paused to reach into his saddlebag and pull out a small purse.

Jerral sneered. "You can't honestly think that is enough to compensate me."

"Here's what I think, old friend. I think you should take the gold I am offering. Then run and find a nice dark place to hide. You tried to send Akiri to his death, after all. He could be anywhere by now. And from what I've heard, he is not the forgiving sort."

Jerral looked around nervously, but quickly regained his composure. "I don't fear Akiri. But right now, you should fear me. Those empty wagons tell me you have enough gold on you to fully compensate me for your treachery. So you had better think about reaching in that saddlebag again, and this time–"

These were Jerral's final words. Before he was even aware that Killian was reaching into his quiver, an arrow thudded deep into the center of his chest. Clutching desperately at the shaft, he fell forward and then rolled onto his side.

It was the signal for chaos. The three mounted men drew their swords and spurred their horses forward into the attack. Ignoring this, Killian shouldered his bow and calmly approached Jerral. After retrieving his arrow, he watched without emotion as the fallen man coughed and spluttered his last few seconds of life pitifully away.

This was Akiri's moment. The sinews of his legs exploded into life, spanning half of the distance between them before Killian reacted to his presence. Even so, the Sylfari was still fast enough to unsling his bow again and notch the arrow already in his hand. But Akiri was prepared for this. With a sharp flick of his wrist while still in motion, he hurled the dagger, and its solid iron handle thudded into the center of Killian's forehead. It was a staggering blow, and more than enough to send his arrow flying wide right.

No more than a heartbeat later, Akiri's shoulder slammed into Killian's chest, toppling him over. At close quarters, it was no longer a contest. The slender Sylfari had no chance against Akiri's vastly superior strength and was easily held in place.

The other six men were still engaged in a furious fight of their own and had not yet noticed this intervention. Akiri pulled Killian sharply to his feet and pressed the sword to his neck.

"Kill them," he commanded, shoving his captive over to one side so that he could retrieve his dropped bow.

The Sylfari hesitated. "Which ones?"

"All of them."

Killian stiffened, but some added pressure from the blade and the resultant trickle of blood was enough to convince him that he had no choice in the matter. In rapid succession, he loosed six arrows into the unsuspecting men. Each shot was precise and caused instant death.

"Very good," Akiri told him, taking the bow with his free hand and tossing it far out of reach.

"I know that you intend to kill me," Killian said, no fear in his voice. "But before you do, allow me to make you an offer."

Akiri grabbed him by the hair and snatched his head sharply back. "What can you offer that I cannot take from you now anyway?"

"Aid," he replied.

"You think to offer me your help? And why would I need it?"

"I know you can take my gold and a horse," he replied. "Which I assume is the reason you are here. But there is something else I possess that you cannot take. It must be given."

"Speak sense."

"Spare my life and I will give you my Shazkra."

Akiri had come across the word, though was unsure of its meaning.

"It is a soul debt," Killian explained. "One you can collect at any time from any Sylfari you chance upon. No member of our race will ever refuse you. It is a valuable thing to have, given the right circumstances, and surely worth the life of a wretched outlaw like me."

Akiri paused to give the offer careful consideration. It was true such things could be useful. And the road ahead would certainly be filled with unknown perils. "If I accept this offer, what will you do?" he eventually asked.

"First, I will thank the gods that you have spared me. After that… I suppose I must hire some new men and seek out fresh opportunities."

Akiri almost laughed aloud. No promises of leading a reformed life. No offers to make amends for past deeds by doing good for others. At least he could not fault the truthfulness of the answer.

He removed the blade from Killian's throat and spun him around. "Very well. Give me this Shazkra. Keep your pathetic life."

Killian sighed with relief and removed a thin chain from around his neck. Attached was a silver teardrop with a single diamond set in the center. "This was given to me by my mother," he said. "Within is held a small portion of my essence. Do not put it on unless you intend to collect the debt. And only do so in the presence of the Sylfari whose aid you need."

"And what would happen if I were to put it on without a Sylfari present?"

"My essence would escape and the charm will be useless. We Sylfari can sense the souls of our own kind."

Akiri looked at the Shazkra for a short time before shoving it into his pocket. "Now I will be having your gold and a horse."

Killian pointed to his mount, which had wandered a few yards away. "Take mine. All I possess is packed away in the saddlebag. Including my gold."

Akiri gave him a long look, then gathered the mount.

"Do not judge me too harshly, Akiri," Killian called, having retrieved one of his fallen men's horses. "I did not abandon the ways of my people easily."

"It is not for me to pass judgment," he replied. "Live as you will."

Akiri spurred his horse into motion and steered it toward the road leading from the village. The panic spawned by the events in the arena was still at a fever pitch. He looked at his hand and made a fist. With his strength returned, he would be much better able to serve his king. But he would be needing far more than brute force to gain the trust of his uncle.

Far above, the dragon called to him. Akiri looked up, smiling. It was…

No, he quickly corrected himself. Not *it… she. She* was free. The bliss of the dragon flowed through him, and for a moment he could almost feel the rush of wind from under her wings on his flesh. Unsure of how it had come about, he knew that they were now connected in some strange and wonderful way.

He concentrated his mind on the road ahead. Unanswerable questions could drive a man to distraction. And distractions could be fatal.

Chapter Five

The guards at both the bridge and the gate took one look at his resolute expression and made no attempt to stop him. It was their lucky day.

Knowing that the journey to Galfaria would take several weeks, Akiri stopped off first at the city of Gothar to collect supplies and suitable clothing. Though his name was well known in this region, his face was far less so, allowing him to ride openly on the road. Also, any bandits would be most unlikely to pick on an armed rider of such fearsome appearance.

The dragon had gone, though he had no idea where. All he knew for sure was that he could no longer sense her presence. His newly regained strength had not faded, though, so he remained content. He considered calling out to her, but bearing in mind the amount of attention this might attract should the dragon appear, thought better of it. He had freed her. That was enough.

The city of Vurna was Acharia's capital, and the surrounding region was widely known for its lush vineyards and fertile farmland. Both the present king and his father before him had managed to keep peace in their land by trading equally with two major powers. Neither Hath on its southern border nor Balnaria to the west was what might be considered an ally, but their dependence on grain put Galfaria in a unique position as a keeper of peace.

His own home of Acharia had no such luxury. Akiri could not remember a year without war. Had their northern border not been on the Almari Sea, the people would have likely starved long ago. The nations on the far north shores feared King Zemel too much to be a threat. Instead, they provided him with a regular supply of wheat and other trade goods.

Akiri *had* heard the stories of how his king had gone mad; not that he believed them for a second. Even if he had not been a loyal servant, he had spent enough time in King Zemel's company to know that he was perfectly sane. Ruthless and sometimes cruel – yes. Calculating and cunning – yes again. But all the time, absolutely sane.

During the journey, Akiri tried to gather as much information on the latest happenings in Galfaria as possible, but with little success. Events of note rarely happened there, so this was not especially surprising. What little he did learn was mostly concerned with the crown prince's forthcoming birthday celebrations. Rumor had it that this was to be a truly magnificent spectacle. Akiri would be arriving in Vurna less than a week ahead of the set date, so he couldn't help but wonder if he might be able to use the festivities to get inside the palace. Peaceful nations were often careless about security.

It was just before midday when he eventually crossed the border into Galfaria. A stiff northern breeze brought with it the promise of winter. The fields he passed had already been harvested, and merchants traveling along the roads were numerous.

Akiri was accustomed to people looking aside whenever he approached. After all, he had been the commander of the Dul'Buhar. One did not seek his attention. Now, his intimidating appearance was attracting more than a few curious glances. Though not actually in hiding, he decided it would be best to pass as inconspicuously as possible.

He stopped at a small village to purchase a heavy wool cloak with a deep hood attached. Wearing it, he appeared much more like a monk than a legendary warrior. Now so far away from Acharia, both his name and face would be meaningless to all but a few. However, those few who were aware of him would be soldiers. And he had no intention of inviting an encounter with the Galfarian army.

He arrived at the gates of Vurna the following morning. The roads had become packed with wagons, horses, and pedestrians the closer he came. It seemed that people were determined to gather early for the prince's birthday celebration.

The city walls, though fairly high, were not particularly thick. Unlike those in the cities of his home, these had not been built with the purpose of repelling an invading army. Here, they were likely designed to keep out nothing more threatening than unwanted individuals and gangs of smugglers.

The main gates were flung wide open, though they were still guarded by at least three dozen soldiers. Most of them were busy making random checks on people and wagons as they entered. Akiri was approached by a young soldier with a friendly smile.

"Here for the celebration?" he asked. "Or just passing through?"

"Both," Akiri replied.

"Name?"

"Akiri." The moment he spoke, he knew he may have made a mistake, but a lifetime of always telling the truth had made it difficult to do anything else. Fortunately, the soldier did not seem to be familiar with his name.

"And where will you be staying?"

"I haven't decided yet."

The young man frowned. "You do realize there are no rooms left at any of the inns or boarding houses?"

"What temples are here?" he asked, hoping that his monk-like garb would now show itself to have been an excellent choice.

"Only two. Tyr Fayne and Imheti."

Akiri nodded gratefully. "Thank you." Tyr Fayne was the goddess of the harvest, worshipped mostly in the north and around Galfaria. Women only. Imheti, on the other hand, was unexpected – a water god of the eastern desert.

"But I doubt you'll have much luck there either, I'm afraid," the soldier told him. He pointed north. "There's a camp outside the wall just beyond the last guard post. That's where most visitors are staying. It's safe enough. But you'll need to be there before nightfall. Any vagrants found inside the city once the gates are closed are fined ten gold."

Akiri smiled. "Again, I thank you."

The soldier smiled back and waved him through.

Akiri was impressed with what he saw. Vurna was a city of elegant design and architecture. Unlike the cold gray stone of Acharian cities, its two- and three-story buildings were colorful and adorned with expertly crafted friezes. Most of the houses also featured spacious balconies fronted with intricate wrought iron railings. Below these, the roads had been paved with red cobblestones, while the broad sidewalks were well maintained and clean.

With wagons and horses clogging each avenue, progress was accordingly slow. But walking would have been little better under the current conditions. Traveling merchants pushing handcarts overflowing with various trinkets and oddities competed with skilled street performers and musicians for space on the pavements, all of them seeking to gather an audience from the crowds passing by. The truth of the rumors was obvious: the crown prince's birthday celebration had indeed attracted all manner of people from far and wide.

In the near distance, Akiri could see the top of a tall spire peeking out above the shops and houses. This had to be the king's palace. He decided to try the most direct approach first, by simply asking for an audience with his uncle. Once he'd achieved that, it would be up to him to make himself believable.

Thirty minutes passed before the palace came into full view. Its tall ivory-colored spires and ramparts were impressive, at least from an aesthetic point of view. But in Akiri's eyes they were also weak and easily breached. By the time he pulled up at the front gate, he had already spotted a good number of blind spots and vulnerabilities. The Dul'Buhar, he knew, could breach these walls in minutes.

A dozen soldiers were guarding the entrance, although no one appeared to be passing either in or out of the palace.

"What do you want?" demanded one of the soldiers, moving closer.

As someone used to being treated with utmost respect by rank and file soldiers, Akiri found his brusque manner more than a touch irritating. "I wish to enter, of course," he told him. "Why else would I be waiting here?"

An incredulous look formed. "You wish to enter?" The man then burst out laughing and turned to his comrades. "You hear that, lads? He wishes to enter."

The other guards joined in with the amusement. Failing to see the reason for this, Akiri said: "I have not even stated my business or identity yet. Is it not your duty to listen and then inform the appropriate person of my arrival?"

The soldier's laughter died. "Listen, monk. Until all the celebrations are over, no one – and I mean, no one – is to be allowed entry into the palace without a royal letter of invitation from King Lanmar himself. And if you had one of those, I'm pretty sure you'd have already shown it to me."

"It is not the king I wish to see," Akiri told him. "It is Tuvarius."

The soldier stiffened conspicuously. "You must have been listening to all those crazy rumors. Don't believe them. There's no one here at the palace by that name. Never has been."

Of all the reactions he might have expected, this was not one that had entered Akiri's mind. King Zemel had told him that Tuvarius was here, so that was where he had to be. His monarch could not have been wrong on the matter.

"You are either mistaken or lying," he said. "I know for a fact that Tuvarius resides here. He is my uncle, and I demand that you pass on my request for an audience."

The soldier gave a low growl and raised a gauntleted fist. "Listen, you. Monk or no monk, I'll pull you down from that horse and pass my boot onto your backside if you call me a liar again. There is no one here by the name of Tuvarius. Got it? Now be gone! Get out of my sight while you still can."

From the depths of his hood, Akiri regarded the man

with contempt. For any member of the Dul'Buhar – let alone the commander – being spoken to in such a way was intolerable. With every fiber of his being, he yearned to jump down from his mount and hand out a harsh lesson in manners to this fool and his grinning comrades. Only the knowledge that such an act would risk seriously harming his cause prevented him from doing so. Gritting his teeth, he rode on. There was now much to consider.

Even allowing for the crowds, finding a stable with room for his horse took far longer than expected. By the time he had eventually located a suitable place, it was well into the afternoon. Now he would need to secure a bed for himself quite soon or face the prospect of leaving the city for the night. It occurred to him that he might hide out somewhere until morning, but this was not something he cared to risk. Discovery would be sure to bring attention on himself, and that was the last thing he wanted, especially now that he was forced to consider more devious ways of entering the royal palace.

Before long, he found his way to a poorer area of the city. Here, the buildings were of a basic design – mostly homes for Vurna's working classes, along with a few taverns and inns. The old and faded sign hanging above the door of a particularly dilapidated establishment read: The Noose and Dagger. As inebriated patrons staggered in and out, the unappetizing smell of stale beer wafted into the street. This was just the kind of place Akiri had been hoping to find: a den of thieves and prostitutes where the kind of information he needed might be found without raising suspicion.

The interior was as expected – a dozen or so tables scattered haphazardly throughout the room, several looking like they had been pieced together from scraps of other furniture no doubt broken repeatedly in brawls. The bar was stained with a combination of ale and dried blood, though this didn't seem to bother the six drunken men talking loudly and boasting of past adventures.

A dozen or so equally drunk customers were sitting around the room, most of them focusing their attention on a young woman dancing in the corner. The sheer blue material she wore flowed with her movements, while a young boy sitting on a stool a few feet away played a sultry melody on a wooden flute.

A young girl sauntered by carrying a tray of beer-filled mugs. She took a moment to notice Akiri and then frowned.

"What's a monk doing in a place like this?" she asked. "Shouldn't you be off feeding starving children or something?"

"I'm just here for a drink."

She eyed him carefully, attempting to penetrate the darkness of his hood. "Then you'd better find somewhere else to quench your thirst, monk. It gets pretty rough in here."

"I'll be fine."

The girl shrugged. "Don't say I didn't warn you."

Akiri took a table near a door at the rear of the tavern. For appearances' sake, he ordered a mug of ale, though only pretended to drink. Judging by the bitter smell drifting up from the dark liquid, it was a choice well made.

"Oi! Monk," a voice called after a little time had passed and people had come and gone.

Akiri could smell the foul breath of the man standing behind him. A hand shoved his shoulder.

"I'm talking to you, monk. Didn't you hear me? Or are you one of them eunuch types that can't speak?"

Akiri turned his head. "I speak, drunkard."

The man staggered forward and slammed his hand onto the tabletop. "Then why don't you tell me what the fuck you're doing here?" He was a full head shorter than Akiri, with an unkempt beard and a mouthful of rotting teeth. A rusted dagger was tucked in his belt. "Answer me, monk."

Akiri's hand shot out, his fingers clamping down in a vice-like grip around the man's testicles. The man let out a loud grunt and fell to his knees.

"Allow me to educate you," Akiri told him in a quiet, even tone. "A eunuch has no balls. They can *speak* just fine. And though I am no eunuch myself, if you do not move on" – he tightened his grip, causing the man to wail and pound his fist on the table – "*you* will certainly become one. Do you understand?"

Unable to say anything, his victim nodded furiously. Akiri shoved him hard to the floor. The man lay unmoving, hands cupped around his groin as he moaned out some unanswered prayer.

With brawls a common occurrence in such places, the spectacle had passed largely unnoticed. Only one man seemed to have taken any real interest. Akiri regarded him from beneath his hood. He was much better dressed than most of the crowd, and the blade hanging from his side was well crafted. His dark hair had obviously been groomed, and his hawk-like features gave him an almost aristocratic look.

Two men dragged the injured drunk from the floor and helped him back to the bar. Before long, Akiri could hear him swearing that he would *Gut that bastard over there like a trout.* His companions were trying to talk him out of it.

"It's bad luck to fight a monk," said one.

"He's no fucking monk," he retorted through grunts of pain. "Bet on it."

"Let it go, Varyn," said the second friend. "You shouldn't have gone over there. Besides, your wife said you had better not get into any more fights."

Akiri considered the situation. He could hear the anger building in Varyn's every word. And someone so drunk and stupid was generally incapable of calming down. This was confirmed when his sharp hearing picked up the sound of a blade being pulled from Varyn's belt.

Only one set of boots was approaching. Clearly, Varyn's companions were not quite so foolish. Akiri waited until the man was only a few feet away; then, just as the knife was being thrust, he spun from his chair. Still twisting to increase the force, his fist crashed into Varyn's jaw, sending him sprawling.

It would be best not to kill him, Akiri decided. Without knowing the local laws, he could find himself in a very unpleasant position. Instead, he stepped on his attacker's wrist and twisted the blade from his grasp.

"You should go now," he said calmly, stepping away and tucking the weapon into the folds of his robe.

Varyn glared up at him with hate-filled eyes. His jaw was shattered, and three of his rotten teeth were now decorating the floor beside him. The two men who had been trying to calm him came over. When Akiri turned to face them, they quickly held up their hands.

"We don't want no trouble," said the man on his left.

Silently, they dragged Varyn to his feet and bundled him out through the tavern door. Akiri sat back down and scanned the room. This second disturbance had gathered a little more attention.

"And to think I was afraid you'd get hurt."

He turned to see the young waitress standing behind him,

smiling broadly. The commotion had caused his drink to topple over; rancid ale was now soaking the tabletop. The girl quickly tossed down a rag and began sopping up the mess.

A few minutes later, she returned with another ale. "And this one is free if you do something for me," she said.

Akiri glanced up. "And what might that be?"

"Let me see your face."

He reached into his robe and retrieved a silver coin worth twenty times the price of the ale. "You can keep this if you can tell me where I might find lodging."

The girl knelt down and gave him a seductive smile. "Show me your face and *maybe* you can stay with me. I've never fucked a monk before."

The idea of bedding this woman was not exactly enticing. Though quite pretty, he was unaccustomed to women of low breeding. However, given his current circumstances, it seemed he might need to lower his standards temporarily. He pushed back his hood.

"Strong *and* handsome," she said with obvious approval. "Are you really a monk?"

"Of course I am."

The girl tucked the coin into her bodice. "I'm Minnie. Stick around. I'll sort you out."

Akiri nodded stoically. "I would like that."

She touched the end of his nose with her finger before returning to her duties. For a moment or two, Akiri grumbled inwardly at such familiarity. As when dealing with the ill-mannered palace guard, he was forced to remind himself that for now at least, he was no longer the commander of the Dul'Buhar. He was simply a servant of the king who had been sent on a mission. And until he got his bearings in this unfamiliar territory, he would need a means of remaining unnoticed. This girl could possibly provide that.

The well-dressed customer he had seen watching him earlier was now smirking in his direction. Akiri pulled the hood back over his head and continued to observe. A minute later, the man rose and crossed over to his table.

"Can I join you?" he asked.

"For what purpose?"

The man raised an eyebrow. "If you're going to pass yourself off as a monk, then you need to do a little better than that." He regarded Akiri for a moment. "Acharian, I'd say, from the accent. A soldier from the way you carry yourself. And a man in need of help, if my guess is correct."

Akiri met the newcomer's eyes. "And you are?"

"My name is Geridia," he said, smiling.

Akiri pointed to the chair opposite. "Please sit."

He did as invited and leaned casually back in the chair. A moment later Minnie returned, a frown on her face. "I'll not be drinking the dog piss you serve here, my dear," Geridia told her. He looked over to Akiri. "And I suggest you don't either. Last time I drank here, I nearly shit myself to death the next morning."

"If you're not drinking, get the fuck out," she snapped back, her eyes darting possessively over to Akiri.

Geridia reached into his pocket and pulled out a copper coin. "Here you are. Now hurry along." He pushed the coin across the table.

Minnie picked it up and placed a hand on Akiri's shoulder. "Don't you go running off anywhere, my handsome one."

He did not look at her, nor did he say anything. After waiting a few seconds unsuccessfully for a response, Minnie moved slowly away, grumbling to herself.

"Now, what help do you imagine I might be needing?" Akiri asked.

Geridia spread his hands. "That is what I am hoping to discover, for the situation is most intriguing." He smiled. "A man walks into the nastiest tavern in the city dressed as a monk. And please don't bother lying. You are no more a monk than I am. He's carrying a sword beneath his cloak, but when some lowlife tries to gut him, rather than use this weapon, he merely breaks his jaw and disarms him." He steepled his hands beneath his chin. "I would say you are a man in need of help."

"And I suppose you are the helpful soul I'm looking for?" Akiri decided to forgo talking around the matter. It was clear that Geridia was no fool.

"Possibly," he replied. "It all depends."

"On what?"

"On what you want, naturally. And what you are willing to do in return."

Akiri studied the man, wondering what his motive might be. If it was gold, he had plenty of that with him, thanks to Killian, but from the way Geridia was attired and the aloof manner in which he presented himself, he very much doubted he had that kind of exchange in mind.

"But these are things we should discuss in more pleasant surroundings," Geridia continued. "What do you say?"

Akiri glanced across the tavern. Minnie was eyeing him closely.

"Oh, don't worry about her," Geridia added. "If you are in need of lodging, I can arrange that. And I can certainly provide you with more appealing company than Minnie. She'll probably try to slit your throat in your sleep and steal your gold anyway."

Akiri considered the offer for a moment and then nodded.

Geridia smiled. "Excellent." He hopped up from his chair. Come, my new friend. Let us seek more civilized entertainment."

Together, they walked toward the door. Minnie called after him, but Akiri paid her no heed. He suspected Geridia was probably right about her motives. More than one soldier from their camp had been lured to his end by a woman like her seeking the gold in his purse.

The sun was nearly down as they wound their way east through the streets. Before long, they were in a far more affluent part of the city. Lavish manors surrounded by high walls dominated the area, and elegantly designed lamps on street corners gave out a warm, reassuring glow. Nearly all of the well-dressed gentlemen and ladies out enjoying their evening stroll seemed to be making a point of displaying their wealth and status by having an unnecessarily large retinue of servants following close behind to cater to their every whim.

"Quite different from Acharia, yes?" remarked Geridia.

"We have many such places there," Akiri responded. "Though built in a different style."

His companion exaggerated a shudder. "Acharian architecture is utterly atrocious. No style at all, in my opinion. All function and very little form. Ah, well, I suppose that's what happens when there is never-ending war in your land."

A stab of irritation shot through Akiri. He did not enjoy hearing his home being criticized – regardless of whether or not it was true. Feeling compelled to rise to its defense, he said: "Clearly you have not been within the palace of

Gol'Naruth. Its magnificence is famed throughout the world."

"Impressive, perhaps. Built to be impregnable from all accounts. But to me it lacks any real elegance. Though admittedly, I have only seen it from the outside."

"Then you should not be so quick to judge."

Geridia held up his hand. "I meant no offense. Each man has his own tastes."

They passed through the residential neighborhood and moved on to a street of shops, most of them dealing in fashionable clothing, jewelry, and other items of high value. In the midst of all these premises, significant by its lack of commercial aspect, stood a two-story building of gleaming white stone. A low hedge surrounded a well-tended garden split down the center by a path of highly polished marble. Just above the oak door was a sign that read: Prince of Polimore.

"This is my absolute favorite place in the entire city," Geridia enthused. He paused to look Akiri up and down. "Though I'm afraid you are a touch underdressed." He flicked a casual wrist. "Little matter. But do please take off that ghastly robe."

Akiri did as instructed, though the travel worn shirt and pants revealed were little better suited.

Geridia regarded him, smiling. "Quite the brute, I see. Yes, indeed."

The door opened a moment before they reached it. A man in a white satin outfit stood just inside. A welcoming smile formed when he saw Geridia, but it quickly faded when Akiri walked in just behind him.

"Please take my companion's robe and stow it away, would you, Lom?" Geridia asked.

Akiri handed the robe over.

"And your sword, if you please," Lom insisted.

"I think I'll keep it with me," Akiri told him, his eyes daring the man to take it.

"It's fine, Lom," Geridia said quickly. "I'll take full responsibility."

Lom's eyes darted from Geridia to Akiri, then back again. "Very well, sir. But please be sure he minds his manners."

Geridia laughed. "Oh, Lom. I would never allow anything to happen here. You know that."

Lom bowed and gestured for them to proceed. "Yes, sir. Of course."

The foyer was decorated with an array of masterfully sculpted statues depicting men and women in various stages of copulation. The murals and paintings on the walls followed a similar theme. At the far end, a broad double door opened into a spacious dining hall filled nearly to capacity with richly dressed men and women. Their laughter and convivial chatter mixed easily with music from a lute being played by a highly skilled musician. The tune was intricate, almost seductive.

Instead of entering this room, Geridia turned left to another door which led through to an outdoor dining area set beneath a large pavilion. The lawn was perfectly manicured and surrounded by dozens of delicate flower bushes. Here it was relatively quiet – occupied by no more than a dozen people. They took a table in the far corner away from inquisitive ears.

The moment they were seated, a young blond boy hurried across the lawn bearing a bottle of wine and two glasses.

"Thank you, Deri," said Geridia. He looked to Akiri.

"Are you hungry?"

"No, not really."

Geridia frowned. "A man with such big muscles needs to eat. Please, I insist." Without awaiting a reply, he nodded to Deri, who scurried away.

"If you don't mind," said Akiri, trying to sound as polite as possible, "why have you brought me here?"

Geridia glanced over to the entrance and his face immediately lit up. "Ah, she's here."

Akiri followed his gaze to see a woman wearing a loose-fitting tunic and pants walking over with long, deliberate strides. A wicked-looking dagger was strapped to each hip. Her shoulder-length red hair was tied in a tight ponytail, which didn't diminish the intensity of her emerald green eyes.

"Where have you been?" she demanded, sliding into a chair between the two men.

"You worry too much," said Geridia. "I was fine on my own." He gestured to Akiri. "You see? I was well protected."

"Protecting you is *my* job," she snapped. "Not some…" She looked at Akiri disdainfully. "Whatever you are."

"My dear, this is…" He raised an eyebrow. "I never did catch your name."

"I am Akiri."

"You see?" said Geridia. "I've been just fine." He smiled at Akiri. "Rena worries so. She thinks the entire city is out to get me."

"You employ a woman as a bodyguard?"

Rena sneered. "Don't tell me… you're Acharian. Fucking savages."

"Rena is quite capable, I assure you," Geridia said. "She has saved my life quite a few times."

"You're wasting your breath," she said, eyeing Akiri with utter disdain. "Acharians only see women as possessions. Things to be used for their pleasure."

"You are wrong," Akiri retorted. "Acharians value their women greatly."

"Yes, I know. As one values a horse or a sheep." She took Geridia's hand. "Come. Let me take you home. You can do better than him."

"You misunderstand, my dear," he told her. "This is not a romantic outing." He regarded Akiri with appreciation. "That is not to say I wouldn't have entertained the idea. But no. I have other business with my new friend."

Rena threw up her hands. "Oh, no! Not that again."

Geridia sighed. "Yes, *that* again."

"You are wrong, Rena," said Akiri. His mind was still lingering on what she had said about Acharian attitudes toward women.

She sniffed. "And what exactly am I wrong about?"

"Though it is true that a few Acharians see their women as possessions, most do not. We are a nation at war. Our women mend the wounded and care for the sick. They work the fields and mind the home. While the men are away, they are all that stands between Acharia and chaos. Without them, we would be lost. That they do not serve alongside men in battle is the only thing I would see as being a shortcoming."

Rena was clearly taken aback. "You would allow women to serve as soldiers?"

Akiri shrugged. "If they are up to the challenge, why not? Many I have known would make perfectly capable commanders. Far more so than some of the incompetent fools I have found myself serving with. A strong arm is one aspect of soldiering, but it is not the most important."

He paused to look her directly in the eye before continuing. "If you were offended by my surprise at you being Geridia's bodyguard, you should know that it was not because I believed you incapable of doing the job well. Far from it. It was that, given his obvious choice in intimate companions, I imagined he would have chosen someone more appealing to his nature."

This suggestion sent Geridia into a fit of laughter. "He's got a point, you know," he giggled. "A nubile young warrior might be just what I need. Yes, I'm imagining it already."

Rena snorted her derision. "Marshum would kill you in your sleep. So you had better get that thought right out of your thick head as quick as you like."

Geridia's amusement faded. "Ah, yes. My dearest love would not appreciate it at all, I think. I can only assume that he was the one who told you I had slipped out of the house." He waved a dismissive hand. "But enough of this. We have business to discuss." He turned his attention to Akiri. "I have a task for you. One I sadly cannot attend to myself. But first I would like to know what assistance it is that you need."

"I need to gain entry into the king's palace," Akiri replied. "I seek a man named Tuvarius."

Geridia's face noticeably tightened. His tone became hushed. "And why would you wish to see *him*?"

"That is my business. Not yours."

"When you need me to help you contact a man like Tuvarius, it becomes my business. No one is granted an audience with him. And I mean no one."

"Why is that?"

"You don't know?" He waited for a reply, but none was forthcoming. "They call him *the mad sorcerer.* Dark magic surrounds that one. Not even the king dares to question him."

"So you can confirm that he does reside at the palace?"

"Oh, yes, it's an open secret that Tuvarius lives there, even though our king publicly denies any knowledge of his existence. Our monarch does not like it known that he relies upon a sorcerer's advice. He feels that it demeans him in the people's eyes. All palace guards are under strict instructions. Any confirmation to an outsider of Tuvarius' presence would be regarded as high treason, punishable by summary execution."

Akiri nodded. That explained a lot.

"If you seek out Tuvarius, all you will find is death," Geridia added.

"Nevertheless, that is my price."

The two men locked eyes. Finally, Geridia blew out an exasperated breath and leaned back in his chair. "Very well. I think I might know a way of getting you inside. But I wish you would reconsider. A man like you could do very well for himself in Galfaria. I can see to it that you remain well employed."

"I have already told you, that is my price," Akiri repeated. "Now tell me yours."

Geridia let out a long sigh of acceptance before beginning. "As you may have guessed, I am quite a prominent man here in Vurna. My primary business is dry goods. Though outwardly not the most exciting of endeavors, it can be remarkably lucrative if one possesses the necessary bargaining skills. My primary competitor is a fat slob of a man named Barsyn Bartone. He arrived here from the north a few years ago and has been a constant thorn in my side ever since." He took a long drink from his glass before moving closer to his main point. "Part of his success has to do with a certain item he possesses that I would very much like to have for my own."

"And you would have me steal it from him?" asked Akiri.

"I would indeed."

"And what is this item exactly?"

"A pendant. From the look of it, a totally unremarkable trinket. But as I am sure you are aware, appearances can sometimes be most deceiving."

"Why is it so important for you to have it?"

Geridia shrugged away the question. "What does it matter? All you really need to understand is the simplicity of our arrangement. Obtain this pendant for me, and in return, I'll gain you secret entry into the palace. There *is* a way. You have my word on that."

Akiri paused to consider the offer for a moment. Lowering himself to becoming a thief was not something that appealed to him greatly. On the other hand, finding a suitable way into the palace without help might prove to be a more than difficult undertaking.

"Of course, if you are so minded, you could always try to sneak inside without my assistance," Geridia added. "But I promise that you will not get beyond the door. Many a thief, not to mention assassins, have lost their lives trying. I am one of the richest men in the city, and it still took me over a year to be granted admittance through official channels for an audience with the king. And *you* want to see the dreaded Tuvarius…" He gave a theatrical shudder.

Akiri nodded. In truth, he had briefly thought of trying to enter under cover of darkness. But that notion was quickly dismissed. He might well be forced to kill a sentry, and that was definitely not the kind of introduction he desired.

"And you are certain you can get me inside?" he asked.

"Absolutely."

"I think this is a bad idea," Rena cut in. "If he's caught, all roads lead back to you."

"If I am caught, I will not divulge who gave me aid," said Akiri. "On this you have my word."

Rena huffed a sarcastic laugh. "And we are supposed to simply believe you?"

Akiri's eyes burned into the woman. "I do not lie. If I say I will keep Geridia's identity a secret, you can most surely believe me."

Though most people wilted under his gaze, Rena did not. "I believe *nothing* you say," she retorted. "Sell-swords are never to be trusted."

"But you are in Geridia's employ. So does that not make you a sell-sword too?"

She burst from her chair, hands resting firmly on the handles of her weapons. "I am not a sell-sword, you great lumbering oaf. I first served Geridia when I was sixteen years old and have been his protector ever since. So you had better mind your damn tongue before I cut it out."

Although unmoved by the threat, Akiri was quietly impressed by her conviction.

"Rena, please sit down!" hissed Geridia. "You're making a scene."

He was right. Several patrons were now looking over in their direction and whispering to one another. Scowling, Rena did as she had been instructed.

"How will I acquire this pendant you covet?" Akiri asked, his eyes never straying from the still smoldering woman.

"That's the hard part," Geridia replied. "He keeps it

around his fat neck at all times. And you can't simply rob him in the street. There are too many eyes about. The only way is to break into his house and take it from him there."

"And how many men guard his home?"

"No more than a dozen, I think. But they are all very well trained."

"So you've sent others to try before me?"

Geridia gave him a guilty smile. "You might say that. Two have failed so far."

"Try six," corrected Rena. "Which is why you should give up on this nonsense."

"I will get this pendant for you," Akiri promised, brushing her objection aside. "But if you do not hold up your end of the bargain…" He allowed the threat to hang in the air.

Geridia clapped his hands like an excited child receiving a much wanted present. "Excellent! Then we have an agreement. That's wonderful."

Just then, three young men hurried over to their table bearing an assortment of plates and bowls.

"So now let us feast," he continued. "You can stay in my house tonight, and I will go over all the details."

Akiri nodded. The meal set before him was unlike anything he had grown accustomed to while living among the Dul'Buhar.

Rena picked up a spoon and sneered over at him. "I think he'd be more comfortable eating with his fingers."

Akiri ignored the gibe and began eating. She was not wrong, however. Only twice before had he used utensils. But then, life for him had always been one of simplicity.

These days, it was becoming far less straightforward.

Chapter Six

Once they had finished their repast, Akiri was taken to his new acquaintance's lavish manor, where he was given details of the pendant's appearance and a layout of Barsyn Bartone's house. Though this was apparently every bit as spacious as his current surroundings, it was pointed out several times by Geridia with almost malicious delight that his business rival's choice of décor was vastly inferior in every aspect to that which he had selected for his own home.

After studying the makeshift map drawn for him, Akiri set about devising the best way to get inside undetected.

"Try not to kill the swine if at all possible," Geridia told him, just before retiring upstairs to his room. "I would love nothing more than to see the devastated look on his pudgy little face once he is without his precious pendant. Oh, and you will also need to be very careful about how you deal with his guards. They are all part of the Hunari Guild, and I certainly don't need them getting involved. If you kill any of them, they will be sure to seek retribution."

Akiri chose to sleep downstairs, near the front door. Rena settled down for the night in a chair close by, unwilling to leave him alone in the house.

The following morning, he left the manor before Geridia

rose and soon found a market where he was able to purchase suitable clothing for the coming night's work, along with a new dagger and a few other odds and ends he might need. He had left his sword inside Geridia's house. Such a bulky weapon was ill-suited to moving with stealth.

In order to verify everything in daylight, he then made a point of walking past Barsyn Bartone's house. It was more or less as Geridia had described, with a ten-foot-high wrought iron fence surrounding the two-story building. Guards stalked the grounds, and a sentry stood at the front entrance. Confirming what he had been told, Akiri could see for himself by the disciplined pattern in which the men patrolled that they were indeed well trained. But no amount of training could prepare them for what was coming. Where six men had previously failed, he would not.

He spent the remainder of his time in a small tavern until it was late in the evening. Now fully prepared, he set off back to Barsyn's manor.

From what he had been told about the man, Barsyn was not one to seek late night entertainment, generally choosing to be in his bed well before midnight. Akiri ducked into the shadows upon nearing the manor. Though the street was reasonably well lit, his skill served to effectively hide him from the few people wandering about. He chosen a section of fence on the left hand side of the house where a small flower garden and a fountain offered some decent cover to make his entrance.

Eight guards split into four pairs were patrolling the grounds, each pair covering a designated area, and within this, each individual never straying more than twenty-five yards away from his partner. It was easy to see why previous attempts had failed. The moment one guard spotted an intruder, the entire security force could be alerted within seconds. But there was an opportunity – a small gap in the rhythm of movement through which Akiri could reach the side of the building unseen if he moved quickly and at exactly the right moment.

He scaled the fence easily, then crept with barely a sound to the far edge of the flower garden. The guard over to his right had his back to him at the moment, but the one on his left did not. He estimated the distance between his last piece of cover – a thick rhododendron bush – and the house to be roughly twenty yards. Once across this short patch of open ground, the shadow of the house itself would give adequate concealment. The black shirt and pants he had purchased, along with some soot collected from the tavern fireplace and now smeared liberally over his face and hands, would make spotting him in the darkness virtually impossible.

The sinews of his legs flexed in anticipation. Timing was everything.

"You ready?" called the guard to his left.

Akiri froze.

The guard to his right waved his comrade over and then removed a silver flask from his belt. Akiri frowned. Drinking on duty. Apparently, they were not quite the professionals Geridia had imagined. This presented a real problem. In just a few seconds, his position would be revealed, and there was nothing he could do to prevent it. The guard would pass only a foot or two away from his hiding place behind the bush. At a distance, he was inseparable from the surrounding shadows, but when close, the sentry would have to be blind not to see the silhouette of a man crouching low. He needed to decide quickly what to do. With great purpose, he drew his dagger.

As the guard approached, Akiri could tell from his manner that he was fairly relaxed and thinking more of his impending refreshment than the possibility of encountering any intruders. He waited until the man's eyes fell directly upon him. The guard stopped abruptly, and for the space of a split second, surprise paralyzed him. An instant later, his eyes widened and his mouth opened to cry out. Akiri leapt up and forward, the leading knuckles of his fingers wrapped around the dagger handle jabbing into the guard's throat. The man gasped and fell to his knees, unable to utter anything more than a series of gasping wheezes.

The second guard was equally caught by surprise. Perhaps he had already taken a few too many reaction-sapping sips from his flask. Whatever the case, he first squinted into the gloom in an effort to establish exactly what had happened before fumbling for his sword. Like his friend, he too then tried to raise the alarm but was too late. The dagger Akiri had thrown was already upon him. It was a long-practiced move designed to stun rather than kill. Just as it had done with Killian, the hilt of the weapon smacked into the middle of the man's forehead, choking off the rising sound. Badly dazed, he staggered back. Akiri covered the distance between them in a flash, and a swift blow to the guard's temple, rendered him unconscious.

Satisfied, he returned to the first guard who was still desperately trying to recover both his feet and voice. A crushing right to the jaw ensured that he would be doing neither for some time.

Akiri paused to listen carefully, but none of the other guards had been alerted; at least not yet. But it wouldn't be long before their companions began wondering where they were and came looking. After retrieving his dagger, he dragged both men into the cover of the garden, then raced to the side of the manor. Still at full speed and calling on every bit of his strength and agility, he ran up the first few feet of the wall, propelling himself high enough to catch the bottom edge of the second story balcony. Soundlessly, he pulled himself up and over the railing. The door at the back offered little resistance, yielding with just a small squeak of protest when the dagger blade slid between the lock and the frame surrounding it. Akiri stepped inside.

He found himself in an unoccupied guest bedroom, just as Geridia had assured him it would be. If the rest of his information was equally accurate, Barsyn would be sleeping four rooms along. This was supported by the fact that, as he had noted earlier, the door on this room's balcony was the only one protected by an extremely sturdy-looking iron outer gate.

Akiri knew he had to act swiftly. If the alarm was raised before his business was done, he might be forced to fight his way out of the house, and that might involve killing some guards. He would try not to, but if it was the only way to escape, he would not shirk from doing so.

He crossed to the bedroom door and peered cautiously outside. For now, the hallway was clear all the way to the far end of the building, but the sound of several men moving about downstairs drifted up a wide stairwell halfway along.

Upon reaching his target, he pressed his ear to the door. He could hear heavy nasal breathing mixed with intermittent snorts and snores. This, he hoped, was Barsyn. The door was locked, but he'd anticipated this and had come prepared. Retrieving a pick and hook from his pocket, he set to work.

It did not take long, though to his ears the clack of the mechanism turning sounded like a series of thunderclaps in the silence. Nonetheless, the continued deep, labored breathing of Barsyn suggested that he had not been disturbed. Gently, Akiri pushed the door open and ducked inside.

All at once, the room fell completely quiet. Akiri's senses immediately started to tingle. The bed situated to his right was empty.

Only the slightest movement of a shadow caught in the corner of his eye saved him from being skewered. Instinctively, he dove low to his left just as the bolt from a crossbow came streaking across the room at chest height. The missile buried itself into the far wall with a deep thud. Almost at the instant it struck, Akiri was racing forward, dagger in hand.

"Guards! Help!" cried the shadowy figure.

Akiri crashed into him, forcing him to the ground. He could feel the man's enormous girth; he had to be at least three hundred pounds. At such a vast size, this could only be Barsyn. He was just as Geridia had described him. His narrow-set eyes flashed wide with fear as Akiri pressed the dagger blade to his neck and cupped a hand over his mouth.

He listened carefully over Barsyn's grunts and muffled cries. An alarmed shout from downstairs carried through the door. "If they enter, I'll cut your throat," he hissed. "So you had better say the right thing. Understand?"

After the terrified man had nodded rapidly several times, he removed the hand from his mouth.

The clamor of boots pounding on the stairs heralded the guards' approach. Although dark enough inside the room to prevent easy identification, Akiri took the extra precaution of pulling the neckline of his shirt up to just below his eyes. A few seconds later the door burst open. Three men stood in the doorway, swords drawn.

"Back off!" the merchant cried out desperately. "He'll kill me if you don't."

The men hesitated, prompting Akiri to press the steel down even harder. The blood this drew had Barsyn waving his hand madly. "I said get back! All of you."

"Tell them to close the door," Akiri commanded.

"Do it!" said Barsyn.

After glancing at each other, the guards backed away and did as instructed.

With the door once more closed, Akiri readjusted his shirt and allowed Barsyn to heave himself to his feet. "If you move, I'll end this right now," he warned.

"You have no fear in you. None at all," Barsyn muttered in an astonished tone. "Unyielding and merciless. By the gods. Who *are* you?"

"Who I am does not matter," Akiri replied coldly. "What *is* important is that I collect what I have come for."

"Then I can only assume it was that dog Geridia who sent you."

Slowly, and with exaggerated movements so as not to alarm his captor, he reached inside his night shirt and pulled out a small pendant. It was unremarkable from outward appearances: just a silver disk attached to a thin chain. "Is this what you seek?" he asked.

"Turn it over," Akiri ordered.

He did as he was told. Just like Geridia had described, the symbol of Ustraya, Goddess of Love and Passion, was etched upon the reverse side. "You can see I am not attempting deception," Barsyn assured him, though he made no move to lift the chain from around his neck. "But before you take this most precious prize to him – and don't bother denying that it was he who sent you – don't you want to know what makes it so special?"

"I don't care what it is," Akiri replied. "Remove it."

He might just as well not have spoken. Still holding the disc between his thumb and forefinger, Barsyn continued regardless. "This was given to me by my dear sister just before I left home for Galfaria." A tiny, faraway smile crept upon his lips. "Lula was quite a talented enchanter. This was the last thing she made before she died. It reveals to me the emotional state of anyone I look at. More than that, it tells me of their innermost desires… at least in a vague way." His smile faded as he scrutinized Akiri. "I see a tempest raging inside you. But controlled by a will of iron. Unbending and determined. Stronger than anyone I have ever encountered before."

Akiri could immediately see how such an item would be invaluable to a man in Geridia's profession. The holder would possess a huge advantage over others when negotiating business deals. Not that any of this mattered right now. "I'll tell you one more time," he said. "Remove the pendant."

"If you would please allow me to say one last thing. After which, if you still want it, it is yours."

Akiri's eyes flashed to the door. He could hear most of the guards gathered immediately outside, muttering fiercely amongst themselves. "Be quick."

"I can feel you are a man with tremendous power and desire. You want something returned to you – something that you have lost and is most dear to your heart. It is an unfinished mission and nothing will stop you. So I ask you to think for a moment. If you hope to continue on this course and attain your dream, there are two things you should consider. Firstly, you have no way out of here. The grounds and the halls are filled with my men. Alone and with naught but a dagger, you have no hope for escape. Secondly, whatever Geridia has offered to pay you, I will double his price. And if it is not gold you are seeking, I will provide whatever else it is you may require. There is nothing that Geridia can give you that I cannot."

Akiri stepped forward. "You have said your piece. Now remove the pendant."

Reluctantly, Barsyn pulled the chain over his head and held it out. "If by some miracle you manage to make it out alive, tell Geridia this is not over. Once I report this theft to the magistrate first thing tomorrow, he is finished."

Akiri snatched the pendant from his hand and shoved it into the pouch on his belt. He then shook his head. "I'm sorry. I'm afraid I cannot allow you to make that report."

Faster than a striking snake, he rammed the dagger up through Barsyn's chin. Such was the force that the blade passed easily right through the man's mouth and into his brain. He died almost instantly, letting out only a muffled grunt before his legs collapsed. Akiri caught him as he crumpled and laid him gently to the floor.

He then raced to the window. In the garden below, only two men were waiting. With the securely locked iron gate barring his way, they obviously considered it most unlikely he would be able to exit this way. He smiled. They did not know whom they were dealing with, or have any idea of the strength he possessed. He yanked open the balcony door and kicked at the gate with all the force he could muster. The first kick was enough to smash open the lock; a second sent the gate flying from its hinges and crashing down on to the lawn below.

The commotion this created was more than sufficient to

galvanize the guards in the hall. The bedroom door flew open, and this time there was no hesitation on their part. At least six of them charged into the room with swords drawn, but Akiri was already in mid-air after leaping from the balcony.

He landed lightly on the grass and set off instantly. The two men waiting there moved in to engage him, but having jumped back in opposite directions to avoid the falling gate, they were badly positioned. Akiri ran straight between the pair of them before either could get near enough to strike. By the time he reached the edge of the grounds, he had already put enough distance between himself and his pursuers to comfortably scale the fence and disappear into the night.

He paused briefly a couple of streets away to listen. There were no further sounds of pursuit; he could now slow to a walk. A sense of satisfaction settled over him. He had managed to acquire the pendant without killing a single guard. And though it was unfortunate he'd been forced to kill Barsyn Bartone, given the circumstances, he had done the right thing.

He threaded his way back to Geridia's manor, avoiding as many people as possible along the way. Only a few pedestrians took any notice of him, and none were close enough to give any kind of description beyond that of a tall dark man dressed in black.

Two guards were on duty at the main gate of Geridia's home; a different pair to those he had seen when leaving early that morning. Akiri halted and asked to be admitted. They eyed him suspiciously.

"Wait here," said the older of the two. He went inside and returned within a minute. A sharp gesture indicated for Akiri to proceed.

The front door was opened by a young woman in a blue house dress. A gasp slipped from her lips as she suddenly found herself confronted by a large, intimidating-looking man dressed completely in black and with his hands and face covered in soot. She quickly regained her composure and gave a formal curtsy. "My master awaits you in the main parlor. Please. This way."

She led him through a door on the left side of the foyer and down a short series of hallways. Upon reaching the parlor, she curtsied once again and hurried away.

Just like the rest of the house, the room was elegantly decorated with fine tapestries and masterful works of art. A fire burned cheerfully in the hearth, while nearby a comfortable sofa and four matching chairs were placed around a low mahogany table. Geridia was lounging in one of the chairs, while sitting close by was a man in his mid-fifties wearing a blue satin jacket and smoking a long, thin gold pipe.

Rena was standing in the opposite corner, flipping through a leather bound book.

"Ah, Akiri!" Geridia exclaimed, clapping his hands together with anticipation. "I am so happy you have returned. And unhurt, by the look of you."

"A touch dirty, isn't he?" remarked the other man, with biting understatement.

"Now, Marshum," Geridia scolded. "Don't be rude to my new friend." He waved Akiri over to join him.

While moving across the room, Rena gave him the courtesy of a sharp nod, and then immediately returned her attention to the book.

Akiri settled into a seat facing the two men. "I have what you wanted," he said without preamble, removing the pendant from his pocket.

Geridia's eyes danced with excitement. "I knew you could do it." Reaching over, he took his prize and held it aloft. "Here it is, Marshum. I told you he'd get it for me, didn't I?"

Marshum was far less impressed. He shrugged. "And now that you have it in your eager little hand, what will you do next?"

"Put that hog of a bastard Barsyn Bartone out of business, of course," he replied. "Oh, how I am looking forward to that."

"Bartone is dead," Akiri told him.

Marshum gasped, covering his mouth. "You… you killed him?"

Geridia sat back, disappointment now clouding his previously bright aspect. "Was that absolutely necessary?"

"He saw my face and stated that he knew you had sent me," Akiri explained. "He also said he intended to go immediately to the magistrate and would see you ruined. As you have yet to fulfill your part of our bargain, I saw no other choice."

Geridia considered this for a moment and then nodded. "I can see you did the right thing. What about the guards?"

"I disabled two. But killed none."

A little of Geridia's cheerfulness returned. "That is good news indeed. It will be bad enough when the magistrate learns of Barsyn's murder, but at least the bloody Hunari won't be involved."

"I've done what you asked," Akiri stated. "Now it's your turn."

Geridia turned to his bodyguard. "Rena, please show our friend where he can get cleaned up, and then prepare my carriage." He switched his attention back to Akiri. "It would be unwise for you to remain here any longer, but I will do as we agreed without delay."

Akiri stood and nodded politely. "Then after tonight our business is concluded."

"This is true," he agreed. "But I still wish you would reconsider. A man such as you could do very well for himself here in Vurna. Especially with my patronage."

Akiri did not waste his breath making a reply. Instead, he simply turned away and followed Rena from the room.

There was only one way of life for him. And it certainly did not involve being a merchant's lackey.

Chapter Seven

Akiri washed away the soot and grime and then rejoined Geridia and Rena in the main foyer, where he retrieved his sword. A carriage awaited them at the front of the house.

"I hope Marshum wasn't too abrasive," remarked Geridia as they climbed in. "He speaks his mind far too often. That's why I've never allowed him to move in with me."

Rena sniffed. "That, and you don't want him to catch you seeking out young men in the taverns."

"Ah. But that's how I encountered Akiri here," he chuckled. "So you must admit that my little vice yielded something good this time."

Their path through the city took them near Barsyn's manor. Here they saw dozens of armed guards walking the streets, stopping pedestrians to ask if they had seen anything.

"You seem to have caused quite a stir," said Geridia, smiling.

Rena was less amused. "Are you certain no one can identify you?"

"Absolutely," Akiri assured her.

They stopped in front of a two-story building, a little smaller but otherwise similar in appearance to the place

Geridia had taken him the night before. A young man scurried to open the carriage door for them. After handing the lad a copper, Geridia led Akiri toward the entrance. Rena remained in the carriage.

"She doesn't much like this place," Geridia explained.

Akiri was about to ask why that was, but then the door opened and his question was answered. A young woman in a sheer silk robe stood just inside. Beyond her lay a spacious common area furnished with elaborately upholstered sofas and chairs. Occupying most of these were well-dressed men and barely dressed women talking in hushed whispers and quiet giggles. A few more were gathered beside a small bar in the corner.

"You bring me to a brothel?" he asked.

Geridia shrugged. "You said you wanted a way into the palace. This is the only way I know."

A tall, ebony-skinned woman wearing an elegant white silk gown and a colorful headscarf sauntered up to them.

"I'm afraid all my boys are currently engaged, Geridia," she said, flashing a welcoming smile. She regarded Akiri. "That is, unless you have need of privacy for you and your friend here. In that case, I think we can accommodate you."

Geridia followed her gaze and gave a sorrowful sigh. "If only… But no. I need to speak with you privately, Quarra." He pointed over to the bar. "You should wait over there, Akiri. I won't be a moment."

After watching the pair disappear down a hall, he took a seat at the bar and took in his surroundings. This was no soldiers' brothel. This was a place where only the very wealthy came to live out their fantasies. The women were likely trained from a very young age in how to best please their customers. Many in society looked down upon them, but a successful prostitute in this type of establishment could earn enough gold to make herself even wealthier than the men who paid her.

Several of the women gave Akiri appreciative stares, though none actually approached him. This was not altogether surprising. He did not have the appearance of a man whose purse was filled with gold, and in their eyes, he would be a waste of their valuable time. He smiled to himself. In truth, he still had much of Killian's gold and could well afford a night of pleasure if he so wished. In fact, many of the beauties here *did* stir his hunger. But this was not the time.

After a few minutes, he heard raised voices coming from down the hall where Geridia had passed, and the merchant soon appeared once more, striding to the bar looking none too pleased.

"I hope you can appreciate how much this has cost me," he said, dropping heavily into a seat beside Akiri. "Quarra was not happy when I told her what I wanted. Not happy at all." He ordered a glass of wine and downed it in a single gulp. "But you will be pleased to know I have now fulfilled my end of our bargain."

"So this Quarra woman will get me inside?" Akiri asked.

"In a manner of speaking… yes." He looked across to see her approaching, anger burning in her eyes. "She will tell you all about it."

On arrival, she did not choose to sit. "You need to leave, Geridia," she told him firmly. Her gaze then switched to Akiri, appraising him carefully. "Well, at least it will be believable. He is more than suitable for the role."

"I think this concludes our business," Geridia said, rising from his seat. "I wish you well, my friend. I honestly do."

He nodded curtly to Quarra and headed quickly for the door. Akiri shot to his feet.

"I suppose the little shit hasn't bothered to explain to you how this is going to work, has he?" Quarra asked.

"We had an arrangement," he stated flatly. "And if he has not–"

"He's honored it well enough," she assured him, her lip curling in disgust. "And perhaps doomed me in the process. I should have never become indebted to that man." She started back to the hallway. "Well, come on, then. I need to get you ready."

Akiri followed the woman until they reached a spacious bedchamber. There, an older man with a slight frame and a balding head was sitting at a table, sipping from a cup of wine and reading a book. He looked up over a pair of wire-rimmed spectacles and regarded Akiri with a curious expression.

"And who have we here?" he asked. "A new addition to the family?"

"In a way," replied Quarra. "I need him fitted. He will be visiting the palace."

"Is that right? Then I suppose I should take a look at what I have to work with."

Akiri stiffened. "Before you do anything, I would like to know how you intend to get me inside."

A quick glance from Quarra sent the man scurrying from the room.

"What do you know about Queen Chelia?" she asked, once the door had closed.

"Nothing."

"The let me enlighten you."

She crossed over to a tall glass door cabinet and opened

a bottle she retrieved from within. The aroma of strong brandy filled the air. "Our dear king is not exactly filled with youthful vigor any longer. So by way of compensation, the queen employs me from time to time to provide her with… entertainment."

"So is that it? I am to be disguised as a whore?" asked an astonished Akiri.

Quarra frowned. "It will be more than a mere disguise. You will be admitted into the palace through a secret entrance and taken to the queen's private bed chamber."

"You are serious? You mean I am to actually pleasure her?" This was becoming harder than ever for him to take in.

"It is the only way that someone like you can ever hope to gain entrance to the palace." She shook her head, rubbing her temple. "May the gods help me. Are you really going to try to see Tuvarius?"

Akiri felt a stab of annoyance that Geridia had told her of his intentions, even though revealing everything had probably been the only way for him to gain her cooperation. "I am," he confirmed. "Do you know where in the palace he might be found?"

"No. But one thing I *do* know very well: If you are caught, they will castrate you, then let you live a while gelded before they kill you – if they're feeling compassionate. Personally, I'd give serious consideration to abandoning this foolishness while you still have your balls."

"I cannot."

Quarra heaved a sigh. "Why did I imagine you might say anything else?"

She paused for a moment, looking straight into his eyes. "Queen Chelia is a highly passionate woman. If aroused sufficiently, she has been known to fall asleep very soon after attaining climax. Assuming you have the skill, this will be your opportunity. Because she fears the king will discover her infidelity, only a few of her most trusted men guard this part of the palace, and they all keep at a very tactful distance. The only one who will be close by is a personal maid. She will greet you and remain in a room opposite the queen's chambers. You should be able to sneak out past her easily enough. As for the rest… well, I just don't know."

Akiri could hear the trepidation in her voice. "I will not implicate you should I be discovered," he assured her.

"I am the one who is sending you there," she pointed out. "So I will be implicated anyway. But I will say that I had no idea of your intentions. So, once you leave the queen's bed, you are on your own."

Akiri nodded.

Quarra went to the door and called for the man to return. "This is Filo. He will be fitting you with appropriate clothing."

Filo folded his arms and tilted his head. "A nice specimen." He snapped his fingers. "Off with them."

Akiri furrowed his brow. "Off with what?"

"Your clothes, of course. I need to see what I'm working with. The queen so loves a nice presentation."

Akiri was not modest about his body; life as a soldier didn't allow for it. This was different, though. He was far from comfortable with the idea of being looked upon as if he were livestock. Nevertheless, it was an indignity he would have to accept if his plan was to proceed. Expressionless, he did as instructed.

Quarra raised an eyebrow and grinned. "You've quite an asset down there, I see. At least you have *that* going for you.

Let's just hope you know how to use it."

Akiri said nothing. He had been with many women. As far as he could tell, they had all been satisfied, though a few had remarked that he was a rather brutal and aggressive lover.

Filo set about his work, taking measurements and jotting them down onto a scrap of parchment. Several times his hands came uncomfortably close to Akiri's penis, and once they even made a fleeting contact. Throughout all of this, the man appeared completely oblivious to any unease he might be causing, and on a couple of occasions actually seemed irritated that the appendage kept getting in his way.

Once finished, he hurried off, clutching his measurements.

"You will stay here and out of sight for the next two days," Quarra told Akiri before leaving. "I will have food brought to you. Do *not* leave this room. No one can know you are here. Is that understood?"

"It is," he replied. "But my horse will need tending to."

Quarra groaned. "Fine. Tell me where it's stabled, and I'll see to it."

After she left, he sat at the table for a time, considering what he would say to Tuvarius once they finally came face to face. How would he convince his uncle that he was not an agent of King Zemel? If Tuvarius was really so adept at magic, would he be able to use this in order to learn the truth? Finally, with no answers forthcoming, Akiri climbed into the far too soft bed.

Chapter Eight

The next two nights passed by without mishap. Once he caught Quarra peeking into the room after she thought he had fallen asleep. At first, he imagined she was simply checking to see that he was staying inside as instructed. But soon her gaze developed an unmistakable look of lust. Akiri found her to be very attractive. Had she acted on her desires, he would not have resisted her. But she had not.

When the time to prepare himself arrived, Filo returned to the room proudly carrying the clothes he had spent the past two days creating. After he spread his handiwork out on the bed for inspection, Akiri blinked, for a moment not knowing whether to laugh aloud or be angry. The entire ensemble was crafted from sapphire blue satin. The shirt had a bright yellow collar and cuffs, along with similarly colored swirling patterns running down each breast. The equally garish pants were clearly tailored for a fit more than snugly enough to fully accentuate his manly qualities.

"What's wrong?" Filo asked, clearly offended by Akiri's look of disapproval.

"Nothing," he replied through clenched teeth. After changing into the clothes, for the first time in his life he actually felt humiliated. He had to resist a powerful urge to throttle Filo for making such ridiculous garments. The idea that anyone would see him dressed this way was almost more than he could stand.

"Very nice," called Quarra from the door. "I'm sure the queen will approve."

"I look like a…" He let out a frustrated growl. "There is not even anywhere to hide a dagger."

"That doesn't matter," she said, clearly amused by his discomfort. "They will search you for weapons before allowing you to enter."

Akiri gave her a sideways look. "And they're too tight. If I so much as bend down, the pants will surely tear."

"No, they won't," assured Filo. "That's good quality material. Try it and see for yourself."

In no mood to be accommodating, Akiri ignored the invitation.

"Besides," added Quarra. "Queen Chelia will have them off you quickly enough."

This did nothing to ease his displeasure.

A short time later, a man wearing a black robe with the hood pulled over his head arrived. Without a word, he waved for Akiri to follow. A carriage awaited just outside the brothel. Sitting in the back was an older man in a fine linen suit. He scrutinized Akiri closely, then nodded with approval.

"I'm glad to see she has sent My Lady a big one this time," he remarked. "Perhaps you'll do better than her last visitor. Poor lad. She very nearly broke him in two."

He folded his hands in his lap and paused, perhaps waiting for a reaction. Akiri merely looked at him impassively.

"In case they didn't tell you, this is how you must conduct yourself," the man continued. "When you are presented to the queen, you will bow and say nothing. You will speak only when spoken to, and you will do exactly as she says. In the morning, you will be taken back to Quarra's establishment, where she will pay you for your services. You are never to speak of anything you hear or see while inside the palace. Should you do so, you will be taken before the magistrate and charged with bearing false witness against the queen. You will be found guilty and executed. Am I understood?"

Akiri nodded.

"You must be the strong, silent type," the man remarked. "All the better. And if your lust matches your body, you might even be invited back."

The palace came into view a few minutes later. After passing through the main gate, they rounded the eastern wing and stopped at a tall iron fence with a narrow gate. Six soldiers stood and watched as Akiri climbed out of the carriage.

"Remember what I told you," the man said before closing the carriage door and whistling for the driver to move on.

Akiri approached the gate.

"Another perfumed toy for the queen," mocked one of the guards. "What's it like to be a whore? I bet it beats doing a man's work."

His remarks drew gales of harsh laughter from most of the other soldiers.

"Careful, Pram," said the man closest. "This one looks tougher than the rest."

"Is that right?" Pram said. "You a tough whore? We'll see. Turn around and raise your arms."

Akiri's every instinct yearned to show these men what

being tough really meant. Only with great self-control did he manage to hold his tongue and do as instructed.

After searching him for weapons, Pram waved a hand. "No blades."

He grabbed Akiri's arm and shoved him through the gate. The palace wall stood around a hundred yards away at the top of a sharp slope. Accompanied by all six soldiers, Akiri allowed himself to be pushed and prodded toward it. Eventually, they came to another gate and a narrow staircase on the other side that descended into a dimly lit passage.

"Head straight down," ordered Pram. "Gertie is waiting for you, so you'd better move your ass."

As Akiri continued, he heard the soldiers behind him talking.

"We shouldn't give these fella's such a hard time," said one. "I'd give anything to fuck the queen."

"Well, how 'bout we dress you up in satin and send you in?" suggested Pram.

This roused more laughter, which faded with each step Akiri took.

As the end of the passage came into view, he saw an elderly woman wearing a simple blue dress. She was standing just beyond an open door with a lantern in her hand. Her eyes ran over him and she smiled.

"It looks like Quarra has got it right this time," she remarked, her tone kindly. "There is no need to be concerned."

"I'm not," Akiri told her.

"Good. I am Gertie, and before we proceed, there are one or two things you should know. In spite of what you have been told, you are to enjoy yourself. Do not feel shy. My queen is not fragile, and she likes it when her lovers take the initiative." She let out a sigh. "By the time most men arrive here, they're usually too scared to utter a sound. But you don't seem to have that problem."

She took Akiri's hand and led him to a staircase a few yards further down. At the end of this lay a long, barren hallway. After a few twists and turns, all of which Akiri committed to memory, the passage came to a sudden dead end. Gertie reached down to press an indention in the stonework. The sharp clack of a mechanism followed as the wall swung outward.

Gertie took a moment to peer through. Then, satisfied there was no one about, she gestured for Akiri to follow.

They stepped into another hallway, but not one that bore any similarity to their previous surroundings. This was a broad passage with highly polished marble floors. Artworks of spectacular design decorated the walls, and gold lanterns placed upon evenly spaced marble pedestals illuminated the way more than adequately.

After a few more turns, they stopped outside a pair of imposingly large doors, each one bearing an intricately carved depiction of a lion.

"This is my queen's private bed chamber," she told him. "No one will disturb you. I will be in the room across the hall."

"There are no guards?" asked Akiri.

"Of course," she replied. "But they stay well clear of here. If any were to actually witness one of the queen's lovers entering her chambers, they would be duty bound to report it to the king. And that would be most unfortunate for everyone." She patted him on the shoulder. "But you needn't worry. All will be well."

Akiri opened the door. With a final glance over his

shoulder at a smiling Gertie, he stepped inside.

The queen's chamber was massive. A glowing hearth to the left revealed a sofa and four chairs set around a small glass table. It was utterly unremarkable. He felt like he had been in dozens of rooms just like it. To the right was a dining area that could easily accommodate a dozen guests. Further back beyond the hearth stood bookshelves and a desk with papers and scrolls strewn haphazardly about the top. The bed itself was by far the largest Akiri had ever seen – at least fifteen feet across and nearly twice as long. It was shrouded in a cloak of sheer silver material and surrounded by golden lanterns held aloft on marble pedestals. A door to the right was partly open, allowing him to see that this was a bathing chamber.

Behind the silver cloth Akiri saw a figure moving toward the edge of the bed. Suddenly he was uncomfortably aware of how ridiculous he must look in his unmanly attire.

"What is your name?" called a soft, feminine voice.

"Akiri, Your Highness." Remembering what he was told, he bowed low.

"And do you know why you are here, Akiri?" she asked.

"I do, Your Highness."

"Is that so? Then tell me."

Akiri considered his words carefully. "I am here to provide you with pleasure."

"And you do not think my king able to do so?"

"That is not for me to say, Your Highness."

There was a long silence before she spoke again. "You do not sound like the others that have come here. Come closer so that I might get a better look at you."

Akiri approached the bed, stopping when only a few feet away. He could see the silhouetted figure of the queen kneeling on the bed, facing him. "Am I to your liking?" he asked.

"Indeed you are. It would seem I have been sent a *real* man this time. A man of strength. And of danger, unless I miss my guess."

"Your Highness is perceptive."

"But it begs the question: Why would such a man be sent to my bed? Someone of such obvious power could possibly harm me."

"I mean you no harm, Your Highness," Akiri replied. "You have my word."

"You have an air of honesty about you that is most refreshing," the queen said. "I will take you at your word." Easing aside the curtain, she stepped off the bed with slow, seductive movements.

Dressed only in a white silk nightgown that did little to cover her ample curves, she regarded him with large, deep blue eyes. A cascade of auburn hair tumbled halfway down her back in loose curls, and her flawless skin bore the lush olive complexion of the women from the far west. Akiri was immediately transfixed by her beauty.

"I wonder why they would dress you in such gaudy attire?" she said, a tiny smile forming on her full lips. "A man of action should not be wearing such things."

She moved in close to run her hands over Akiri's chest, where his heart was pounding wildly. She was far, far beyond anything he might have been expecting. It felt like an eternity since he had been with a woman. Every aspect of the queen was perfect – from her sensual touch to the sweet scent of honeysuckle she carried, and even the way she simply looked at him with those enormous eyes. All of this and more sent his passions into a raging inferno.

Her hands drifted slowly down, and he felt himself becoming hard. By the time the tips of her fingers were tracing the outline of his shaft, the strain was almost painful. The queen licked her lips and moaned softly.

"Definitely a man of action," she sighed, the promise of pleasure dripping from each word. Taking a step back, she slid the nightgown from her shoulders, allowing it to shimmer its way down her body and gather gently at her feet.

"Do you find me beautiful?" she asked playfully.

Akiri nodded. "You are stunning, Your Highness."

Her breasts were full and perfectly shaped, and though tall, her curves were in exact proportion to her height. The small area of hair between her legs had been neatly shaped to form a strip an inch long and no wider than a man's finger.

Remembering what Gertie had said, he stripped off his shirt and moved in closer. Before the queen could react, he wrapped a powerful arm around her waist and pulled her roughly to him. She gasped, though whether this was in surprise or delight, he wasn't sure. For a moment, he ran his fingers through her hair, then with a firm jerk, pulled her head back and kissed her deeply.

She responded eagerly, her tongue searching for his and her hips pressing hard against his aching member. When their lips parted, her eyes were closed and her breathing was rapid.

"A real man at last," she gasped in what was barely a whisper.

Scooping her up into his arms, Akiri carried her over to the bed. His lust was driving away all other thoughts. Pausing only to remove the last of his clothing, he moved in beside her, propping himself up on one elbow to loom over her naked form, delighting in every inch of her beauty.

For the briefest of moments, it was obvious to Akiri that she reveled in his adoration, but impatience quickly overcame her. Wrapping her arms around his neck, she pulled him down to her waiting lips. No further words were needed. The fire of passion was all they knew. Still clinging to him, she rolled so that she was the one on top. It was the first time Akiri had experienced a woman assuming the dominant position in lovemaking, but he willingly went along with her desire. She straddled him just above his eager manhood and he felt the heat radiating from between her legs.

Looking down at him one final time, the queen cupped his face in her hands and then slid slowly down until he was fully inside her. Throwing her head back, she let out a wild scream of ecstasy.

The pleasure was shared equally. Never before had Akiri known a woman who filled him with such erotic bliss. He was soon utterly lost in the oblivion of lust.

He had no idea how long their lovemaking lasted. It was raw and primal – like a raging tempest. The explosion of his seed erupted inside her, brought her to a climax that made her entire body shudder for more than a full minute. Even when it had passed, she refused to let Akiri withdraw for several more minutes while her body continued to jerk erratically.

Finally, she rolled beside him and looked into his eyes. He could see that her passion was still burning fiercely. It was little wonder that the king could not satisfy this woman.

She kissed his chest, smiling impishly. "I hope you are not completely spent."

Before Akiri could answer, she began making her way

down, kissing and lapping up the love sweat that now covered them both. In only a few seconds, her skillful lips and tongue had him fully erect once again.

For hour upon hour, they continued in this way. Never had Akiri known a woman fired with such unyielding lust; it felt as if the very life force within him was being drained away. By the time she was eventually exhausted, he knew that he could not have continued any longer even if she had demanded it of him. He couldn't help but wonder at the caliber of men who had passed through her bed before him. How many of those had possessed the stamina to satisfy her lust?

"I hope you will choose to return," she said, throwing an arm over his chest, mercifully with a contented smile now on her face.

He watched her closely until her eyes closed and her breathing became regular and deep. With great care, he then lifted her arm from his chest and slipped out of the bed. The thought of putting the ridiculous clothes back on brought a frown to his face. But it was either that or wander the palace naked.

On reaching the door, he glanced back over to the bed. The queen had not stirred. He peered into the hallway and listened closely. The door across the hall leading into Gertie's room was closed. He had thought about using her to discover where Tuvarius' quarters were, but realized such a move might risk alerting the guards. Even so, unless he wanted to wander aimlessly, he needed to find someone to guide him. That much was certain.

After softly closing the queen's door, he made his way to a broad archway at the far end of the hall. More doors lined the walls at regular intervals. Akiri paused at each one, but they were all empty guest rooms. It seemed Queen Chelia had ensured that the entire wing was empty of any potential prying eyes.

He moved on, eyes and ears both constantly alert. The next hallway he came to was lined with open archways leading into various parlors and rooms designed for entertainment. Halfway to the end, he heard hushed whispers coming from a room to his right. Crouching low, he peered around the corner of the entrance and saw a young man talking to one of the house maids. Drawing back again, he continued to listen. Apparently, the youth had arranged a secret rendezvous.

"Your mother will have me whipped if she catches us," whispered the girl, a slight tremor in her voice.

"What do you think she'll do to me?" said the boy. "She'll disown me for sure."

"She will not."

"Of course she will. She doesn't care a lick about me. All she cares about is my older brother and securing his place in the royal court. To her I'm just the bastard she had by accident after her husband died. This would give her the excuse she needs to rid herself of me once and for all."

"That's dreadful," remarked the girl, with no small measure of pity. "But why risk so much?"

"Because I love you."

There was the brief sound of the two lovers sharing a passionate kiss.

"I can't," she said, her breathing rapid. "Not here. Not like this."

"But don't you love me?"

"I do." Her voice became firm. "And if you truly love *me*, you will not treat me like a common whore. This is not a suitable place. And I will not do it."

"I… I'm sorry," the boy stammered. "It's just that you drive my passions wild. I didn't mean to… well… you know."

"It's all right." Her tone softened. "Be patient. If the gods want us to be together, they will provide a way in the end. But for now, we can't risk being seen. I have to go before I'm missed. You should wait here for a few minutes."

Akiri backed away and ducked inside a small ballroom. This could be the opportunity he was hoping for. A few moments later he heard the girl hurrying away. He waited until the creaking of a door further down told him that she was now out of sight, then made his way back to where the boy was still waiting.

After a few minutes, the youth left the room. Akiri was on him in an instant, wrapping a thick arm around his throat and covering his mouth. The boy was slender, though not frail, and only slightly shorter than himself. At first he twisted and struggled, but Akiri tightened his hold and dragged him back into the room.

"Be still and you shall live," he whispered.

The boy soon realized that he was up against someone far too powerful to resist and gave up the fight.

"If you cry out, I will snap your neck," Akiri told him. "Do you understand?"

His captive nodded furiously.

He uncovered the youth's mouth. "What is your name?"

"Daresh," he replied. "Please don't hurt me. I haven't done anything wrong."

"Perhaps. But would your mother feel the same way?"

The boy stiffened. "You saw?"

"Of course I did. And if you want me to keep your secret,

you'll tell me exactly what I need to know."

"Yes. Yes. Of course."

"Where can I find Tuvarius?"

Although terrified, the youth said nothing. Akiri tightened his grip further. "Answer me."

"Why do you want to find *him*?"

"That is not your concern. Tell me… now."

The added steel in Akiri's tone was sufficient to loosen his tongue. "If I do, you must promise not to say a word about who told you. Or who you saw me with… not to anyone."

"*That much,* I can promise."

The words flowed from the youngster's mouth. "The doors at the end of this hall will take you into the king's receiving chamber. Directly behind the throne is another door that leads to the north tower. Tuvarius resides somewhere up there. That's all I know. Honestly, it is."

Akiri could hear no deception. Satisfied, he tightened his hold, completely cutting off the youth's air supply. He struggled uselessly for a few seconds before falling limp. Akiri placed him in a nearby corner, knowing he would remain unconscious long enough for him to be well away.

As instructed, he followed the corridor to the end and passed through the pair of large arched doors leading into the receiving hall. Though it was currently empty, it was easy to visualize the kind of scenes that would often take place in this vast chamber. This was where the king would greet foreign nobles and other important guests. Massive columns reaching all the way up to the thirty-foot-high ceiling flanked a walkway of polished crimson tiles. At the far end of this, imposingly placed upon a dais, stood a magnificent gold and ivory throne. Decorating the walls were huge tapestries depicting men proudly bearing the royal crest while performing various acts of heroism. This was a room with two purposes only – to inspire awe and boast of the king's wealth.

Relieved and more than a little surprised to find that there was no one about, Akiri hurried behind the throne and through the door that Daresh had indicated. The narrow corridor he stepped into was starved of light; just a few burned down nubs of candles offered any relief to the dark. The air was much colder, a direct contrast to the splendor he had just left behind. He pressed on, eventually coming to a flight of spiral stairs.

The stairs rose for more than one hundred feet before ending in a narrow chamber with a raised portcullis-like iron grille at the entrance. Through an identical opening on the wall directly ahead he could see another ascending stairway. This was where he would have expected to find guards. But there was no one. Only a rickety wooden chair tossed carelessly against the wall.

He paused for a moment to listen behind him. Not a sound. Cautiously, he stepped inside and started toward the next set of stairs.

He knew after taking only three or four paces that he had made a bad mistake. A brief, high-pitched squeak of metal cogs jerking into action sounded a warning from both the front and back of him. But it was a warning far too late even for someone blessed with Akiri's rapid reactions. He barely had time to spin around before both portcullises dropped simultaneously, slamming shut with a force that shook the entire floor.

Had he triggered some hidden device?

He tried to lift both barriers, but even his tremendous

strength could not budge them. A search of the walls for a release mechanism produced nothing. Feeling like a rat in a cage, he had to accept that he was trapped.

Very soon he heard the stomping of approaching boots from below. Akiri cursed his carelessness. Now he would need to fight his way out. Though without any kind of weapon and confined to such a small space, it was a fight he might not be able to win.

The soldiers halted just before they came into view. Then, from the far side of the other portcullis, he heard a door groan open. The footfalls that approached were lighter and less rapid. Just one person.

He remained out of sight.

"Why have you come here?" demanded a deep commanding voice.

Realizing he had been heard, Akiri stepped into the light. "I seek Tuvarius." There was no sense in lying at this point.

"And why would you do such a foolish thing? Has Zemel become so desperate that he would send *you* to deceive me?"

Being identified so easily startled him. "King Zemel did not send me," he said, trying hard to keep the lie from his voice. "I came here of my own accord to talk with you."

"And this is how you choose to introduce yourself? Sneaking around the palace like a thief?"

"I could see no other way. The guards at the gate refused me entry. And they told me that you were not to be found here."

A mocking laugh sounded. "A falsehood easily disproved. The guards tell people merely what they are ordered to say. In reality, though few ever see me, just about everyone living in Vurna is aware of my presence. Indeed, from what I am told, many of them fear me greatly."

Akiri was quick to agree. "As you say, I soon learned the truth. But that did not make gaining an audience with you any easier. I was forced to adopt more devious means. I had hoped to catch you alone; that a private talk might convince you of my true intent."

"Which is what exactly?"

"To know who my father was."

"Your father is dead. That is all you need to know."

"You're wrong! I need to know more. I need you to tell me *how* he died."

There was a long pause before Tuvarius spoke again. "Go with the guards," he ordered. "Do not try to escape."

The portcullis leading downstairs slowly rose again. A moment later six guards appeared, swords drawn. Akiri kept his hands firmly to his sides as one of them produced a set of shackles.

"That won't be necessary," Tuvarius' voice instructed. "They would not hold him anyway, I suspect."

One of the other guards regarded their prisoner with a broad smirk. "He doesn't look so dangerous to me. Who dressed you up? Your husband?"

"Akiri," called Tuvarius. "If that man utters another word, you have my permission to kill him."

He grinned viciously. "Thank you, uncle. I would enjoy that."

Suitably warned, and no doubt alerted by the familial reference, his tormentor wisely refrained from saying anything further.

The soldiers escorted him back down the stairs and through the receiving hall, then along a series of broad corridors. After a time, the splendid décor disappeared and they entered an area with unadorned walls of gray stone.

Here they placed him in a room containing half a dozen cots, a table, chairs, and an empty water basin. Most likely a disused guard or servant quarters, Akiri considered.

He wasn't sure what he had been expecting, but this wasn't it. He could hear through the closed door that two of the soldiers were remaining on duty immediately outside. Escape was now certainly possible, had he a mind to, but having come this far, that would not serve his purpose. Content to see how things developed, at least in the short term, he stretched out on one of the cots and closed his eyes.

He drifted into a light sleep – though always with one ear cocked to be fully alert in an instant if danger threatened. Several hours passed before his rest was interrupted, and then only by a young girl bringing him a bowl of steaming beef stew and a cup of water.

"Lord Tuvarius said to tell you that he will be with you shortly," she said, before hurrying away again.

Akiri eyed the food with suspicion. Experience had taught him never to eat from the table of an enemy, and he was not about to ignore that rule now, even though he was pretending to be here on a perfectly innocent mission and should not be regarding his uncle as an enemy. Tuvarius might take this refusal to eat as an insult, but that was a risk he was willing to take.

When the door opened once more, a man dressed in a black robe stepped inside. Though not as tall as Akiri, he had an equally solid build. His silver hair was neatly trimmed to his shoulders and held in place by a black circlet around his brow. From out of a face creased by many years of toil and worry, hazel eyes bored into Akiri.

"I'll be fine on my own," he said, casually waving away the two guards at his back. They obeyed without hesitation.

Akiri rose to his feet and gave the man a polite nod. "Are you Tuvarius?"

"Who else would I be, boy?" he replied. "I honestly didn't think Zemel would be this stupid. To send you, of all people." He shook his head. "Am I really supposed to believe that you have sought me out simply to reunite with your family?"

"I sought you out because I want to know the truth," Akiri replied.

"The truth? What truth? That you serve a mad tyrant? That he murdered your father and betrayed the Tul'Zahar?" His voice dripped with hatred.

"Yes, if that is the truth. I want to know everything about where I come from."

Tuvarius sneered. "And so you sneak into the palace and risk death in order to discover this. What kind of fool do you take me for?"

Akiri searched for a convincing response, but none was forthcoming. His uncle was not believing his story. Not a single word of it. "If you are so sure that I am lying, why allow me to live?" he asked.

"Oh, I am sure enough, Akiri. I have watched you for many years. Your dedication to King Zemel is absolute."

"It *was*. That much is true. But no longer. I am exiled."

"For what reason?"

"I was convicted of murdering General Kirlon Galliani, along with two of his lieutenants."

Tuvarius leaned forward. "And were you guilty of this?"

"They all died at my hand, yes. But I did not murder them. The general paid a large amount of gold to have me assassinated–"

"Let me guess," Tuvarius cut in. "As the Dul'Buhar

commander, you exercised your right to execute him. Am I correct?"

Akiri was taken aback by how perceptive his uncle was. "Yes. But the general's family is very powerful. They used their influence to have me convicted."

"I see. And I suppose rather than ordering your execution, Zemel exiled you instead, citing your past service as a reason for his clemency." He chuckled. "Very clever. But it will do him no good. The Scepter of Xarbaal is beyond his reach… and mine too. He will never again taste its power."

Akiri cocked his head, feigning ignorance. "What does the Scepter of Xarbaal have to do with any of this?"

Tuvarius burst into laughter. "Years under the dark magic of Zemel has not made a good liar of you, nephew." He walked over to the door. "And though I do not sense his foul corruption within you, I am now most curious…"

With a sharp movement, he pulled open the door and waved the pair of guards inside. "Kill him," he ordered.

Akiri tensed instantly. The two soldiers rushed in, swords at the ready. He could tell by their approach that they were well trained. But they were not Dul'Buhar.

They struck from both sides at once, the first soldier jabbing straight at his lower body, the second swinging his blade in a neck high horizontal sweep. Akiri reacted instinctively, ducking low and bouncing forward on his haunches. One blade shot behind him and the other passed over his head with more than a foot to spare. In the same fluid movement, he spun sharply left and thrust out a leg. The rock-hard base of his heel collided with the first soldier's knee, forcing it violently back against the joint. The dreadful agony contorting the man's face was all he needed to know the blow had done its work. Although barely able to keep his balance, he made a weak second attempt to stab at Akiri's body, but it was far too slow to present any danger. Akiri was already behind him, using him as a shield from the second soldier and driving both fists into his kidneys. An instant later, he wrenched the sword from the gasping man's hand and pushed him aside.

With the fury burning in his eyes temporarily obliterating his discipline, the second soldier swung his blade in a wild downward arc. Akiri had all the time in the world to step aside from this clumsy attack. A loud clang echoed as the man's steel struck against the hard tiles. Badly off balance and with his arm fully outstretched, he had no defense to offer as Akiri's blade sliced deep across his forearm. Roaring in pain he reared back, but even before his dropped sword had fully settled onto the floor, a second strike directly into his heart settled matters.

The first soldier was trying his best to support himself on one leg well enough to fight on. Seeing his comrade fall, his fingers fumbled for the handle of a small dagger strapped to his belt. It was brave, but it was also to be his final act in this world. Akiri thrust his sword into the man's neck so hard that it protruded through on the other side by nearly a foot.

The gurgling gasp of his fallen enemy was a welcome sound, and the blood as beautiful as the most magnificent sunset. Jerking the blade free, Akiri swung around to the corner where Tuvarius was watching with interest. A tiny smile on his lips plainly said that he was not afraid.

"Not bad," he remarked. "Not bad at all." He lifted his right hand. "*Imobio!*"

As Akiri started to move toward him, he suddenly jerked

to a stop, as if an invisible hand had wrapped itself around his entire body and was holding him in place with unrelenting power. He struggled to break free, but even with his great strength, it was futile. He glared helplessly at his still smiling uncle.

"And just how have you managed to fill your *merkesh*?" Tuvarius enquired, moving closer and extending his hand so that the palm hovered directly over Akiri's heart. He closed his eyes. "Ah, I see now. Yes. So tell me. When did you encounter a dragon?"

Akiri remained silent.

"Not that it matters. But it is clear that you have. And it was this contact that gave life to your *merkesh*. Unfortunately, it is stunted. The result of Zemel's foul magic, I would assume." He scrutinized Akiri steadily. "Have you never wondered where your great strength comes from?"

Akiri, still grunting with the effort of trying to free himself, paused for a moment. "It comes from the bond I held with the king."

Tuvarius nodded. "But as you are aware, that connection has been broken. And though you are damaged, the dragon has returned your strength." He sighed. "Unfortunately, I can see that you understand nothing of what I say. A great pity."

The grip on Akiri tightened. Almost immediately, he felt the crushing weight robbing him of consciousness. His heart thudded ever more loudly in his ears as darkness crept in.

Chapter Nine

When the stirrings of consciousness returned, the first thing Akiri heard was the sound of rats scurrying about. He breathed in cold, dank air filled with the stench of decay and death, and as his sight gradually returned, he could make out that he was inside a room with a single door. The dull gray of the stone, the rusted chains, the desiccated excrement shoved into the corners – everything about the cellar confirmed its true nature as a prison.

He had been chained to the wall with his hands stretched up over his head. The tips of his fingers soon confirmed that he had been secured with Sylfari shackles. Apart from literally ripping off his own hands, there was no possible way to break free from them.

That he still lived suggested that Tuvarius must have plans for him, and considering the situation, those plans included torture. Not that it would serve any purpose. No amount of pain would make him betray his king.

The door opened, and a figure wearing a crimson robe entered. Though the hood was pulled up and hid his visitor's features, the scent of her perfume told him at once that it was Queen Chelia. She stood in silence just inside the doorway for a full minute before turning away and leaving.

He wondered what thoughts had passed through her mind as she looked upon him. There was no doubt that he felt some regret for the trouble he must surely have caused her. She was a woman of deep passion, and by far the most skilled lover he had ever been with. But ultimately, she had merely been a means to an end. It was important to remember that. He could not allow his emotions to cloud his mind.

Several more hours passed before the door opened again. This time it was Tuvarius. After placing a lantern in the center of the cell, he stood there regarding Akiri closely in the dim light.

"You have the look of your mother," he eventually remarked. "But the spirit of your father."

"Whatever you came here to do, just get on with it," Akiri told him defiantly.

"In time." Tuvarius shook his head and chuckled. "I have to admit that when my *wards* told me you had entered the palace, I was most surprised to find you in the company of the queen. Trust me when I say that she was none too pleased to discover who you really are. It has taken no small measure of persuasion on my part to convince her that you should be allowed to keep your cock attached to your body. You must have shown her something very special indeed to have upset her so badly." He waved a dismissive hand. "Little matter. She has no wish for her dear husband to find out about her secret rendezvous, so she will not trouble us any further."

He crossed the room, his gaze probing deeply into Akiri's eyes. "So much damage. I fear you may never regain what you have lost."

"I am not damaged," he snapped back.

"Of course you are. Your *merkesh* only enhances your physical attributes. True magic is lost to you."

Akiri sniffed. "I care nothing for magic. A keen mind and sharp steel are all I require."

"Your father would not have agreed. He was a truly powerful Tul'Zahar. Only the beast Zemel rivaled his strength. Sadly, whatever power Zemel used to bind you to him may prevent you from ever experiencing what I speak of. Only time will tell, I suppose." He produced a key from his sleeve.

Suspicion gripped Akiri. "What is this? You are releasing me?"

"Of course," he replied, smiling. "What did you think was going to happen? I merely needed you contained until I had a chance to settle things with King Lanmar."

"Then why did you have those men attack me?"

"A test. Nothing more. And of course, one that you passed most easily. But that made it necessary to hold you here until I could explain what had happened. The men you killed were part of the king's own guard."

"Then he should train his guard better. They were easily overcome."

"Perhaps *you* can train them during your stay with me," Tuvarius suggested.

Akiri furrowed his brow. "Are you saying that you will allow me to remain here in the palace?"

Tuvarius reached up and unlocked the shackles. "For a time, certainly. At least until you are fully convinced of the futility of your intentions." He raised his hand. "Please don't bother lying to me any longer. I know Zemel sent you. And I also know that you will not leave or attempt to kill me until you have the information you came here for. After all, even the legendary Akiri can't obtain information from a dead man. But understand that in the unlikely event that you were able to discover the Scepter's location, it would still do you no good. You cannot acquire it. No one can."

Akiri was uncertain how to reply. This could be a ploy to have him admit what up until this point Tuvarius was only suspecting. Now free of the shackles, he waved a careless hand. "I care nothing about this Scepter. Keep the secret if you wish."

Tuvarius laughed. "You truly have much to learn. A blind man could see through you in an instant. Did the Dul'Buhar teach you nothing of subterfuge and intrigue?"

"The Dul'Buhar do not lie," he replied proudly. "We have no need for such skills."

"But you are no longer a part of them," Tuvarius pointed out. "And if you are to survive in this new world you face, there are other skills you will need beyond those you have been taught." He snapped his fingers. Almost at once, a young servant boy hurried in carrying a folded robe. "Cover yourself with this for now. We can't have you wandering around the palace in those ridiculous clothes."

Akiri accepted the garment and slipped it on. "Tell me, uncle. If you are so certain I am an agent of King Zemel, why not kill me and be done with it?"

Tuvarius shrugged. "Good sense might say I should. Perhaps I'm just a sentimental old fool who doesn't wish to have the blood of his brother's child on his hands. Then again, perhaps King Zemel is not the only one with plans for you."

He led the way up a flight of stairs and through a series of corridors, passing by kitchens, storerooms, and servants' quarters. Once back in the main area of the palace, Akiri was taken to a guest room in the east tower. Though by no means as lavish as the queen's chambers, it was still far more comfortable than anything to which he was accustomed. A plate of beef and fruit lay on a table near the window, along with a bottle of wine. The bed looked soft. Almost certainly too soft, Akiri suspected.

"Do not leave this room until I summon you," Tuvarius instructed. "The mother of the young lord you assaulted while looking for me is demanding your head, and has the wealth and power to be granted her wish. I fear it will take me some time to calm her down." He began laughing. "Between her and the queen, I don't see how much more difficult you could have made this. Though I must admit, I envy you your liaison with Her Majesty. I hear tell she is every bit the passionate woman."

A few minutes after Tuvarius left, a young girl arrived with a fresh set of clothes. It was with enormous relief that he was able to shed his current garb, though the new garments provided were still a little tight-fitting for his large frame.

He remained in the room for the better part of two days. Throughout this time, Tuvarius did not appear once, though he did send word that his nephew should remain patient. Akiri did not mind in the least. Patience was something he had in abundance.

Tuvarius was definitely not the sort of man to act without thought, and he had already demonstrated quite effectively that his magic was powerful enough to be lethal. Akiri had fought battle mages in the past and knew how weak they generally were. Weak and cowardly. Hiding behind fire and ice while using superficial glamour to frighten the faint of heart. But Tuvarius was different. He had felt the man's power, and it was unlike anything he had experienced before. Of course, he was well aware that there were at least a few genuinely powerful sorcerers in the world. King Zemel was one, but most shunned a public profile, and it was rare for ordinary people to actually encounter them. This was likely the reason why Tuvarius had gained such a sinister reputation.

When his uncle returned, he bore a grave expression. "Tell me, just how many people *did* you kill before you came here?" he demanded.

Akiri was sitting at the table, reading. He closed the book. "If you mean since I've been in Galfaria, only one. Well, three, if you count the soldiers you set on me. But you already know about that."

"So you did murder Barsyn Bartone," he spat. "Wonderful. You have now managed to complicate matters even further." He planted his hands on his hips. "Explain yourself. And be sure to tell me the truth."

"I needed a way to get inside the palace," Akiri explained. There was no remorse or apology in his tone, only a statement of fact. "Killing him provided that means."

When he added nothing more, Tuvarius huffed a disdainful laugh. "I don't believe it. You are actually protecting that cur Geridia? Fool! How do you think I know it was you?"

"You mean Geridia has spoken of my involvement?"

"Of course he has. The man has no spine at all. Once the Hunari Guild got hold of him, he–"

"The Hunari Guild?" Akiri cut in. "Geridia led me to believe that they would only become involved if one of their own was killed."

"That might be true normally. But Barsyn Bartone was a

very prominent man, and there has been much talk in the city of his killing – talk that is potentially very damaging to the Guild. And Bartone had written in his journal several times how much Geridia coveted his pendant. It was not such a great leap for the Hunari to trace the killing back to him. After they actually caught him in possession of it, he had little choice but to confess everything. He has now named you as the killer in the hope of avoiding his own execution."

Akiri's eyes narrowed. "And do you think he will succeed?"

His uncle flicked a hand. "He has no more hope of saving his worthless life than those two soldiers had of defeating you. If all else fails, I will see to the wretch myself. But the problem with the Hunari Guild remains. Apparently, they now feel that you have damaged their reputation and have come to the king seeking justice."

"What will happen?" Akiri asked.

"You will be called to answer for your crime."

"And if I am found guilty?"

"You don't understand. You have already been found guilty. Only sentencing remains."

Akiri stood and nodded. "Then you are saying there is nothing to be done."

"No, I am saying that you have been found guilty. You must now go before the king and plead your case. You must convince him why your head should not be on a pike by morning." He went to the door and gestured for Akiri to follow. "I hope your mind is as sharp as your sword."

He followed his uncle to the receiving hall. King Lanmar had taken his seat on the throne. Though his gray hair and deep wrinkles told of his advanced years, his broad shoulders and regal posture bespoke a man of vitality and strength. He was draped in a golden cloak, while a crown adorned with both diamonds and blood rubies rested proudly on his head. Beside him stood Queen Chelia. Her hair was tied into a series of tiny braids with silver strands woven within. The sleek sapphire dress she wore shimmered in the light cast down by twin crystal chandeliers that dominated the ceiling. Six of the king's guards stood on either side of the royal couple, each one bearing a tall onyx-tipped spear and wearing a longsword on his belt.

Facing the monarchs stood three men clad in leather armor bearing the emblem of a clenched fist embossed on the breast. Akiri assumed this trio was here representing the Hunari Guild. Kneeling at their feet was Geridia, his face heavily bruised and his once elegant clothing now torn and stained with blood. He looked down at the floor as Akiri approached.

But it was the queen who caught his attention. Her expression was impassive, but her eyes were burning brightly and never left him for an instant.

Tuvarius motioned him to a spot beside the Hunari and then stepped up to join the royal couple on the dais. There was absolute silence for a long moment as the king regarded Akiri. He found the monarch's gaze oddly unsettling, as if he was digging deeply into his soul. Not even King Zemel had made him feel this uncomfortable.

Finally, the king spoke. "You are Akiri?"

He bowed. "I am."

"You will address my husband as *Your Highness*, dog," snapped the queen.

The king smiled over to his wife. "Calm yourself, my love. Low born cannot be expected to understand etiquette."

"I apologize, Your Highness," Akiri said. "I meant no offense."

"It is not me who you have offended, young man," the king returned. "You have committed murder. In spite of that, seeing as you are the nephew of my most trusted advisor, Lord Tuvarius, I would be inclined to show mercy. But unfortunately, the Hunari have taken exception to your crime. You have embarrassed them."

The Hunari standing to the left of Geridia bowed low. Shorter than his companions, he was the only one of the three wearing a red sash around his waist. "Your Highness, I am Volar Markasa, Captain and Regional Commander in Vurna. I assure you that this is about far more than simply our reputation. This is about achieving justice for our late client. We have provided you with all the proof you need. All we ask is that you use your great wisdom to pronounce a fitting sentence on this… Akiri."

"Your concern is appreciated, Captain," said the king, "as is your desire to seek justice." His eyes returned to Akiri. "And what have you to say?"

"Nothing, Your Highness," replied Akiri. "If my guilt is not in question, then there is nothing left for me to do but accept my fate."

King Lanmar raised an eyebrow. "Brave words indeed, considering the consequences. And do you feel what you have done warrants death?"

"Many things men do make them deserving of death, Your Highness. I am no different. But I would question the motives of the men who seek to mete out justice upon me. Regardless of who actually delivered the fatal strike, it was most assuredly the Hunari Guild's incompetence as much as anything else that was responsible for the death of Barsyn Bartone."

"That is a lie!" shouted Volar.

Akiri diverted his attention. "Then Captain, please explain how a lone intruder was able to overcome a large team of your supposedly highly trained men and gain entry to a house that you were responsible for securing. And how did this intruder manage to escape so easily from inside, once the alarm was sounded? Should my death be required, so be it. But I would hope very much that it results in word of your failings becoming common knowledge." He locked eyes with the captain. "*That* would certainly be justice."

Veins bulged from Volar's neck. "You will not sully our reputation with falsehoods. The Hunari Guild is trusted throughout Galfaria with the safety of her most important citizens."

"Not for long, I suspect," remarked King Lanmar. "Akiri is correct. Bartone's death was indeed caused at least in part by your failure to adequately protect him. Should this become public knowledge, many nobles might think twice before continuing to place their lives in the Guild's hands."

"And I will ensure that it *does* become public," added Tuvarius. "If that is my nephew's wish."

Akiri smiled inwardly, but remained expressionless. "It is, uncle."

Volar's eyes darted from a grinning Tuvarius back to the king. "Your Highness, may I request a moment to speak with my men?"

The king gave a curt nod and a wave of his hand. Volar immediately led the other two Hunari a short distance away where they huddled together and began talking in urgent hushed whispers. Akiri glanced at Geridia, his eyes still downcast and his narrow shoulders slumped forward. He looked utterly defeated.

The Hunari returned a few minutes later. After shooting Akiri a hate-filled look, Volar bowed to the king.

"We have discussed the matter, Your Highness," he began. "And we are now agreed that justice would not be best served by the death of Akiri. At worst, he was merely a tool used by Geridia. It was Geridia himself who planned and instigated the murder of our client. Therefore, it should be he who pays the price."

The king rubbed his chin. "And you do not feel that Akiri also bears responsibility? Though he has not made any admission of guilt, was it not stated in your petition that you had proof it was he who dealt the fatal blow?"

Volar cleared his throat. "Upon further consideration, we have found that this is not proven as decisively as first thought. Akiri was a guest in Geridia's house. It is likely he implicated Akiri in order to protect his long-serving personal guard, Rena."

"So you are now saying it was this Rena person who got past your men?"

"Not in the manner suggested, Your Highness. It was already known to us that she was our client's lover, and we had instructions that she should be allowed to pass. It wasn't until after the deed was done that we discovered what had happened. There is no way we could have prevented it."

Even in his cowed condition, this was too much for Geridia to bear. He jerked to his feet. "That is not true and you know it!" he shouted. "Rena has never so much as spoken to that pig."

Volar let his hand fly, striking the merchant across the jaw and sending him crumbling back to the floor. "You will not speak."

"And do you know where Rena is?" asked Lanmar.

"Not at present, Your Highness. But we will begin the search at once."

"Leave her alone!" pleaded Geridia. "She has done nothing wrong, I swear." This outburst was met by a swift kick to the stomach. He curled up, gasping for air.

The king turned to his queen. "And what do you think of all this, my love?"

Akiri could see Tuvarius tense.

Chelia smiled sweetly at her husband. "I think the Hunari are all liars and rogues, my dearest. As for this Akiri person, I consider him to be nothing more than a brute and a murderer. But as the accusations against him have been recanted, I see no other choice but to free him."

Lanmar reached over to take hold of her hand. "My thoughts sound like music when spoken from your lips." He turned to Akiri. "You are officially declared guiltless. As for Geridia, the sentence is clear. I also order the apprehension of Rena, his co-conspirator. I trust the Hunari Guild can handle this?"

Volar nodded. "It will be done. I would ask only that Geridia's sentence be carried out at once. I would not wish to have him spreading lies that could damage our good standing."

"That is acceptable," said the king. He waved his hand dismissively. "You can go now. This has already taken up too much of my time. My son's sixteenth birthday is nearly upon us, and I would have this matter concluded."

Akiri and the three Hunari all bowed in acknowledgement while a sobbing Geridia was dragged away by two of the king's guard.

Tuvarius whispered something into Lanmar's ear before stepping down from the dais and motioning for his nephew to follow. As they left the hall, Akiri caught Queen Chelia passing a brief look of anger in his direction. It was almost imperceptible, but she clearly hated him.

"Very good," said Tuvarius approvingly once out of earshot. "Your mind is quite sharp. It was clever to use the Guild's reputation against them."

"A result of my training," said Akiri. "We learn to exploit our enemy's weaknesses."

His uncle smiled. "I can only assume that you hope to do the same with me. And who knows? Perhaps you will even succeed. We shall see."

Chapter Ten

Tuvarius led the way up to his quarters on the north tower, a quite plainly furnished room containing a bed, two tables, and several bookshelves. Numerous chests were piled up in the room, some of them casually left wide open to reveal yet more books and a few crumpled clothes.

"This is where I spend most of my time," Tuvarius told him. "I enjoy the solitude. Not to mention the fact that it gives me an air of mystery. Useful when you are trying to stay out of sight."

"And why would you want to do that?" Akiri asked.

His uncle snorted a laugh. "Do you think you are the first to be sent here by Zemel?" Grabbing a bottle and two cups, he sat at one of the tables. Once Akiri had joined him, he opened the bottle, allowing the sweet scent of plum brandy to fill the room. "Almost from the moment I arrived here, he's been trying to get to me. In truth, I never expected him to send you. Too risky, and so very unlike him. The madness must be growing."

"King Zemel is not mad," Akiri retorted.

"Of course he is," Tuvarius snapped back. "He may not always appear to be, but if he still desires the Scepter after such a long time, then he most surely remains unsound of mind." His tone softened a little. "However, if it helps to ease your own thoughts, nephew, he was not always that way."

Akiri refused to believe him, and there was nothing Tuvarius could say that would sway him.

His uncle gave him a sad smile and poured the brandy. "To have the son of his chief adversary serve him was to be his final revenge." He downed the drink in a single gulp and immediately poured another. "I once served King Zemel in the same way you do. In fact, I was one of the very last to see what he had become. Your father tried to tell me, but like you I refused to accept it. It wasn't until the wars began that I finally came to realize the truth."

Akiri pushed the brandy aside. "And what truth is that?"

"That he is possessed. You see, when Zemel returned from the east, bearing the Scepter of Xarbaal, he assured the Tul'Zahar that the legends they had heard were unfounded. He insisted it was nothing more than a trinket – a ceremonial object of no significant power. He even went so far as to suggest that it might not be the original Scepter. And at first, nothing appeared to be amiss." His eyes darkened. "But then the rumors of war started. Zemel was convinced that the King of Merina to the south was plotting to attack us. He even had strong evidence to support this claim."

"Merina *did* attack us," Akiri jumped in.

Tuvarius sniffed. "Of course. What else could they do? Zemel had assassinated their king."

Akiri looked at him incredulously. "That is a lie."

"I thought so too when the King of Kalmar first made the accusation. Only your father was able to see the truth immediately."

"Is that why he betrayed his king?" Akiri asked.

"First of all, it was Zemel who betrayed *him*," Tuvarius retorted sharply, struggling with his anger. "But no. Serhan did nothing at first. He shared his concerns with me, but I dismissed them. I told him that even if it were true, I was sure Zemel had good reason. After all, before he was crowned king, he had been a Tul'Zahar himself. As was his father before him."

This revelation took Akiri slightly aback. "But the Tul'Zahar were riders of dragons. King Zemel has outlawed their existence."

Tuvarius' fury was showing clearly on his face. "I know that all too well. He did so because even now he fears the return of our order. Dragons gave us a powerful connection to magic. A fully trained Tul'Zahar atop his dragon was capable of…"

His voice became briefly distant, as if recalling a fading memory. "We were truly powerful. Feared and loved in equal measure." He then stiffened and his eyes burned. "Only through betrayal was Zemel able to withstand us."

"You might believe that King Zemel betrayed the Tul'Zahar," Akiri said. "But I know full well it was *they* who attacked their own nation. They allied themselves with the other five kingdoms in order to conquer Acharia."

"Yes, that is true," Tuvarius agreed. "But they did it to save Acharia from a far worse fate. Zemel had become totally mad with power. He wanted to conquer the world and was prepared to kill anyone who questioned him. I witnessed the aftermath of his insanity. An entire village was burned to the ground and the dismembered bodies of its people left scattered about like fallen leaves."

"War is brutal," Akiri pointed out. "Sometimes one must act without mercy to be victorious."

"I know that, but what I described was not a foreign village. These were our fellow Acharians he slaughtered. A village elder had requested that they be allowed to keep a larger portion of their harvest; it had been a brutal winter and the needs of the army had taxed them beyond their limits. They were close to starving. Zemel replied by sending a hundred men to wipe them from the face of existence." He met Akiri's gaze. "It was only then that your father decided to take action."

Akiri huffed. "I have never heard of such a massacre."

"Why would you have?" replied Tuvarius. "Zemel may be mad, but he is also very clever. The soldiers responsible for razing the village and murdering its people were themselves put to the sword soon afterwards. I only discovered this by chance."

"And how do you know it was the king who ordered all of this killing?"

Tuvarius gave a mirthless chuckle. "Zemel himself told me. He had become so possessed by the power of the Scepter that he cared nothing for what the Tul'Zahar thought. He no longer saw himself as a man but as a god. It was your father's hope that when he took the Scepter and hid it away, Zemel would be released from its hold and regain his sanity. Sadly, it did not work out that way. Instead he flew into a terrible rage and vowed our destruction." Tuvarius folded his hands on the table and lowered his head. "In the end, he achieved his wish."

Akiri regarded his uncle. There didn't appear to be any attempt at deception. The sadness in his eyes and the barely perceptible tremor in his voice made his words highly convincing. But there had to be more than this to the tale. King Zemel would never slaughter his own people, and he was most definitely *not* insane.

Tuvarius shook his head. "You still doubt the truth of what I am saying, but consider this – the only thing preventing Zemel from wreaking unspeakable havoc across the entire land is his loss of the Scepter. Without the power this gave him, he can be contained by a determined foe. Which is exactly what's happening. Acharia has been locked in a state of war for decades, yet still he persists in his lust for more conquest and power. Should you succeed in your mission, Akiri, he will become unstoppable. You will then see for yourself the most loathsome horrors unleashed, and realize too late that I am speaking the truth."

"And do you intend to stop me, uncle?"

"I haven't yet decided. For now, I am content to have you here." He rubbed the bridge of his nose. "I must rest for a while. Return to your room. I will tell you more about your father later."

Akiri rose. He wanted to hear more. Not because he believed his uncle's words, but so that he might find a hole in the story. Something to prove that the man was either lying or delusional. But it was clear Tuvarius would say no more until he was ready to do so.

A guard standing at the entrance to the tower escorted him back to his chambers. He had heard the history of how the wars had started many times. The Tul'Zahar had betrayed the king and tried to steal his throne by joining forces with the five bordering nations. Treachery such as that *had* to be renounced. The seeds of betrayal couldn't be allowed to flourish. Traitors had to be ground down into the dirt. Broken. King Zemel, through his great courage and strength, had eventually prevailed and cast them down. Since that time, the lands to the south had been under his control, their kings and queens mere vassals, but this had not brought about peace. Fresh armies and allegiances were constantly being formed elsewhere, and the rebellions had been never-ending.

Until now, Akiri had never thought to question this account; but after seeing the conviction in Tuvarius' eyes and hearing the pain in his voice, confusion was slowly creeping into his mind. He still wasn't convinced, but for the first time in his life he couldn't help but wonder if there might be more to the story than he had been permitted to know. Something was stirring inside him. Something that he didn't like. He might not be the Commander of the Dul'Buhar any longer, but he was still Akiri.

He was lost in his thoughts when the door cracked open a few inches. Almost immediately the sweet scent of honeysuckle drifted through, telling him that the eyes peering in at him were those of Queen Chelia. A moment later she entered, still wearing the elegant sapphire dress that hugged her curves so perfectly. Flashes of the night they had spent together caused his desires to stir. With an effort, he pushed them aside.

She closed the door behind her and paused for a moment, her expression tight with barely contained anger. "I should have you whipped to death for what you did."

"And what did I do?"

"You used me," she snapped back. "You shared my bed so that you could gain entry to the palace. Do not bother denying it."

"I do not deny it, Your Highness."

She glared at Akiri, fists clenched for a menacing moment. With a burst of energy, she then spanned the room with rapid strides until she stood directly in front of him.

With surprising speed and force, she let her hand fly. He could have easily avoided it, but he allowed the blow to strike him across his cheek. He didn't flinch. That earned him a second slap.

"What kind of man are you?" she demanded, the hint of a tremor in her tone.

"I am Akiri, Your Highness. Nothing more."

She met his eyes. For a moment, he thought that she would strike him again, but instead she reached up and pulled him to her, kissing him with crushing desire. The contact, though brief, was more than enough to fuel the fire of his passion. As she tried to back away, he wrapped his arm around her waist and pulled her hard up against him. Her head jerked back with the force of the movement, and a tiny gasp slipped from her mouth. This time their kiss was even more urgent and fiery, her tongue searching desperately for his. Her fingers danced their way downwards, seeking out the growing bulge between his legs. Akiri held her back.

"Come to me tonight, Your Highness," he said, his tone set firm.

After taking a step back, she smoothed her dress and glowered at him. "You dare to command me?"

"It is an invitation, Your Highness. Not a command."

He wanted her every bit as much as she seemed to want him, but he was also well aware of how dangerous it was to risk this in the middle of the day, when prying eyes might easily discover them.

The queen straightened her back and lifted her chin. "I will consider it," she told him, and then spun on her heels and walked with graceful strides to the door.

Akiri watched her every move with appreciation. She was

a worthy queen, but he knew he had to proceed with great care. He did not want to think for even a moment of the complications that would arise should the king come to hear of their meetings. In truth, he could not recall any other woman who would have caused him to risk so much. He hoped he would not live to regret his rashness.

Chapter Eleven

That night the queen came to his bed.

Her lust for him was unrelenting, and their lovemaking lasted until the first light of dawn crept over the horizon. By the time she left, he was completely spent and soon fell into an uncharacteristically deep sleep.

When he woke it was well into morning, and he gave himself a silent reprimand for his slothfulness. Normally, this would be followed by a self-imposed punishment involving extra training and overnight guard duty. No Dul'Buhar was above discipline, the commander more so than anyone.

"But you are no longer commander of the Dul'Buhar," called a child's voice from across the room.

Akiri sprang up from the bed, wondering how anyone could have entered the room without him noticing. Whatever the answer, it had clearly happened. Sitting on a chair near the unlit fireplace, dressed in a simple cotton shirt and trousers, was a small boy no more than eight years old. Red hair fell to his shoulders in tiny curls, framing a chubby face that was covered in freckles. His bright blue eyes sparkled as he smiled innocently.

"How did you get in here, boy?" Akiri demanded. "Who are you?"

The youngster laughed. "Such pride to think that no one can sneak past the mighty Akiri." He clicked his tongue. "It will be your undoing if you are not careful."

There was something odd about this child. Both his manner of speech and his posture were not at all like one expected of a small boy. Sitting with back straight and hands resting easily in his lap, he bore a confident demeanor normally reserved for those with experience of power.

"Who are you?" Akiri repeated.

"You are everything I dared hope you would be," the child said, still ignoring the question. "You will do *very* nicely."

Akiri took an imposing step forward. "Tell me who you are, boy."

"Boy? Is that the form I have taken?" He sighed. "It's been a long time, and I fear I am out of practice." He slid from the chair and looked down at himself. "Yes. I suppose this isn't exactly the best way I could have presented myself. Small and weak." He looked up and regarded Akiri. "Nothing like you. Nothing at all."

"Enough of this nonsense," Akiri growled. He took another, more rapid step forward, intent on forcing some answers out of the youngster, but that was as far as he got. Before he could take another stride, in a blinding flash of movement, the boy was suddenly standing behind him, next to the bed.

"Do you intend to hurt me?" he asked. "If so, you'll need to do much better than that."

"I am in no mood for your childish games," Akiri told him, trying hard to conceal his surprise at this amazing display of speed.

"Quite right. I will now introduce myself." The boy

bowed low, extending both arms. "I am Vazhta, messenger and servant of Mishna, Mistress of the Light and Goddess of Wisdom. And it is my sincere honor to meet you."

"So, a spirit demon," Akiri muttered. He didn't believe for a moment that this abomination had been sent by Mishna. The gods cared nothing for mortals or their prayers. He despised the way the temples continued to make regular sacrifices to beings who did nothing to aid those who worshipped them. If they were ignored, perhaps they would just fade away into oblivion.

"I can see that you find my claim preposterous," Vazhta continued. "But there is no reason for you to trust me, I suppose."

"I have no desire to banter with spirits."

"I am not a spirit," he retorted, frowning. "They are foul creatures who serve no one. Formless and without clear intent. I am definitely not a spirit." He lowered his eyes, as if in deep contemplation. "But now that I think about it, I am not entirely certain what you would call me. A demon, perhaps? That might be more fitting. Although the word implies that I am evil. But I can assure you that I am not."

"I care nothing for your character, and if you are a messenger of Mishna, then you have wasted your time revealing yourself to me. I have no use for the gods or their minions."

Vazhta giggled with delight. "I can see why she has taken notice of you. Most people are terrified when they meet me. But not you. There is no fear at all." He waved his hand. "Forgive me. I digress. My mistress knows of your plan to seek the Scepter of Xarbaal. When Tuvarius had it in his possession, he should never have allowed it to remain intact; but at the time he would not listen to reason. Now, after many years, an opportunity has come again to make things right."

Akiri's interest was suddenly captured. "Are you saying you know where the Scepter is hidden?" he asked, a little too quickly.

"Alas, no. Tuvarius is still the only one who knows of its location. And he has not been forthcoming."

Disappointment surged in Akiri, raising a sneer. "So you would have me learn of its whereabouts from him and then acquire it for you. Why doesn't Mishna do this herself? She is a goddess, isn't she? Or are you lying about being her messenger?"

"Mishna cannot be directly involved. Which is why she has enlisted your help."

"Then you can tell her that my help is not hers to enlist," Akiri stated. "I do not serve the gods. Nor will I be tricked by some demon spirit into betraying my king."

Vazhta waved it away dismissively. "I'm afraid you have no choice in the matter. You *will* serve Mishna. The King of Acharia must not be permitted to use the Scepter ever again." His blue eyes abruptly darkened, as if a deep shadow had fallen upon them. "Should you test my mistress' resolve in this matter, the consequences will be most severe."

"You do not frighten me, demon. Leave before my patience is exhausted."

"You have been warned, Akiri."

In the blink of an eye, the boy vanished.

Akiri stood absolutely still for the best part of a minute, glaring at the spot where the spirit had been. Every instinct he possessed told him not to trust anything it had said. Even if this Vazhta did in fact serve Mishna, it made little difference. The motives of the gods were seldom in keeping with the best interests of those in the mortal world.

A moment later there was a soft rap on the door, and a servant entered carrying a tray of porridge, fruits, and a portion of ham. After placing it on the table, she curtsied politely.

"King Lanmar has commanded that you join him in his personal study within the hour," she said, and left without waiting for a reply.

Akiri wondered what the king might want with him. It was unlikely to be anything to do with the queen's infidelity, as the message would have undoubtedly come from a group of heavily armed soldiers, not a servant girl.

After finishing his meal, he washed himself in a small basin and dressed in a pair of plain brown trousers and a white shirt he found inside the wardrobe, along with a pair of leather boots.

Outside the door, two guards were waiting to escort him to the king. The palace was truly immense. Even though Akiri had seen quite a bit of it by now, he soon realized that it was far more expansive than he had imagined. At almost every corner they turned, he saw people hard at work decorating and cleaning, presumably for the upcoming birthday celebration. It took them nearly fifteen minutes to thread their way through the multitude of corridors and halls before eventually arriving at the king's study.

The room was neither as lavish nor as large as Akiri had expected. Though far from shabby, the furnishings appeared a touch worn, and the tall bookshelves that lined every wall ensured that there was very little scope for stylish décor. A fire smoldered in a small hearth on the left, while on the opposite side of the room stood a modest desk. King Lanmar was seated behind this, poring over a tall stack of papers. He glanced up briefly and pointed to the chair just in front of him. Akiri took a seat and waited in silence while the monarch continued with his work.

Eventually Lanmar pushed the papers aside and leaned back in his chair. "I know who you are, Akiri. And I must say your presence here troubles me a great deal."

"Why is that, Your Highness?"

"The commander of the Dul'Buhar is dangerous company. I find it unsettling to have you walking freely about, in the home where my family lives. Were it not for the assurances of Lord Tuvarius, I would have you removed at once."

"I mean you no harm, Your Highness. You have nothing to fear from me."

Lanmar regarded him closely. "I have heard the tales of your order, and of your exploits in particular. They are the stuff of legend. When word of your exile reached me, I never imagined that you would come here. And when you did, to my even greater surprise, I discover that you are in fact Tuvarius' nephew."

"That you should hear of my exile from so far away is surprising, Your Highness."

"I make a point of keeping an eye on warring nations. Though Acharia is far enough away not to threaten our borders, the actions of all nations have an impact on trade. It is through trade that my kingdom maintains its stability."

"If you have summoned me for information, I'm afraid I cannot provide you with any," Akiri stated firmly.

King Lanmar steepled his hands beneath his chin. "You continue to give your loyalty to someone who has exiled you?" He waved a hand before Akiri could answer. "It makes no difference. I do not need information. Not even

King Zemel's reach extends this far. His thirst for conquest will be his undoing long before he ever becomes a threat to me. What I want to discuss is the matter of what you did to my guards when you arrived."

"I had no choice in the matter, Your Highness."

"I know this. Lord Tuvarius explained it very clearly to me. Even so, I must admit I was not pleased that he sacrificed two of my men. I hand-picked them. Every guard who serves within these walls is completely dedicated to safeguarding the royal family. To lose even a single man is a blow not easily taken."

"If you are looking for compensation–"

"I am looking for security for my family," the king responded, cutting him short. "Unarmed, you dispatched two of my best guards as easily as if you were fighting children. This tells me that the stories about you are true, at least in part. That being so, while you remain in my palace, I would have you train my men."

This was clearly not a request, and the look in the king's eyes was once again making him feel oddly uneasy. It was little wonder that King Lanmar was able to manipulate his neighbors and keep his nation secure.

"As you wish, Your Highness," he said.

The king nodded sharply. "Good. Captain Tamson of the palace guard will come to see you later today." He allowed his gaze to linger for a moment longer before returning his attention to the papers. "You can go now."

Akiri stood and crossed the room. He was reaching for the door when the king spoke again.

"Oh, one other thing, Akiri." Lanmar looked up to meet him eye-to-eye. "If you are to continue bedding my wife, please see to it that you are discreet."

Akiri tensed, uncertain what to say.

The ghost of a smile passed briefly over the monarch's face. "Do you think I would not know what goes on within my own home? My queen is young and filled with the fire of passion. Understandably, at my age, I lack the energy to meet all of her requirements; therefore, I do not begrudge her having them fulfilled elsewhere. But this is a very private matter for me. You will mention nothing of it to her, nor to Lord Tuvarius. Neither must know I am aware of her infidelity."

Akiri had no idea how to reply. He settled for simply bowing his head in acceptance of the king's wishes and leaving the room as quickly as decorum allowed. Clearly, Lanmar was a man of great complexity and inner strength. Akiri had seen other men go wild with jealousy over what the king seemed to calmly accept as being a fair acceptance of his wife's basic needs. It was not uncommon for soldiers to duel to the death after finding themselves a cuckold. He had never experienced this feeling himself, and hoped he never would.

He found Tuvarius waiting for him when he reached his chamber, an impatient frown on his face. "What did he want?" his uncle demanded.

"He asked me to train his guards while I am here."

Tuvarius sighed heavily. "I wish he had waited."

"Why?"

"My hope was to determine if your *merkesh* can be healed," he told him. "This will be a time-consuming process. And besides, the king's guards are already more than adequately trained."

"I would disagree. They are slow and clumsy."

"You say this because you are made strong by the power

within you," Tuvarius pointed out. "Without it, you would have been slain."

"Perhaps," Akiri agreed. "But my greatest weapon is not my strength. It's my wits. I have fought men who, without possessing the power of the Dul'Buhar, have still provided me with a great challenge. When the mind is sharp, the sword can be a little less so."

"Now you sound more like your mother. Did you know she was once an adviser to Zemel's father, and widely regarded as the brightest mind in all of Acharia? Serhan used to say that she could penetrate even the mysteries of the heavens if she set her mind to it."

A faraway smile inched up from the corners of his mouth. "Your father loved her dearly. And she him in return. It was because of her that he was able to rise to the head of the order. Her tutelage and encouragement were the key to his success."

"What did she teach him?"

Tuvarius tapped the side of his nose with his finger. "Wisdom, my lad. Wisdom." He pushed himself up. "Now come. I would like to get started."

"With what?"

"I told you. I want to see if your *merkesh* is beyond aid."

Akiri stiffened. "I have no desire to use magic. So there is no need for you to bother."

"There is every need for it. As a warrior, do you not want to have every tool possible at your disposal?"

"And as an enemy of King Zemel, why would you want me to have them?"

"That isn't your concern." Tuvarius started for the door. "Of course, you can always just sit here and wonder what you might be missing out on."

Akiri knew he needed to be close to his uncle if he were to discover the location of the Scepter. Grumbling with displeasure, he reluctantly stood up. "Very well."

Back in the north tower, Tuvarius had Akiri sit quietly while he rummaged through an old battered chest, eventually producing a small blue crystal about the size of a man's fingernail. He pressed it into Akiri's palm and pulled up a chair directly facing him and sat down.

"Magic exists everywhere," he began. "In the air, the earth, and in every fiber of everything you see. For most people, it remains unnoticed and unused; but for those who learn to harness its power, it can create wonders beyond the scope of your imagination."

Akiri was unable to hold his tongue. "Magic is useless," he scoffed. "For all but a few it is a crutch so they do not appear weak. I have seen the battle mages. None would last more than a few seconds against the Dul'Buhar."

Tuvarius spat. "Battle mages! Is that what you think magic is? But you are right about one thing; many use it as a crutch. Only a chosen few have the talent to use it to its full potential, and they are counted as being the most powerful – and dangerous – beings ever to breathe free air. Your father's knowledge of magic was unparalleled, and he was the mightiest of all the Tul'Zahar. He could have easily matched you in strength and skill with a blade. Against him, you would have been no better than the guards you killed. That is, if his dragon didn't rip you to shreds first."

"Yet for all their power, they still fell," Akiri retorted. "In the end, magic did not save them. And it would be most foolish to underestimate the Dul'Buhar."

"I do not underestimate you, Akiri," Tuvarius assured him. "In fact, I am sure that if Zemel had not corrupted your *merkesh*, you would have become as formidable as your father. And that is no small compliment. Demons trembled at his coming."

His final words sent a picture of the spirit flashing through Akiri's head. "You speak of demons. Have you ever seen one?"

Tuvarius eyed him strangely. "No. Have you?"

"One came to me in my chamber today," he said, certain that his uncle would see through a lie. "At least, I think it was a demon. It claimed to be the messenger of Mishna."

Tuvarius immediately sat up straight. "What did it look like?"

He described the boy who came to him and recounted their conversation. "I didn't believe what it said," he concluded. "But I thought perhaps you would know more."

"I only know that if the creature was telling the truth, then you are in danger. Attracting the attention of the gods is not something you want. If Mishna has her eye on you, you must be very wary indeed."

"I do not fear the gods."

"Then you are a fool." Tuvarius stared down at the floor for a short time. "If this Vazhta returns, you must tell me right away. I do not like the fact that he was interested in the Scepter."

"Could he retrieve it?"

"If he is truly the messenger of Mishna and he discovers its location, then yes."

"Then you should tell me where it is."

Tuvarius snorted disdainfully. "For the Scepter of Xarbaal to be in the hands of the gods would be bad enough. To give it to a mad man like Zemel would be…"

"And if I promised to destroy it?"

"Then you would be lying."

"What would happen should Mishna acquire it?"

Tuvarius leaned back in his chair. "I honestly don't know. The god Xarbaal tried to use its power in an attempt to cleanse the world of all mortal life. It took the combined efforts of all the other gods to defeat him. In the hands of a human, the Scepter would drive them mad. But in the possession of a god…" He sighed. "Nothing should have that much power. Not even Mishna."

"But Vazhta said it should be destroyed."

"And that may be the reason he came to you, but I cannot risk it being a deception." He heaved another sigh, his inner conflict clear. "I must think more on this. For now, let us continue what we started."

He leaned in close to place his hands on Akiri's shoulders. "You may find this a little uncomfortable at first."

Before Akiri could object, a sharp pain shot into his chest. He felt heat radiating from deep inside, pulsing and throbbing in time with the beating of his heart. His eyes lost focus, until he could see only tiny flashes of white light dancing all around. The strength in his limbs began to ebb and his concentration to pull away, but then Tuvarius released him and normality returned.

"The damage is extensive," his uncle said. "I doubt you will ever be whole. But I may be able to help in some way."

"To what end?"

Tuvarius shrugged. "It might enable you to cast simple *wards* that would protect you from weaker forms of magic. Or it might increase your physical prowess. We won't know until we try."

"Try?"

"I can't guarantee that what I do will help. But you have

my solemn word it will not do you any harm."

Akiri considered this. "Then I agree."

Although it was painful, Akiri easily bore the discomfort as they continued for a time. It was during a brief respite that a sudden loud banging sounded on the door. Tuvarius grunted with irritation before answering.

A man in his mid-thirties with a shaved head and grim demeanor stood in the doorway, a well-made sword hanging from his belt. His build was lean, though Akiri could tell at once that he possessed deceptive strength. Though not in armor, the king's crest was stitched into his loose fitting shirt. His confident eyes and proud stance told of a man who demanded respect – and had most likely earned it.

"You just couldn't wait, could you, Captain Tamson?" Tuvarius growled.

Tamson met his gaze firmly. "I was commanded by the king. Perhaps you would like to tell him that his orders are an inconvenience to your plans, Lord Tuvarius."

"Careful, Captain. Your disrespectful tongue is liable to get you in trouble."

"You are to come with me," he said to Akiri, ignoring the veiled threat. "My men are waiting."

Akiri crossed over to the door, pausing to give his uncle a polite nod. Tamson eyed him with undisguised hostility before leading the way down from the tower. They walked in silence until they were nearly at the bottom.

"I was far from pleased when King Lanmar told me about this," Tamson said.

"Would you not have your men well-trained?" Akiri asked.

"They *are* well-trained," he shot back.

"The two I killed could have certainly used more instruction."

Tamson's hand drifted to his sword. "If you say one more word about that…" The threat hung in the air.

Akiri grinned. "You might consider learning to control your anger, Captain. You have no idea what type of enemy I might be."

"I know full well who you are. And what you are: Akiri of the Dul'Buhar… King Zemel's most feared killers. You were exiled, were you not? So tell me, why should I take instruction from a man expelled from his own order and exiled in disgrace?"

"Because your king has commanded it," Akiri replied without emotion. "But I will strike a bargain. Clearly, you would like revenge for the death of your men. I will allow you an opportunity to take it. You and I will fight. I will be unarmed. Should you kill me, so be it. But should I emerge the victor, you will then forgo your vengeance and allow me to do what your king has asked of me."

A wicked grin was barely visible on the captain's lips. "You may regret those words."

"Perhaps," said Akiri. "We shall see."

They continued walking in silence again until reaching a large, open-air courtyard where more than two dozen men were waiting, every one of them dressed in leather armor and carrying a wooden practice sword. As one, their eyes fell on their new instructor, all of them radiating hate and fury.

Akiri frowned heavily. "Is this how you have them train? With wooden swords and light armor?"

"Unlike you, I value the lives of those who serve under me," Tamson responded.

"Then they should be training with the tools they will be using when faced with a real enemy."

"Before any of that, there is the matter of your bargain

to settle," Tamson remarked. Striding over to the corner of the yard, he drew his sword and placed the scabbard carefully on the ground.

The scowls on the faces of the men quickly turned to malicious grins as they realized what was about to happen. Everyone backed away until they were up against the wall.

Akiri watched the captain's movements closely. He was agile and, in spite of his height, well centered. His relaxed grip on the sword handle and the way he now stepped slowly toward the center of the yard showed that he was a man of great skill and experience. Akiri never underestimated an opponent. Though confident that he would prevail, he had no intention of sustaining a serious injury in the process.

He moved forward, matching Tamson's steps exactly. The captain's eyes were fixed on Akiri's hands at just above waist height. A good strategy, particularly when facing an opponent skilled in unarmed combat. They circled several times while sizing each other up. Then, in a flurry of action, Tamson struck.

The tight sideways sweep of his blade forced Akiri to lean back. He gauged the movement precisely, allowing the tip to pass harmlessly across the front of his body, falling short by less than an inch. Tamson quickly followed this up with a solid thrust that would have skewered most foes. But Akiri saw it coming well in advance and stepped sharply to his left. He could have easily landed a good blow to his opponent's jaw, but that would have left him wide open. And not knowing the captain's ability to sustain punishment, he chose instead to shift backwards and ready himself for another assault.

"You move well," remarked Tamson. "But I still think the reputation of the Dul'Buhar is somewhat exaggerated."

Akiri ignored the insult. A rudimentary tactic. He was never driven to rage.

Tamson struck again, this time bringing his sword in a long downward arc while at the same time sliding to his left. The natural thing for Akiri to do would have been to move back and to his own left to avoid the descending blade. But he had been trained to make use of the unexpected whenever possible. Instead, ducking low, he leapt to the right and then dove in closer. Caught completely by surprise, Tamson was in no position at all to defend himself as a sharply rising Akiri rammed a solid uppercut to the tip of his chin.

Out of instinct more than anything else, the captain raised his blade defensively as he stumbled back. He had taken a blow that would have felled most men instantly, and it was a testament to his resilience that he had not gone the same way, but he was barely managing to keep his footing. Knowing that the fight was already as good as over, Akiri pressed home his advantage, sweeping Tamson's legs completely from beneath him. He landed heavily, flat on his back, with the air whooshing noisily from his lungs. Before the man had any possible chance of recovering, Akiri straddled his chest, wrenching away his blade and tossing it out of reach. Tamson struggled briefly, but it was quickly apparent that he would never be able to dislodge the far heavier frame of Akiri.

"You have lost, Captain," Akiri told him. "There is no need to take a beating to prove your courage."

Tamson glared furiously. He was obviously a man who had experienced very few defeats in combat, if any at all. However, after a few seconds, he relaxed and nodded sharply. "Very well. I yield."

Akiri rose and offered his hand to the captain. Reluctantly, he allowed Akiri to help him up.

"You are indeed skilled," Tamson admitted. "I have never encountered anyone who moves as you do. And your speed… it is almost unnatural."

"The Dul'Buhar begin their training at a very early age," Akiri told him. "And it continues throughout our lives." He was not going to let slip details of the power that gave him his marked advantage. "I can teach you and your men certain techniques. But I will be here for only a short time; not long enough to make any real difference."

Tamson's anger was already subsiding, replaced by a commander's desire to better his men's skill. "Then perhaps you could instruct me in your training methods so that I may pass them on after you leave."

Akiri nodded. "Yes, that might be more practical. But just for today, I think I would like to work with your men directly."

He spent the rest of the afternoon instructing the guards in hand-to-hand combat. It felt good to lose himself in the purity of battle, though he dearly missed the much greater challenge of pitting himself against his fellow Dul'Buhar. The palace guards were indeed tough. They would easily measure up to any of the most hardened soldiers in King Zemel's army. What they lacked was the steely focus of the men in his order… his *former* order, he quickly reminded himself.

By the end of the day, they seemed to have all but forgotten that he was responsible for the death of their two comrades, even bidding him a fond farewell when Tamson told him it was time they returned to his quarters.

"You are not as I expected," the captain remarked once

they arrived. "I was told that the Dul'Buhar are mindless killers. You are something quite different."

"I *am* a killer," Akiri admitted. "But we are anything but mindless in what we do."

Tamson nodded. "I can accept that. It would be advantageous if you were to stay here permanently, though I know you will not. I can see in your eyes that you have a great purpose ahead, so I will not waste time trying to persuade you. Instead, I will give you a word of warning: Do not trust your uncle. Tuvarius has his own agenda. Whatever that may be, my instincts tell me that it will serve only his benefit. I know that he is your kin, but darkness surrounds that man."

He turned and left without waiting for a response.

Chapter Twelve

For the next few days, Akiri passed his mornings with Tamson, outlining a training regimen for his men and demonstrating how best to employ it, while the afternoons were spent with his uncle, who seemed determined to heal Akiri's ailing *merkesh*.

The queen continued with her nightly visits. Akiri found it mildly amusing that she took such great care to be discreet when her husband was already fully aware of her liaisons. He wondered what this said about the king's feelings for her.

He had learned through the limited amount of conversation he shared with the queen that she was the daughter of King Vralos of Marciona, a kingdom far to the west. King Lanmar's first wife and mother to his only son had died several years before, and it was only after a respectable period of mourning that he had elected to marry Chelia in a mutually beneficial arrangement. Trade in Marciona was stagnant and desperately in need of the commerce that Galfaria could provide. In return, Chelia's hand in marriage came with a substantial dowry, together with the promise of another heir – though thus far, she had yet to provide him with one.

On the day of the prince's birthday, the entire palace was

alive with activity. Tamson sent word that he would be too heavily occupied with duties for their daily session, leaving Akiri uncertain how to spend his time. No one had invited him to attend the opulent celebration banquet – not that he had any desire to do so anyway. He considered going into the city. He was more than a little curious to discover what had happened to Quarra; and as far as he knew, his horse and the rest of his belongings were still in her care.

Eventually, he decided simply to remain in his room until the next day and avoid the entire affair. He had found a book on ancient lore to read when Tuvarius appeared. His posture was bent and he looked weary. He plopped heavily into a chair near the window.

"Nothing will please me more than when this day is over," he said, blowing out an exaggerated breath. He glanced over to his nephew. "Did no one send you a change of clothes?"

Akiri sat down in the opposite chair. "Thankfully, no. I have never enjoyed these types of gatherings. Fortunately, the Dul'Buhar are not welcome guests at most social functions."

"That was never the case with the Tul'Zahar," Tuvarius told him. "Our presence was requested at every significant occasion. It was considered a badge of honor should we choose to attend. I once suggested to your father that we charge gold to make appearances. He rejected the idea, naturally. He said there was no amount of gold in the land that could make him suffer some of the asinine events arranged by nobles." He looked around the room and his mouth twisted into a frown. "Don't tell me there's not even a bottle of wine here."

"I'm afraid not."

Tuvarius heaved himself up. "Then let us make the climb to my room. I have plenty there. Some excellent whiskey as well."

The halls were teeming with people as they made their way to the north tower, though the sight of Tuvarius and Akiri caused most to hastily clear a path. Tamson had told Akiri that his uncle was greatly feared… and for good reason. Akiri knew that Tuvarius had also gone to some lengths to cultivate this fear. He made no secret of his ability to use powerful magic; he had displayed these skills on several very public occasions.

Upon reaching his quarters, Tuvarius retrieved a bottle of whiskey and two stout glasses. They were soon comfortably settled in chairs while his uncle told tales of his youthful exploits. Akiri could not help but notice a change in his demeanor. He seemed ill at ease, and looked as if he were expecting something to happen. Every so often, he would pause his tale to cast his eyes about the room, as though checking to see if anyone was listening.

"Tell me more about the Dul'Buhar," he said eventually, after talking uninterrupted for more than an hour, pausing only to take another drink from his glass or replenish its contents from the bottle.

Akiri thought for a moment. He had never told stories about the order before. No one dared to ask for such details. And in any case, the Dul'Buhar did not engage in such frivolity.

"Come on," Tuvarius pressed. "After all that bloody war, you must certainly have something to tell."

Accepting the situation, Akiri began speaking of the time he and three of his men had infiltrated an enemy stronghold in order to assassinate its commander. At the end of the story, his uncle simply stared at him, a deep frown on his face.

"You must forgive me if I do not tell an entertaining tale," Akiri said. "I am a soldier, not a bard."

"It's not that," Tuvarius assured him. "I just can't help but wonder what might have become of you had things been different."

To Akiri, this felt like an insult. He felt a flash of anger. "I live the life for which I am best suited. I am… I was… the commander of the Dul'Buhar, feared and respected by both friend and foe alike. My blade has tasted the blood of countless enemies, and my actions have saved the lives of many Acharians who would have otherwise fallen to the swords of those who seek to destroy us."

"But you could have been so much more," Tuvarius insisted. "I hope you still can be." He drained his glass and quickly refilled it. "Or perhaps I have become unrealistic in my old age. More than likely you'll end up serving the man who murdered your father for the rest of your days."

"What happened to you after the Tul'Zahar fell?"

Tuvarius rubbed his face and took another drink. "What does it matter? My dragon was slain, as were my comrades. What I did after that is of little consequence." He shoved himself to his feet, gripping the edge of the table for balance. "But I am reminded of a promise I made to your father… not that he was alive to hear my oath."

Stumbling over to a chest near his bed, he retrieved a sword held in a scabbard of polished black leather. The figure of a dragon inlaid in gold ran down most of the scabbard's length, while the handle of the sword inside it was solidly crafted and the pommel capped with what appeared to be a large diamond.

Tuvarius gazed at the weapon for a long moment, his eyes glistening with barely contained tears. "This was your father's. I managed to acquire it after he died."

He cleared his throat and sniffed, his expression once more that of an old man who was filled with too much whiskey. Moving back to the table, he unceremoniously tossed the sword to Akiri. "When I heard you had been spared, I swore to give this to you should we ever meet. So there you are." He plopped awkwardly back down into the chair and snatched up his glass.

Even though it was still inside its scabbard, Akiri could tell that this was a weapon of perfect balance crafted by a true master. The diamond was the only sign of extravagance to be seen. Everything else about the sword was purely functional… and perfect. A true instrument of death.

He stood, a tiny smile on his face. The song of steel filled the chamber as he freed the magnificent weapon. The blade was unblemished, with not even the faintest scratch or the smallest nick marring its edge. The only markings were the stamp of the maker just below the hilt. Akiri's eyes shot wide on recognizing the mark of Zerbia.

"This cannot be," he whispered.

"Of course it can," Tuvarius told him. "You hold in your hand a weapon made by the greatest swordsmith in history."

Akiri ran his hands down the length of the blade, careful to keep near the middle. If this had truly been made by the great Zerbia, then even the slightest touch on a cutting edge was likely to remove a finger, no matter how long the blade might have lain untended. "I thought all those crafted by him were lost."

"Obviously they are not," Tuvarius said. "Your father was given the scabbard as reward for saving the life of

Queen Lucial, mother to the beast Zemel. And the sword, just before he was made head of the order." He chuckled softly. "You should have seen him wield this weapon. In his hand it was almost like a living, breathing creature."

Akiri raised the sword to eye level, glancing along its cutting edge. "It is difficult to believe that you would part with something so precious."

He swung the weapon in a series of intricate arcing patterns. It felt like an extension of his own arm. Even a novice swordsman would be deadly with this masterpiece of steel in his hand. But in *Akiri's*…

He found himself laughing with joy as he continued to swing the sword in ever increasing complex motions.

"That's enough," called Tuvarius. "There will be time for that later."

It took tremendous effort for Akiri to stop and sheath the sword. He sat down, unable to tear his eyes away from it. "I am in your debt," he said.

"In more ways than you know."

His uncle reached across the table to touch the jewel set in the pommel. Almost at once, a faint light glowed from within. Akiri stared in wonder as the face of a woman appeared. Her smile was warm and loving, and her eyes kind. "Who is she?" he asked.

"That is your mother, Lady Leona. Your father often summoned her image before going into battle. It was already ingrained into the jewel when I acquired the sword."

Akiri continued to watch as the image slowly faded. "Do you know if she still lives?"

Tuvarius spread his hands. "Who knows? It's possible, but I doubt it. Zemel let you live out of revenge, and because you are useful to him. He would have no such reason to keep your mother alive for so long, except perhaps to use her against you somehow."

With the aspect of his mother now vanished, unfamiliar images flashed through Akiri's mind. He felt strange emotions stirring. With a shake of his head, he placed the sword on the table. Everything was suddenly different. "I don't want this," he said.

"Then throw it away. It is yours. I have held it for far too long."

Akiri's eyes remained fixed on the diamond. A painful mixture of anger, guilt, and sorrow was raging inside him. But why? He had seen trusted comrades tortured, small children put to the sword, and witnessed countless other atrocities, the likes of which would break most men. But he had never shed so much as a single tear. Yet here he was on the brink of weeping, simply from seeing the face of a mother he could not remember.

"I see that Zemel did not rob you of everything," Tuvarius remarked.

His uncle's words were enough to shock him into regaining his composure. He squared his shoulders and placed a hand back on the sheathed sword. "You are right. It *is* mine. I will not allow a forgotten ghost to deny me of such a treasure."

"She may be a ghost, Akiri. But she is not forgotten."

He looked at the jewel again. No. She wasn't. Although the image had vanished, her presence seemed to be growing stronger every minute. Waves of urgency rushed through him. He could not continue like this. He needed to be back where he belonged.

"Is there no way I can convince you to tell me of the Scepter's location?" he asked.

"Are you so eager to leave? Don't you want to know

more about where you came from?"

"The only thing I want to know is why you insist on this game. You hope to cloud my mind with doubt. But you must know it will not work."

Tuvarius smiled. "It has already worked, Akiri. Though it may be some time before you are ready to admit that. I keep you here because the moment you know where the Scepter is hidden, you will march off to your death. You cannot acquire it. It is beyond the reach of mortal men. Only a fully trained Tul'Zahar astride a dragon might be able to retrieve it, and even then it would be a formidable task. By keeping it from you, I am saving your life."

"I need no one to save me," he retorted.

"We all need someone to save us from time to time," Tuvarius said. He lowered his head and briefly closed his eyes, his voice becoming almost a whisper. "But I fear there is no one left for me." Suddenly he looked very old and tired.

Akiri had seen behavior like this many times before – how in the blink of an eye the deeply buried emotions of a drunken man could come flooding to the surface. Was this a good time to press a little harder?

He leaned forward. "Perhaps I can be the one to save you, uncle. All you need to do is tell me where the Scepter is hidden. Sooner or later it will be found anyway – if not by King Zemel, then by the gods. Tell me, and I can retrieve it. You must trust me to do what is right."

A deep and lengthy sigh fell from Tuvarius' mouth. "I agree with you about one thing, Akiri. It will not stay hidden forever. I should have destroyed it when I had the chance. Now I am faced with the consequences of that choice. It is a heavy burden to bear. One that I often feel too old to continue carrying."

Akiri waited in silence, feeling that to speak any further might work against him. His uncle was already teetering on the edge, pushed there by a combination of drunkenness and deep emotional reflections.

Minutes passed before Tuvarius spoke again, each one more unbearable than the one before. "Very well. I *will* trust you, Akiri. I must believe that you will eventually do what is right. You are, after all, my brother's son. Blood will surely win in the end."

He pointed toward the far wall. "If you would just step over there, I will deliver what you seek."

There were no trunks in that part of the room, nor any other type of furniture, and the wall itself appeared to be nothing but plain stonework. Nevertheless, Akiri did as he was told, confident that he would not be wasting his time.

Tuvarius eventually extended his arm to point at a spot just to Akiri's right. A single word came from his mouth. "*Ouvenit!*"

At once, an opening about twice the size of a man's hand appeared in the solid wall. "Take what is inside," Tuvarius instructed.

His excitement rising, Akiri reached in and pulled out an envelope sealed with wax. The instant his hand was clear of the opening, the wall became solid once more.

"Understand that the moment you open this letter, there will be no turning back. Your destiny will be set. Where it will lead, I do not know. But risking the madness of Zemel may well be the least of the evil unleashed upon the world." He passed a weary hand across his brow. "I can only hope that when your moment comes, you will do better than I."

Akiri stared at the envelope for a few seconds longer. Although normally a man with boundless patience, his desire to open it right away was almost unbearable.

"Thank you, uncle," he said, pushing it deep into his pocket. "I assume you know this means that our time together is now at an end."

"Of course I do," he replied. "And now that you have what you want, I hope it serves to do more than plague your heart with doubt." He groaned as he pushed himself to his feet. "I wish your mother were here right now. She would know the words that elude me at this moment. As she is not, I will merely say farewell, and be done with it." With a sharp nod, he turned toward his bed.

Akiri watched as he carefully laid himself down, the man's joints cracking with each movement. "Farewell, uncle."

There was only one more thing left to do here, and then he would leave the memory of this place far behind.

He took a seat on the steps just outside the door and immediately broke the envelope's seal.

Chapter Thirteen

Akiri sat silently for more than an hour. Tuvarius had been right in his assessment. Whatever happened next would set in motion events from which there could be no turning back. In his mind, he mapped out every step he would take. Once he had decided on a plan of action, he stood and returned to his uncle's door. The deep regular breathing told him that he was in a drunken slumber. This would make the task much simpler.

He pushed open the door and saw Tuvarius lying on his bed, still fully clothed and with one leg dangling to the floor. Pulling out the dagger he kept hidden beneath his shirt, Akiri crept soundlessly to the bedside. It was a pity such a life would not meet its end in battle, he considered.

The thought was quickly dismissed. Delay could be damaging to his resolve. In a single swift motion, he plunged the dagger directly into Tuvarius' heart. His uncle's eyes shot open and he let out a sharp gasp. Then it was over. His body fell limp, and his eyes glazed over with the empty stare of death.

Akiri bowed his head. "Goodbye, uncle," he said quietly. He regretted that the killing was necessary, but he dared not risk the Scepter's location being learned by another from Tuvarius' lips.

After cleaning his blade on the sheets and tucking it away, he hurried over to an old chest that was shoved against the wardrobe. Inside this he found the small purse of gold coins he had noticed on an earlier visit. It wasn't much, but it would probably be enough to purchase supplies and a decent horse if necessary. That was all he would need.

He returned to his room and changed into a comfortable set of clothing suitable for a long journey. With his father's sword attached to his belt, he entered the hall.

As he made his way through the palace, the guards he encountered nodded to him respectfully. He could not help but feel a sense of pride in knowing that what he had passed on to them had improved them as soldiers, making them far more capable of protecting their king and his family.

For a moment the queen flashed into his thoughts. He would miss the nights they spent together. It was unlikely he would ever encounter another woman quite like her. He was very tempted to seek her out, if only to set eyes upon her one last time. But that would be a foolish move. He needed to be well away from the palace by the time Tuvarius was discovered.

As expected, the corridor leading to the queen's private chamber was guarded. When approaching, he gave the two men a friendly wave.

"You're not supposed to be here," said the guard standing to his left.

"I know," he replied. "But the truth is I just don't like crowds. Especially when it's a lot of chattering nobles all competing for the king's attention. You wouldn't object if I used this way to sneak outside for a short while, would you?"

The guards looked at each other uncertainly. After a moment, the older of the two shrugged. "What does it matter? The queen isn't down there anyway. Just tell the guard at the passage entrance that Drayke said to let you pass."

"Thank you. I really do need to get some fresh air."

The man smiled. "I wish I could come with you. We'll be standing here with nothing to do all night long."

Akiri slapped him fondly on the shoulder. "It could be worse. At least there are no hordes of drunken guests in this part of the palace to make your life difficult."

He moved on to where the secret passage led outside. Two more guards stood at the exit, but Akiri's friendly smile and the mention of Drayke's name was more than enough to set them at ease. They allowed him to pass without objection.

Once beyond the palace walls, it was immediately obvious that the public celebrations were just as enthusiastic as those within the royal house. All the street lamps were decorated with streamers of red and gold, as was the front of virtually every building he passed. Unsurprisingly, with so many people packing the thoroughfares, movement was slow. Loud music mingled with a non-stop cacophony of shouting and whistling was further enlivened by the staccato pop and crackle of fireworks. The people of Galfaria unquestionably had a special place in their hearts for their king.

Navigating his way to the brothel took Akiri more than an hour. When he arrived, he could see the windows were flung wide open, allowing the sounds of merriment from Quarra's patrons to flood into the street. Apparently, business was especially good that night.

Inside, it was almost impossible to move without brushing against someone, and he was relieved when he spotted Quarra near the bar. She was talking and laughing with an older man clad in expensive silks, ostentatiously displaying his wealth with a ridiculous amount of gold and jewelry about his person. Her bright smile instantly faded as she spotted Akiri approaching. She whispered something into her client's ear, and brushing her hand across his plump cheek, she moved across to head him off.

"What do you want?" she demanded.

"I assume that you still have my belongings?"

She snorted indignantly, but without replying, she led him through to the back and into the room where he had stayed when he had first arrived. Quarra rummaged through a dresser until finally producing a small pouch of gold coins.

"I had to sell your horse and sword," she said. "This is what's left of your gold. It took nearly everything I had to keep the queen from throwing me into prison." She tossed the pouch over to him. "I should never have let Geridia talk me into helping you. Now he's dead, and I'm penniless."

Akiri frowned. This would slow him down. He needed a horse and supplies, and it was most unlikely he would find an open shop or livery. Apart from Quarra's brothel, every business in the city seemed to have shut down for the celebration.

"Geridia's death was unfortunate," he told her. "But as you are still alive and your establishment is thriving, I am certain that you will recover your losses in time."

"Just get the hell out of here," she retorted, her eyes sending spears of hate into him.

Akiri inspected the pouch contents. After a brief calculation, he removed a few coins and tossed the rest of the gold back. "I have enough for my purpose. Take this as compensation."

Her surprise showing, Quarra placed the offering on a nearby table. After bowing to her, Akiri headed for the door.

"Is it true?" she called after him. "Did you kill Geridia yourself?"

He paused. "No. But I did nothing to prevent his death, either. His fate was sealed from the moment he first spoke to me."

He did not wait for a response. Quickly leaving the room, he pushed his way through the crowd and back onto the street. Geridia had only himself to blame. He would still be alive had his overwhelming greed not blinded him to the simple fact that he would always be the prime suspect for the theft of Barsyn Bartone's precious pendant. Or, as it turned out, his murder. But what Akiri had just told Quarra still held true. It was his own success that had ultimately doomed the man. There was little chance of Geridia ever finding anyone else with even the smallest hope of penetrating Barsyn Bartone's security, so the situation that followed would never have arisen. However, once they had met by chance and their deal made, the die was irrevocably cast.

How many fates had he altered merely by crossing their paths? For sure, many who would have otherwise lived were now dead. On the other hand, there were a great number of Acharians who owed their continuing existence to him. If the stories of the gods were to be believed, then he would one day be called to answer for his deeds. Many men feared what might come on their judgment day, but not he. He feared nothing. The gods least of all.

After a fruitless search for a livestock trader that was open, he settled for striking a bargain with a passerby and paying twice what the animal was worth. Food and supplies would have to wait until he was well away from this place. Once Tuvarius' body was discovered, there was sure to be a search party sent out for him. But with a day's head start, he should easily be able to avoid any pursuers.

The guards at the main city gate took no notice of his departure. Their attention was focused almost entirely on those still trying to enter the city. He left the road and followed the city wall west until the point where it turned north. Straight ahead, the moonlight illuminated a tree line about a half mile away. From there it was only twenty miles to a small village where he could pick up some of the supplies he needed. He spurred his horse to a trot. Every yard he traveled brought him closer to getting his old life back… and closer to banishing all the unwanted doubts forever.

It wasn't long before he felt a strange presence. He didn't understand what it was at first. Then a distant cry from high above announced the return of the dragon; or perhaps she had never left and had merely been waiting for his reappearance.

He could feel her raw emotions coursing through him – a combination of concern and relief. She was happy to see him again. He was pleased, too. Having such a creature as an ally would be a great advantage. Then, almost immediately, a sinking thought occurred. King Zemel had outlawed dragons. They were all to be killed on sight. But surely, he reasoned, if he returned the Scepter, the king would be glad to make an exception. Or would he? Nothing could be certain.

The dragon let out a piercing screech as though she could feel the conflict troubling Akiri's soul. They were truly connected. That might prove an issue with what was to come, he considered. But *to come* meant it was a problem for another day.

Chapter Fourteen

Tuvarius stared out of the window. His eyes were looking down upon the lights of the city, but his mind was elsewhere. Even the pounding on his door did not shake him from his trance-like state.

"Lord Tuvarius," called a woman's voice from outside his chamber.

The pounding became louder and more urgent.

Finally, he became aware of the noise. After letting out a deep sigh, he turned. But before he could answer the door, it swung open. Just beyond the threshold stood an older woman with silver hair and sharp angular features. She wore an extravagant white satin gown, with scores of tiny jewels stitched into swirling patterns down the front and blood rubies down the sides – a fitting display of wealth for the celebration now consuming the entire palace. She had apparently breezed by all of the guards he had put in place to discourage unwanted visitors. This was a woman not accustomed to being kept waiting. He couldn't help but admire that.

"What do you want, Lady Folsa?" he asked, making no attempt at all to hide his irritation.

"You know full well what I want. Is it done?"

Stepping away from the door, he gestured for her to enter. "Come see for yourself."

She hesitated. "I… I don't need to actually see him."

"I insist," he said.

Reluctantly, she did as he instructed. She was barely inside the room when the heavy door boomed shut behind her, making her jump like a startled bird. After taking a moment to settle herself, though still breathing far too rapidly, she advanced toward the bed with tiny nervous steps. The body lying on it was soaked in blood, and more was dripping steadily onto the tile floor. Then, her eyes shot wide and a cry of total anguish flew from her mouth.

"No! By the gods, no." She fell to her knees beside the bed. "You were supposed to kill Daresh. Not Shemil."

"Indeed," said Tuvarius. "But should it matter which son of yours is dead? Clearly you had too many."

She sprang to her feet, tears of fury and sorrow streaming down her face. "What kind of monster are you? I told you explicitly that it was Daresh I needed to be rid of."

Tuvarius chuckled. "You hire me to kill your son and then call *me* a monster?"

"You have no right to judge me. He was preventing Shemil from taking his rightful place. Then after I found out about that whore of a servant girl…"

He silenced her with a sharp move of his hand. "You wanted him dead because you found him inconvenient. And that *whore of a servant girl,* as you call her, is worth a hundred of you. Not that any of this matters in the slightest."

Still standing close to the door, he produced a key from his pocket and turned the lock. The ominous clacking of metal was enough to send Lady Folsa trembling. "Why are you afraid, My Lady?" he asked when facing her again.

"Surely you do not believe all the rumors about me?"

It was obvious that she did. Every one of them. Her haughty demeanor vanished in an instant. "Let me go and I'll pay you whatever you want," she begged.

"Will you?" He clicked his tongue. "What a pity you did not offer me more in the beginning. Now I'm afraid you have nothing left to give."

"You are wrong. My family–"

"Your family is now controlled by Daresh," he said, cutting her short. "Or I should say, Lord Daresh Folsa. It was good of you to give him your late husband's name. Though I strongly suspect this was not done out of any great kindness, but merely to ensure that no one would ever know he was born a bastard. However, bastard or not, he is the one who now controls your family's wealth. Which means he can easily pay me a great deal more than you are able."

Lady Folsa's face was now terror-stricken. "That's impossible. Daresh would never do such a thing to me. Not to his own mother."

"On that score, you would have been right until only a few days ago," Tuvarius told her. "But once I informed him of your treachery, I was surprised at how ruthless the lad could be." He cocked his head. "I think the prospect of being free to pursue the woman he loves might have helped to steel his resolve as well. I have never understood why the nobility is incapable of seeing the merit in a person if there isn't a title before their name. I suppose that is one little mystery I shall never solve."

Panic seized Lady Folsa. She made a sudden dash for the door and tried desperately to force it open. Tuvarius was unmoved. While she continued to tug and kick, he merely shook his head and took a seat at the table. After a minute or so, she gave up and collapsed to her knees.

"Please," was all she could gasp out through a series of uncontrollable sobs.

"Normally such a display might sway me," he said. "But then I remember why you have come here. You wanted to see the body. You wanted to be certain he was gone." He waved his hand in an elaborate circle. "Look now. Look and see that all is well."

Unable to resist his command, Lady Folsa's eyes shifted upwards. A gasp of astonishment slipped out. There, standing beside the bed, was her son, Shemil. He was smiling warmly. There was no trace of blood on him. He was whole.

"This… this cannot be," she whispered. "You were… dead. I just saw you."

He chuckled softly. "Dead? Do I look dead to you?"

"But… you were covered in blood. Lord Tuvarius said… he said…" She covered her face. "No. I don't believe it. You're trying to trick me."

Shemil crossed over to his mother and leaned down to place his hands tenderly on her shoulders. "You see? I am warm and alive. This is not a trick."

Slowly she looked up, her face soaked with tears. "Is it really you?" She touched his cheek with her fingertips. "My darling boy."

He lifted her to her feet. "You have been through so much, mother. You need to rest now."

She threw her arms around him. But after only a few seconds her legs began to weaken and her vision blurred. "Yes. I think you're right," she murmured. "I'm sorry. I don't know what's come over me."

Shemil helped her to the bed and gently laid her down. "Sleep now, mother," he said, taking her by the hand. "All is well. I am here with you."

As her eyes closed, a fragile smile crept upon her lips.

Tuvarius continued holding Lady Folsa's hand until all traces of life had completely drained from her body. Blood still dribbled from the cut he had made to her jugular, mingling with that of her son lying beside her.

"Quite the gruesome sight," came a child's voice from near the window. "But why so much effort? You could have simply stabbed her through the heart, just like Akiri believes he did to you." He laughed softly. "Mortal eyes are so easily fooled."

Tuvarius scowled over at the small figure standing in the shadows. "What do *you* want?"

"Honestly? I was confused. I wondered if you might help to clear my mind."

"Ask what you will and be gone."

"Just one question. It should not prove to be too difficult to answer. Simply this: why did you give the location to Akiri and yet withhold it from me? One might wonder if it wasn't entirely… *personal*?"

"You know perfectly well why," he snapped.

The boy shook his head and sighed. "Mortals and their petty desires. You would risk everything just to curry favor in the hope of receiving some bauble? Quite pitiful, really, when you think about it."

"And yet you are no better," Tuvarius reasoned. "You seek approval and status in your own way, all in a desperate bid to feel the love of a creature that is incapable of giving it. I would say that makes you far more pathetic than I."

"Careful," he replied, his voice taking an edge. "Do not forget who I am. This form is only for your benefit. Should I anger, I may reveal my true self."

Tuvarius huffed. “Do as you will. I do not fear the likes of you. I have slain your kind before.”

“Yes, you have,” he conceded. “But that was long ago. You do not think you could challenge me now, do you?”

As the boy finished speaking, the air suddenly became cold and the light from the lanterns dimmed. Tuvarius pulled his robe tightly around him, his breath now coming out in misty clouds. But none of this had affected his confidence. After sneering at the creature and retrieving a bottle from his cabinet, he said: “If your intention is to intimidate me, you are wasting your time.”

The air and lights returned to normal. “You are right, of course. Any attempt to frighten you is pointless. I think I am spending far too much time with mortals. You and your petty ways are beginning to rub off on me.”

“Then why do you insist on plaguing me with your presence?”

He let out a wild laugh. “I will be leaving you soon enough. Now that Akiri has set out on his mission, he has become my main concern.”

“I hope he guts you,” Tuvarius said.

“That is always a possibility. I suppose I will need to be extra careful.” He regarded Tuvarius for a moment. “Were you able to heal him?”

“And if I was?”

“Oh, nothing really. I was simply being curious. As his fate is already set, I was wondering why you bothered.”

Tuvarius looked at him sideways. “You should know very well that no one’s fate is totally fixed. Least of all the son of Serhan.”

A knock sounded at the door. Tuvarius heaved himself up and allowed four guards to enter. They gazed at the bodies in shock.

"Is that…?" began one of the men.

"It is," said Tuvarius after calmly returning to his seat. "Take them to the cellar and inform Lord Daresh Folsa that his mother and brother are both dead."

The man hesitated. "What happened?"

"The same thing that will happen to you if you question me again," Tuvarius snapped. "And once you've spoken to Lord Daresh, go to the stable and have a wagon prepared for me. I will be leaving at first light."

"Should I inform the king of this, My Lord?"

"His Majesty is already aware of the situation." He waved an impatient hand, jerking the men into action.

As they carried away the bodies, Tuvarius glanced over to the window. The boy had vanished.

Events had been set irrevocably in motion. Years of planning were finally coming to fruition. Unfortunately, the one thing he had not counted on was Akiri himself. This was no lost child searching for the meaning to his existence. He was all that was best in his father, combined with the high intellect of his mother. But his dealings with Akiri had come to a close for the time being. Whatever was to be was beyond his control.

He was still thinking on this when the door flew open and Queen Chelia stormed inside. He cursed himself for forgetting to re-lock it.

"Where is he?" she demanded.

"If you are speaking of Akiri, he has gone."

The queen's face was bright red with fury. "I don't believe you. He would not have left without at least seeing me first."

"Take care, Your Highness. You cannot afford to allow your emotions to rule you. Akiri was a pleasure for you to enjoy. Your husband… and your king… that is where your heart belongs."

"Do not talk to me as if I am some lovesick child."

"That was not my intention, Your Highness. I was simply reminding you of your station. Passion can often be confused with true love. I assure you that Akiri understands this very well. Even if he felt something deeper for you, he would never allow it to interfere with his duty."

He looked her over carefully. Then a revelation washed over him. "Ah, I see it now. You are with child. Akiri's child? Of course it is. What am I thinking?"

Chelia said nothing.

"I think it is for the best that he is gone, don't you?" Tuvarius continued. "As for you… you must go to your husband's bed as soon as you are able. This very night if at all possible. The king *must* believe the child to be his own."

"Will you at least tell me where he went?"

Tuvarius smiled. "If you knew, would you seek him out?"

"Please. Tell me." Her voice had lost its steel, but she was not betraying the anguish Tuvarius knew she must be feeling.

"Akiri hopes to return home," he said. "More than that I cannot say. But should destiny be on his side, I suspect his name will be heard in these halls again… one day."

Queen Chelia stood in silence for several seconds. Then, slowly, acceptance washed over her face, and she nodded. "Thank you, Lord Tuvarius," she said, her voice quiet. "I will say goodnight now. I am sorry if I disturbed you."

He rose and bowed. "You could never disturb me, Your Highness."

After the queen had left, Tuvarius considered how this could complicate matters for her. He was sure that the king knew of her trysts, but he had no idea how he would react to the possibility of another man fathering a child with his wife. Chelia was resourceful and clever and, in a way not apparent to most people, she was extremely ruthless.

The older prince would need to step very carefully from the day the child was born.

Chapter Fifteen

With freshly purchased supplies, Akiri stayed on the road heading west. He could remain concealed far more easily if he chose to travel through the heavily forested areas, but speed outweighed stealth in a situation like this. It would take time for a search party to be organized, and more time still for them to determine which direction he had taken. Tamson was no fool, so any search party would consist of a dozen men at the very least, and the more men in the group, the slower they traveled. Akiri had seen maps in the palace and knew there were no garrisons between himself and the border, meaning that even though he would need to stop and rest his horse now and then, so would his pursuers. They would not have the advantage of simply exchanging tired mounts for fresh ones at each outpost.

When he needed to halt, he found a small clearing a few yards away from the road. He had seen few other travelers, which was hardly surprising considering the number of people gathered in Vurna for the celebration. He was far from alone, though; he could still feel the dragon's presence throughout. She was constantly there, circling high above him as he traveled.

He closed his eyes and tried to imagine what it must be

like to soar freely above the clouds. Tuvarius had described it as *wildly exhilarating, yet at the same time gloriously peaceful.* Sitting firmly on the ground, it was hard to comprehend a combination of such directly opposing emotions. Even so, when he recalled his uncle's stories about the way the Tul'Zahar rode into battle astride their mighty dragons, his heart pounded with blood lust. Why would King Zemel not want such powerful creatures on his side? He cursed himself for the thought, even as it was still entering his mind. The king had his reasons. It was not for him to question them.

Knowing that the sound of his horse might alert any passersby of his presence, Akiri decided he might as well light a small fire. At least that way he would not draw unwanted attention by appearing to be on the run.

A few minutes after the flames had taken hold, he heard the beating of wings overhead A minute later, the dragon landed at the edge of the clearing. Her crimson scales shimmered in the light of the fire as she paced slowly about the perimeter, her eyes fixed on him.

Akiri watched the creature intently. Her thoughts were a jumble of curiosity and trepidation. Just like himself, she seemed unsure of how or why they had become connected.

"Come closer," he said, a smile creeping onto his face.

She ceased pacing and let out a low growl.

"Yes. I'm sure you are fierce. But I need no warning." He held out his hand. "Come."

This time the dragon took a cautious step forward, her serpentine tongue flicking from side to side. She circled again before eventually inching closer to the fire. Akiri could feel it relaxing… *her* relaxing.

"Am I supposed to give you your name?" he wondered aloud. Tuvarius had told him that his father's dragon had been named Ragnir, though little else, aside from Serhan's great affection for the creature.

The dragon shook her head, like a dog shaking water free from its fur. Akiri could imagine what she might look like once fully grown. He knew little about their life cycle. This one was clearly young, though how young he couldn't begin to guess.

Akiri regarded her, still smiling. "I think I'll call you Kyra. It means *fire jewel* in the language of the ancients." He nodded with satisfaction. "Yes. That suits you well."

Kyra cocked her head for a moment, then let out a soft purring grumble. Akiri took this to be a sign of approval.

"So, Kyra, what do you want from me?" he asked. "You are free. Surely there are others like you somewhere in the world."

The young dragon merely blew a breath of hot air and dropped onto her side. Akiri continued watching her. Having a dragon with him would certainly have its advantages. Even a young one was a deadly foe. But there was a downside too. Her presence would make it impossible for him to pass unnoticed. The mere sight of Kyra would be enough to create panic. There was also the matter of King Zemel's law to consider.

Kyra soon closed her eyes and fell into a light sleep. He could feel that she was far more at ease now. He focused his mind on her, and for a moment, he felt something beneath the raw emotions, but it was elusive. Leaning back on his elbows, he rested his chin on his chest. One thing was certain – life had become rather more complicated.

Later, with the sun beginning to peek over the horizon, he remounted his horse. Kyra took position beside him and kept pace as they moved back onto the road.

"You should keep out of sight," Akiri said. "You draw too much attention."

Kyra shook her head and grumbled a growl.

He was about to speak again when the dragon abruptly halted, her body stiff. A split second later he heard it as well. Around a bend in the road a hundred yards or so ahead, men were approaching on horseback. Armed men. Kyra spread her wings and flew straight up in the air, disappearing quickly above the treetops. Akiri spurred his horse forward. It was too late to hide. In any case, the men were approaching from the wrong direction to be coming from Vurna. Best to simply ride on past them if possible.

A few moments later, they came into view: six riders on horseback and an ox pulling a wagon. They were not soldiers, but all were armed and wearing chain mail shirts. As they neared, he could see that three of their number were badly injured, with blood soaked bandages wrapping their wounds. In the back of the wagon was a woman, shackled and gagged.

Akiri recognized her.

Rena.

The Hunari Guild must have caught up with her, he realized. The cuts and bruises that covered her face and arms, together with similar damage showing on most of the men, said that she had not been taken without offering a stern fight. Akiri steered his horse to the side of the road to allow them a wide berth. The Hunari barely took notice of him. But Rena saw him clearly enough. She glared hatefully.

Akiri looked back at her unblinkingly. It was a pity she would have to pay the price for Geridia's greed. She had merely been a pawn caught up in the middle of events beyond her control.

Once the procession had passed out of sight, he continued on. Not that he got very far. Soon Kyra swooped back down, landing in the road ahead and clearly intent on barring his path.

"Move," Akiri ordered.

She gave a low rumble, but refused to get out of the way. Waves of emotion from her began passing into him, but he couldn't understand what she was trying to tell him. Then, like a flash of light, an image of Rena popped into his mind.

"What about her?" he demanded.

Kyra hissed and spat, her tongue flicking back and forth. Akiri tried to move around her, but she nimbly kept herself in his way.

He sighed. "What would you have me do? I'm probably being hunted as we speak. I cannot afford a delay. In any case, Rena's fate is not my affair." He looked down at the determined creature and grunted irritably. "Why do you care what happens to her?" Then it struck him. "Can you see into my thoughts?"

The young dragon began pacing the breadth of the road, her eyes darting repeatedly from Akiri to the direction in which Rena had been taken. Could it sense his guilt? Was that how the great beast knew that he was partly to blame for Rena's plight? Or was that just his guilt talking even louder than any telepathic link they might share?

"I'm not going back for her," he insisted. "Now move out of the way."

Kyra paused in her pacing to blow what sounded like an exasperated breath from her nostrils. Akiri saw the muscles in her legs tense for a moment. Then, in a flash, she raced past him, letting out a feral roar. It was clear what she intended to do. Spitting a curse, he turned his horse and spurred it to a run after her.

The dragon was fast, easily faster than a human, but Akiri's mount was able to catch up before they reached the Hunari.

"I'll do it, damn you," he called out. "Stay hidden."

Sliding to a halt, Kyra allowed him to pass and then ducked into a nearby brush. A further string of curses flew from Akiri's mouth as he galloped on. No man short of King Zemel could alter his path once he had set his mind to it, but somehow Kyra had managed to do exactly that without even possessing the ability to speak. *This is just what I need*, he thought savagely. *A dragon with a soft heart.*

As the wagon and group of riders came into view, Akiri drew his sword. At least he would have the chance to use his magnificent new weapon. The prospect of this went some way to lessening his frustration.

On hearing the beating hooves of his horse bearing down on them, the Hunari turned to face the potential threat, but Akiri was upon them before they could organize any kind of defense.

He met the two riders on the right hand side of the wagon head on. One mighty blow from his blade almost cleaved the first man totally in half, clean from his shoulder to his hip. Even allowing for its maker's reputation, Akiri was surprised at how easily his sword sliced through the thick chain mail and bone. For all the protection the mail offered, it might as well have been crafted from parchment. A similar thought must have been passing through the second man's mind. A look of astonishment was still fixed on his face when Akiri jerked his blade free and then ran it through the center of his chest.

With so much blood spraying through the air, Akiri's face and arms were soon spattered in red dots. His battle lust surged. With his free hand he seized his dagger and hurled it at his next victim. With absolute accuracy, the blade flew over the top of the wagon and buried itself hilt deep into the man's neck. Barely five seconds had passed since first making contact and already only three Hunari remained, two of whom were previously injured.

These three were gathered just a few yards ahead of the wagon, all clearly still startled by the incredible speed in which their comrades had fallen. The only uninjured man held a massive hammer in his right hand. From his posture, Akiri guessed him to be the commander. He was about to spur his horse into a charge to deal with this opponent first when a shadow moved in the corner of his eye. Before he knew it, something hard struck him across the back of the head, sending him tumbling from the saddle. Though landing awkwardly, he was on his feet in an instant searching for answers.

What had happened was soon apparent.

Rena leaped down from the wagon and grabbed the sword of a slain Hunari. Akiri kicked away the shackles she had thrown at his head. For a moment he thought she was going to attack him, but then she let out a primal scream and charged at the remaining enemy instead.

The Hunari commander urged his horse forward to meet her, but Rena ducked just as he swung his weapon. Sliding past on her knees, she rose up and shoved the tip of her blade into his rib cage. Without pause, she was on her feet and headed straight toward the remaining two men.

Akiri saw that the commander, though injured, was far from finished and already turning his horse to attack Rena from behind. He rushed in, swinging his sword with tremendous force. The Hunari was able to bring up his hammer in time, but it did nothing to save him. Akiri's steel bounced off the weapon, sending a shower of sparks flying. Even before the last one of these had faded, he had spun to one side and rammed his sword through his enemy's back.

Rena was already engaged with the final two. Desperately, they hacked down at her, but their injuries were slowing their actions. She easily avoided the strikes, lithely ducking and weaving around their horses, her blade slashing and finding its target virtually at will. Akiri could see that she did not need any assistance and was intrigued as he watched her skillful attacks. He had seen a fair few women wield swords in the past; some had been quite good. But Rena carved her foes to pieces with a precision and power that rivaled the skill of any man he had faced save his own Dul'Buhar when sparring with them. The two Hunari were ultimately sliced to ribbons, both succumbing to their mounting injuries and blood loss. They slid from their mounts within moments of each other.

With victory complete, she spun to face Akiri. "You killed Geridia," she spat at him. The air of menace in her voice would have frozen the hearts of most men, particularly after having just seen her in action.

"No," he corrected. "I did not kill him. You have my word on that. But nor did I do anything to save him. That much I admit to."

His words did nothing to calm her anger. "You think by helping me I will spare you?" She looked down with scorn at her slain victims. "I would have escaped and killed these inadequate fools without your assistance. They only managed to capture me in the first place through sheer luck. And even then I dispatched three of them for their trouble. So I owe you nothing."

Akiri gave her a half smile. She was fierce and brave. And what she said about escaping was probably true. He guessed she had slipped her shackles some time ago and had only been waiting for the right time to strike.

"I had no intention of saving you," he told her. "The decision was made for me. So you are correct. You owe me nothing. Should you seek to avenge your master, I am here."

With a snarl on her face, Rena took a pace forward. "You ruined my life. And now I will take yours. I only regret there is nothing you love that I can take as well."

As if in response to this threat, a piercing cry came from above. Rena jumped back, sword at the ready. Knowing what Kyra intended, Akiri groaned. A moment later she flew in from over the treetops, landing heavily between the pair of them with teeth bared. The muscles in her shoulders rippled, ready to burst into life.

Rena nearly fell over as she quickly jumped back. Her eyes grew wide and her jaw fell slack. At first, she was completely dumbstruck and only slowly regained her composure. "What is that… beast?" she gasped.

"You don't recognize a dragon when you see one?" asked Akiri, slightly amused.

"There are no dragons in Galfaria," she said, still backing away.

"Clearly this is not true. Now it seems you have a choice to make. Though my companion insisted that we save you, it is obvious she has no intention of allowing you to harm me."

"Your companion?" she repeated incredulously. "That's impossible."

Akiri scowled. "Why do you insist on stating what is plainly incorrect? I had given you credit for more sense than that. Or has grief for your friend dulled your wits?"

This was enough to bring Rena's aggression surging back. Spreading her stance to form a solid base, she held her sword out in front of her. "If that thing comes at me, I'll gut it like a fish."

Akiri chuckled. "She means you no harm. Though I can feel that she intends to protect me. As long as you do not attack me, you will be quite safe."

"So you fear to fight me then," she taunted.

"I fear nothing," he said, though without betraying any anger. "The Dul'Buhar embrace death when it comes."

"You're a liar," she snapped. "You are no Dul'Buhar."

"You have heard of us? That's good. And you are correct. I was exiled from the order. But make no mistake, I have forgotten nothing of my time as their commander."

Rena suddenly looked uncertain. "Then it seems I am forced to retreat."

Akiri sheathed his sword. "You are free to do whatever you wish, but I suggest you decide quickly. The Hunari Guild will undoubtedly be out for revenge when they discover their men have been slain. I advise you to head south across country. The terrain there is rocky, and it will be difficult for them to track you."

She frowned. "What about you? Why are you leaving Vurna? Did your audience with Tuvarius not go as well as you hoped?"

"I also advise that you mind your own affairs," Akiri warned. "Look after yourself and forget about me."

It crossed his mind that there was a risk she could disclose his location. From here, a good enough tracker might well be able to follow him the rest of the way. The thought of killing her flashed through his mind, but almost instantly, Kyra spun to face him and let out a loud hiss.

Akiri glared back at her and let out a sigh. "You must stay out of my mind, beast."

Rena threw him a quizzical look. "It hears your thoughts?"

"As I said, mind your own affairs."

"You are a most unusual man, Akiri. One that I wish I had never met. Know that if I ever see you again, you will *not* be greeted as a friend." She turned away and began to rifle through the Hunari's packs.

Akiri regarded her for a moment before crossing over to his mount. Kyra was immediately at his side. "You and I need to come to an understanding," he muttered under his breath.

The young dragon let out a low rumbling growl. Akiri felt that she was amused by his irritation, which only served to inflame his mood further. After mounting his horse, he urged it to a quick trot. Kyra took to the sky and was soon out of sight.

Akiri brooded. This was becoming a problem. He could not allow the dragon to continue influencing his actions. He had a mission to complete, and was not in a position to stop and save everyone in need of help he happened upon. He did not fear death. But he also had no wish to throw his life away on some fool's quest. If the Hunari been carrying bows, or had there been more of them, things might have turned out far worse.

He looked up at the empty sky. "You hear me? You will not interfere. If you try, I will send you away."

Waves of silent laughter struck him. This time, a single word sprang into his head.

No.

Still grumbling to himself, he focused his attention on the road. The mere thought of Kyra coming to harm or being distressed was sufficient to produce uncomfortable feelings of anxiety.

"You will obey me," he muttered. "I'll find a way to make you."

Chapter Sixteen

Akiri continued west along the main road leading to the border with Balnaria. He had marked no signs of pursuit, no dust clouds in the distance or other telltale giveaways, but he was not yet ready to believe they were safe.

Kyra was always near, though she spent the majority of her time amongst the clouds. At night she would join him by the fire. He was becoming fond of her company. While lazing by the fire on the night before they reached the border, he tried once again to touch her. He had attempted to do so on several previous occasions, but she always backed away. This time was no different.

"Dragons are such curious creatures," came a childlike voice from just beyond the firelight. "Don't you agree?"

Akiri immediately thought of Vazhta. "Show yourself, demon," he snapped, jumping to his feet.

"Demon?" the voice said. "Why would you call me that?"

"I have no patience for your games. Show yourself."

"Of course. Forgive my discourtesy."

The figure who stepped into the light was not the one whom Akiri had expected to see. It was a young boy with dark curls and a bronze complexion. He also appeared to be several years older than Vazhta. His tan trousers and shirt were both simple and ill-fitting – most definitely made for someone much larger. He beamed at Akiri and dropped down beside the fire.

"Who are you?" Akiri demanded, accentuating his words by placing a hand ominously on the hilt of his sword.

"My name is Hagrik," he replied. "I am the emissary of Mishna."

"Is that right? And what of Vazhta?"

Hagrik's face turned instantly sour. "He is no servant of Mishna. He is a liar and a trickster. You don't want to get mixed up with him. That much I can promise."

Akiri sneered. "But I suppose it's perfectly safe for me to place my trust in you."

"Indeed it is," he said, his smile returning. "Though I doubt you will. But that doesn't matter. Please sit. Let us talk."

Akiri hesitated. He had been hoping not to encounter any more of these creatures. Kyra, however, seemed unconcerned and ignored Hagrik's presence completely. Finally, he did as asked and re-took his seat.

"Why are you here?" he said.

"I am here to convince you to turn the Scepter of Xarbaal over to me once you have acquired it."

Akiri huffed a disdainful laugh. "Then you are wasting your time."

"I know that you intend to give it to King Zemel," the youth responded. "And I am fully aware that you are his most loyal servant. But consider this. Should he ever possess the Scepter again, it will undoubtedly consume him. It has already clouded his mind. Further exposure would drive him to a place beyond redemption."

"Like the others, you think to shake my resolve," Akiri said. "But you will not succeed. If the Scepter will help my king to end the wars, I will see that he has it."

"It will not end the wars," Hagrik told him. "Your king will defeat his enemies, but he will not stop there. He will continue with his conquests until he is completely enslaved by the power of the Scepter. When that happens, he will fall under the control of Xarbaal and be forced to release him from his prison. With Xarbaal free again, war amongst the gods will inevitably follow. And so will utter devastation. The petty battles that you mortals wage will seem like nothing more than a small squabble between children by comparison."

"So you would have me pass the Scepter to Mishna instead?"

"Exactly! She will keep it safe and far away from the hands of those who would think to use its power."

Akiri chuckled. "If I do that, then it would be Mishna who controls the fate of the world. Why would I want that to happen?"

"Because if Xarbaal acquires it, he will kill everything that lives in the mortal world. It was only through the combined strength of all the other gods that he was prevented from achieving this the last time."

"If they have stopped him once, why could they not do so again?"

Hagrik rested his arms on his knees and lowered his head. "They no longer have the strength. As the eons have passed, they have become weaker. As the mortal world expands, they diminish."

Akiri threw back his head in a loud burst of laughter. "You must think me a fool. If the gods are diminishing, I would welcome it. And if what you have told me is true, I would never give the Scepter to Mishna. I would see it destroyed first."

Anger flashed across Hagrik's face. "You *are* a fool. You cannot destroy it. No mortal can. If you tried to do so, it would kill you. You must do as I say. Only through the wisdom of Mishna can your world be saved."

"And what has this so-called *wisdom* ever done for my world?" Akiri demanded. "I think your mistress will have to do without her prize. Now leave me… before I become curious as to what might happen should I pass my blade through your neck."

Hagrik stood, his hands planted firmly on his hips. "You are a stubborn one. It baffles me why Mishna has taken such a keen interest in you."

Akiri rose and drew his sword. The light of the fire danced off the steel, giving it a magical appearance. Slaying a child was not something he would normally consider, but this was no child.

"Tell me, demon," he said, a vicious grin forming. "Is your body real? Or is it just an illusion?"

Hagrik took a step back. "It is quite real, I assure you. Conjured, yes, and at great cost and no little difficulty, but no mere illusion. But as I see you intend to make good on your threat, I will depart. By way of a parting gift from me to you: do not under any circumstances allow Vazhta to take the Scepter of Xarbaal."

"Of that you can be certain. He will no more touch it than you will."

Hagrik sniffed. "We shall see, Acharian."

His final words were still hanging in the air when he disappeared in a flash of white light.

Akiri sheathed his sword and sat by the fire. Two demon spirits had now plagued him, both of them claiming to be the servant of Mishna. One of them was clearly lying. But which one? He had no experience in dealing with such creatures. Many sorcerers had lost their lives trying to harness their power, and many a warrior had been tricked into sacrificing his life by a demon's destructive lies.

Kyra growled and flicked her tongue. Akiri could feel that she was hungry. He rummaged through his saddlebag and produced a portion of salted pork. After sniffing suspiciously at the offering, she backed away.

"That's all the food I have," Akiri told her. "If you want something else, you'll need to find it yourself."

Kyra spread her wings wide and flew straight up, disappearing in seconds.

Stretching out beside the fire, he shut his eyes. The demon's words echoed in his mind. The tale of Xarbaal, the god of death, was well known. His hatred for the mortal world had driven him into attempting to extinguish every trace of life within it. But the other gods joined together and imprisoned him for all time within The Cave of Silence. Only the Scepter he once wielded could free him. Akiri had always thought such tales to be nonsense, no more than stories to tell children at bedtime. But now… perhaps there was truth to the legends after all.

He forced all this from his mind and allowed himself to drift, but his sleep was far from peaceful. Images of childhood invaded his dreams; they felt like memories, though he could not say exactly when or where any of them might have occurred. He saw his mother's face: she was smiling at him in the way only a mother could. She was trying to tell him something, but frustratingly he could not hear her voice. A strange sadness washed through him. He longed to remember the sound of her voice and to feel her kiss on his brow. But like everything else, they remained just out of reach.

On waking, a single tear fell down his cheek. He collected it on the tip of his finger and stared at it in surprise. He had not shed tears since… he couldn't remember when. As he flicked the tear away, he noticed that Kyra had returned and was dozing by the fire. Blood stained her talons and around her jaws, though there was no trace remaining of her kill to tell him what it might have been.

After a quick breakfast of the pork that Kyra had rejected earlier, he made ready to leave. As he mounted his horse, Kyra took to the air. With each day that passed, he found himself becoming more and more comforted by her company. Even the solitude of being away from the Dul'Buhar was now far less unsettling.

The Scepter's hiding place indicated in Tuvarius' message would take him more than a week to reach. The Temple of the Blood Moon had been abandoned centuries ago, and since then only the very bravest of adventurers had dared to go there. Of all those who had risked their lives seeking out the temple's treasures, not a single one had escaped with his life.

"I will be the first," Akiri promised himself. He spurred his horse to a trot.

The Temple stood on the banks of the Great Mol'Sanath Lake. Its waters had been poisoned by evil magic, and it was said that if so much as a single drop of it touched your lips, a slow and hideously painful death was certain. Complicating matters even further, foul creatures were reputed to lurk in the forest surrounding its shores – beasts of unimaginable hunger and savagery that devoured all who ventured away from the temple road. But Akiri feared no beast. And he would not be turned into a coward by myths and legends.

Soon, he would be back where he belonged.

Chapter Seventeen

As his destination grew closer, Akiri began to feel as if his every move was being watched. Perhaps it was Hagrik or Vazhta, he considered, possibly even both. Whatever the case, Kyra was acting increasingly on edge. Whenever he stopped at a village for fresh supplies, he felt her urging him to turn back.

The only populated area close to the Temple of the Blood Moon was little more than a dilapidated trading post calling itself Plenty. To Akiri, it seemed an ironic name, given the dire state of the place. The earth everywhere was bone dry, and what little vegetation that managed to struggle through to the surface was sickly and stunted. The people matched the surroundings. Unwashed and ragged, they barely noticed him as he rode by. He could feel Kyra calling even more urgently than usual for him to avoid this place.

"I do not wish to continue blind," he muttered. "If there is something to be learned here, then I should find out what it is."

He tied his horse to a post outside Plenty's only tavern. The sign above the door was faded to the point that the words written on it were no longer legible. There was no music coming from inside, only the grunts and coughs of drunken men.

It was a little before midday, but the dreary overcast sky made it seem far later. Akiri opened the door and was immediately struck by the foul reek of stale beer, vomit, unwashed bodies, and urine, all mingled together to form a sickeningly poisonous vapor. He fought an instinct to cover his nose. The stench of a soldiers' camp during a long campaign could be bad. But that was like the scent of spring flowers compared to what he was now experiencing.

A dozen disheveled men sat at the few tables, but only a handful bothered to glance briefly at the new arrival before returning their attention to the apparently far more important matter of their drinks. A barman at the rear was propped on a wooden stool, busy sharpening a small dagger.

"If you have no coin, get the fuck out," he called over, without looking up.

Akiri took a seat at the bar and slapped a copper down. This was instantly snatched up and a mug of bitter smelling ale shoved in his direction.

"What can you tell me about the Temple of the Blood Moon?" Akiri asked.

The barman sneered. "I might have guessed. Another sad fool come seeking his fortune. Well, believe me, you had better turn back. Not that you'll listen. You're probably just like all the rest. You think you'll be the one to make it where all others have failed. The Watcher tends to the stupid and the brave pretty damn quick and with equal measure."

"The Watcher?" Akiri looked down at the unappetizing liquid inside the mug and pushed it away.

"You go meddling around near that bloody temple and you'll find out quick enough who that is, believe me."

Akiri took out another copper. "I'd like to find out now."

The barman hesitated for only a second before accepting

the coin. "Fine. The Watcher guards the entrance to the temple. Before you can step foot inside, you must defeat him."

"But *what* is he?" Akiri pressed.

The barman shrugged. "How should I know? I've never been stupid enough to go there."

Akiri leaned in, his voice hard and unyielding. "I think a copper is worth a bit more information than that, don't you?"

The barman didn't seem the least bit intimidated. "You asked me a question, and I answered it. I'd say I earned my coin. So either drink your ale or get out."

"Now, Toby. Don't be rude."

The voice came from by the door. Akiri turned to see a man in his early thirties, dressed in purple and gold finery, standing in the entrance. His black hair was oiled and pushed back in the fashion of the eastern lords, while a ruddy complexion and brightly sparkling blue eyes only served to set him apart from the rest of Plenty's depressingly rundown inhabitants.

"Give him back his money," he continued. "You know nothing worth paying for."

The barman's eyes were instantly downcast. "Yes, My Lord." He pushed the copper across the bar and backed away.

"That's better," the newcomer said, giving a satisfied nod. "I wouldn't want visitors here to think we lack hospitality." He crossed over to the bar and bowed. "I am Lord Marshio Lowd. Welcome to Plenty. Though I'm afraid the name is a trifle… misleading."

Akiri regarded the man. His good manners and friendly disposition were obviously meant to be disarming. "I am Akiri."

"Akiri, you say? Well, Akiri, what brings you here on such a dreary day?"

"I seek information about the Temple of the Blood Moon."

"So you're an adventurer. How marvelous." He gestured to the door. "Come. Join me at my home for some decent food and drink."

"I am seeking only information."

Lowd gave him a bright smile. "Then join me and you shall have it."

Akiri followed the man outside and down the main avenue for a short distance until reaching a modest, single-story dwelling. Though not lavish, it was of significantly superior construction to any of the other buildings he had seen. The narrow front yard was well tended and surrounded by a low fence.

"I considered building myself something a touch more extravagant," Lowd informed him. "But it seemed such a waste to bring anything of real beauty to this awful place."

"What do you do here?" asked Akiri.

"Why, trade of course. Even here there is gold to be made. Though I miss my home."

As they approached the front door, Akiri noticed that the stones beneath his feet were veined with silver. Upon closer inspection, he saw that they continued in the same manner all the way around the house.

"That is the true wealth of this wretched place," remarked Lowd, noticing his interest. "Were it not for the legends about those living in the hills to the north where the mines are, you would not be able to spit without hitting someone seeking their fortune."

"You mean the lycan?"

"So you've heard the stories."

"Everyone has," Akiri replied. "A comrade of mine said that he had once encountered one."

Lowd raised an eyebrow. "Really? And he lived to tell of it? He must have been quite a warrior." He opened the door and swept his arm in a gesture of welcome. "But we can talk inside."

The interior of the house was ornate. Fine artworks set in silver frames decorated the entrance hall, and a delicate crystal chandelier hung from the ceiling. The floors were of black marble with silver engravings polished to a mirror-like shine.

Lowd led him through an oak door and down a series of short hallways. Eventually they reached a sitting room with a hearth and several comfortable chairs. Silver lamps lined the walls, and a small cabinet stood in the far corner.

"Please sit," said Lowd, pointing to a chair near the hearth. He crossed to the cabinet and poured two glasses of brandy. "So you believe in lycans?"

"The man who told me of it would not have lied."

Lowd placed the glasses on a small table and then took a seat. "Where did this encounter take place?"

"In the southern regions."

"That is good. But rest assured, there are none of them around here. There may have been many years ago, but if there were, they are long gone." Chuckling, he picked up his glass and held it under his nose. "Of course, try telling that to the locals."

Akiri suppressed a look of doubt. Over the years he had found that, though folk from small communities were often suspicious of strangers and more prone to superstition than city dwellers, the knowledge they had of their own area was for the most part highly accurate. If someone other than a member of the Dul'Buhar had told him of an encounter with a lycan, he would not have believed it. But in this case the man not only would not lie, he was incapable of doing so.

"How can you be so sure they are no longer around?" he asked.

"Because in the ten years I've lived here, I've never seen a single one. And nor has anyone else, to my knowledge. What keeps the lycan superstition fresh around here is that every once in a while someone from Plenty mysteriously disappears. Then the rumors really begin to fly. But if you ask me, those that vanish are simply running away, probably heading east in search of a better life. I mean, can you blame them for wanting to escape the misery of this rat hole?"

"So why would anyone attribute their disappearance to a lycan?"

Lowd took a sip of his drink. "Because of that damned temple, of course. Kyzeech, goddess of the hunt, is said to have lived in it once, and that's more than enough to convince the simple minds around here." He smiled. "But I didn't bring you here to discuss the past. You wanted information, as I recall."

"I do," Akiri affirmed. "And I suspect you want something from me in return."

Lowd winked over the rim of his glass. "Perceptive. And as it happens, yes, I do want something, but that can wait a moment. You wanted to know about the Watcher, and I am happy to tell you what I know of him, free of charge."

He took another small sip of his drink before continuing. "The thing looks like a human, but he is most definitely not. What he actually is, no one knows. But he's old… ancient, in fact. His speed and strength are beyond measure, and his hide is as hard as stone, able to turn aside even the sharpest blade. But for all this, he is not invulnerable. About five years ago, a band of treasure hunters faced him. Only one of them was able to flee the scene, and though terribly injured, he made it this far before dying. He told me that one of his companions had managed to hurt the beast. Apparently, its back is soft and fleshy. If you can find a way to get behind the creature, then you might stand a chance. But beware its embrace. Apparently, its preferred method of killing is to crush its opponents to death."

"Is that all you can offer?" Akiri said, frowning.

Lowd drained his glass and sat it on the table. "That was for free, but considering what you face, I assume that any information I pass on would be of value."

"What about inside the temple?" Akiri pressed. "What is that like?"

Lowd spread his hands. "That remains a mystery. No one has ever defeated the Watcher to find out. But if you become the first to gain entry, there is something I want."

Akiri stiffened. "If it's the Scepter, you are wasting your time."

Lowd furled his brow. "Scepter? No, no, no. I want a medallion. Some say it hangs on the main alter. Assuming there is even an altar in that place. Most of it is stories and rumor. But maybe, just maybe, this story is true. And if it is, it would be worth a great deal to me. It's crafted in the form of a wolf's head and has two glittering ruby eyes. Such a thing should be easy to recognize, yes?"

He rose and crossed to the far wall where he lifted a painting to reveal a small safe. After unlocking it, he removed a white cloth. "Obtain the medallion for me, and I will reward you with this."

He unwrapped the cloth to reveal a diamond roughly the size of a hen's egg. Its perfect facets captured the light and sent rays of brilliance shooting in all directions.

"If this medallion is so valuable, why would I agree?" Akiri asked. "What is preventing me from keeping it for myself?"

"Obviously you could, but as a trinket it holds little worth beyond the obvious gold weight and the stones. But to certain people, it is priceless. And before you ask, no, I am not about to tell you who these people are or why they covet it." He held out the gem so that Akiri could get a better look. "But think about it. With this, you could live the rest of your life in comfort."

Akiri had no need for vast wealth, but the diamond would make a worthy gift for his king. "If I find this medallion you speak of, I will bring it to you," he promised.

Lowd wrapped the jewel and smiled. "Excellent. I shall be waiting here with it, but I suppose I should be honest with you, warrior: I have made this offer many times before, and every time I have been left disappointed. But perhaps you will be different?"

"I like my chances." Akiri stood. "If there is nothing more you can tell me, I will go."

Lowd glanced down at Akiri's untouched brandy and sighed. "Quite right."

They walked to the door and parted at the front gate. Akiri could feel the man watching him as he walked away. There was something about this Lord Marshio Lowd that bothered him. The diamond he had offered was worth a king's fortune – many thousand times more than one would normally be prepared to pay for a trinket. But what did it matter? The motives of a lesser lord in some ramshackle village were of no interest.

Once beyond the borders of the town, the sun broke through the overcast sky, and soon large patches of blue were visible. He cleared his mind and focused on the task ahead, wondering what manner of creature the Watcher could be. There were many things in the world that had superior strength and speed, but none he could think of came in human form and had skin dense enough to repel or deflect steel.

Like the sun overhead, Kyra's relief that he had left Plenty was also now coming through clearly. Two words from her entered Akiri's mind. Though simple, they took him aback.

Nasty place.

Was she learning to communicate with him in actual language, or was he learning to better understand her? Either way, it was a special moment.

"You're right," he said, grinning. "A very nasty place."

Chapter Eighteen

He hadn't traveled far before conditions changed again. The road had become increasingly soft and muddy, and though it was still several hours before dusk, the sun had disappeared behind the clouds to produce an even denser gloom. Akiri's keen eyes penetrated this well enough for a time, but as the stench of decaying leaves and boggy earth increased, an unnatural fog descended, drenching his hair and clothing. A dead silence added to the sense of foreboding.

Kyra circled nervously above.

"Calm down," he told her. "Fear serves nothing. I will defeat whatever lies ahead."

He barely heard her screeching reply. It was as if the air was devouring her call.

The temple almost caught him by surprise when its outline appeared in the mist. Akiri was struck by the sheer scale of the structure. Four looming towers spaced at least a hundred yards apart seemed to climb up forever. As he drew closer, he saw that the towers were connected by a massive wall crowned with iron spikes. A series of amazingly lifelike reliefs decorated the façade, depicting various wild beasts. Immediately above these, his eyes were drawn to a line of strange-looking glyphs in a language he had never seen before.

Set between two of the great towers was a black marble colonnade that ended in a broad open archway. The head of a wolf had been carved into the keystone of the arch, its eyes set with rubies that somehow managed to flash and sparkle vividly despite the gloom.

The absence of a gate seemed odd for a place rumored to be so well guarded. Akiri allowed his senses to sharpen. Along the colonnade he saw number of discarded swords and broken shields. Some were relatively new, while others were badly rusted and decayed by time.

Kyra began spiraling into a slow descent.

"No," Akiri told her. "Do not follow me."

Kyra replied with a deep rumbling growl. *Danger coming.*

A moment later, from beyond the archway, a lone figure clad in a sleeveless gray tunic and short trousers came into view. At first glance, it appeared to be a man, but as Akiri looked more closely he saw that it was anything but human. Its face was narrow, with eyes sunk deep into its skull. Though equally as tall as himself, it looked thin and frail – not that he would allow this to deceive him. Its flesh was deathly pale and marked with deep scars that spider-webbed every inch of its face and arms. The creature regarded Akiri curiously for a moment and then cracked a crooked smile, revealing sharp, jagged teeth.

"Something new, I see," it said, its voice thin and hollow. "Not the same rabble that usually comes calling at my door. What business have you here?"

"I seek what is hidden within the temple," replied Akiri.

The Watcher flicked his wrist. "That much I gathered. But there are many treasures there. Far too many for one man to carry alone. What exactly do you seek?"

"That is my business, creature."

"If you intend to pass, then it is my business too," he retorted firmly. "Many have tried to enter. Only one has succeeded. And he did not come seeking plunder, but to leave treasure behind for safe keeping. He was a man much like yourself: strong and determined." The Watcher glanced skyward. "And he too had a dragon. Albeit one much older and larger than yours."

"I come for what that man left behind," Akiri told him. "What he placed here did not belong to him."

"Nor does it belong to *you*. Not unless you are Xarbaal in disguise."

"It belongs to my master," Akiri stated.

The Watcher chuckled. "I was told about the mortal king who would make himself a god. And you would serve such a fool?" He clicked his tongue. "Humans are such odd creatures."

"And what manner of thing are you?"

He shrugged his bony shoulders. "I have been called by many names. Some call me the Watcher, but I do not like that name. I prefer *pishaac*."

Akiri raised an eyebrow. The pishaac were thought to have vanished long ago. Once a proud race of desert dwellers, they were fierce in battle and cunning beyond measure, especially when preying on travelers stupid enough to wander too close to their lands. But the physical descriptions he had encountered during his studies did not in any way resemble the being that stood in front of him.

The pishaac laughed. "I can see that you doubt my word." He looked down at himself. "I must admit I have changed a great deal over the centuries."

"What happened to your people?" Akiri asked, the scholar within him bringing his curiosity to the fore.

"As humans invaded our beloved desert, most of us journeyed east to seek a new home." There was a longing in his tone that bordered on despair. "The few who remained behind were mostly hunted and killed."

"Do you not wish to join with your people again?"

"I sought them out once. I wandered for a hundred years, but found no trace of them."

"So why are you here?"

The pishaac took a step forward. His movements were fluid and measured. "I was bound to this temple by the goddess Kyzeech and set the task of guarding the treasures held within." His mood had suddenly darkened. "I do not wish to speak of this any further."

Akiri dismounted. "Then we shall not. But I must pass."

"You will have to earn the right of passage, and even if you are to prove successful, your dragon will not be able to join you. Beasts cannot enter the temple."

Akiri followed him through the archway into a large open courtyard, on the far side of which he saw iron gates leading into the temple itself. In the center of the courtyard stood a marble statue of a wolf with its head thrown back, in the act of howling. The moss-covered granite floor was badly cracked, and there were dark stains everywhere – presumably blood from the previous victims who had dared to challenge the pishaac.

Akiri glanced over his shoulder to see that Kyra had landed and was pacing nervously about just a few yards outside the entrance. He sent her thoughts of reassurance, though it did little to calm her.

"I have never understood those beasts," the Watcher

remarked. "Why would such proud creatures choose to serve humans?"

"Maybe it is not a choice," offered Akiri. "Perhaps it is simply in their nature."

"Perhaps," he agreed. "A pity we will not have the opportunity to consider the matter further."

Akiri took note that the pishaac was carrying no weapon – a disadvantage he had no intention of sharing. The song of his blade reverberated off the courtyard walls. "Do you have a name?" he asked.

He cocked his head. "Of course I do. But why would you wish to know it?"

"The tale of this should be told properly," Akiri replied. "If your people are nearly gone from this world, then your name should be passed down."

"So you imagine yourself victorious," he said, a hint of amusement creeping through. "That is good. And though I think my name will not leave this place, I will tell you anyway." He gave Akiri a low, sweeping bow. "I am Orn."

Akiri bowed his head. "And I am Akiri."

"Akiri… it means the *cast out*, does it not?"

"It does," he affirmed. "And your name means *gentle one.*"

Orn cracked a smile. "I am impressed. More is the pity that your life will end here."

Akiri broadened his stance. "We shall see whose life ends today."

"Indeed we will."

The pishaac's expression hardened. The cracking of joints echoed around the courtyard, the sound abnormally loud as he clenched his fists tight. Akiri watched his opponent's feet as he shifted his weight forward, warning him that a frontal assault was coming. It also suggested that this was a creature of considerable speed, much like the soul shredder he had encountered just prior to his exile.

Orn charged in. His fist flew at Akiri's jaw, and he was barely able to twist his head away in time. This creature, he immediately realized, was even faster than the soul shredder had been. Considerably so. After making a rapid sidestep, Akiri swung his blade in a neck high sweep. He expected Orn to duck or move away. Instead, he merely raised his forearm and blocked the blade with his flesh. It felt as if the sword had struck granite. He was stinging from the impact when a mighty blow thudded into his midsection, driving the air from his lungs and sending him stumbling back; it took enormous effort to remain on his feet.

Orn raised an eyebrow, clearly impressed that Akiri was able to withstand the power of his punch. "It has been a long time since I faced anyone who might present an honest challenge to me," he remarked. His eyes shifted momentarily to the point on his arm which had blocked Akiri's blade. A tiny scratch was barely visible. "And your weapon… I have not seen the like of that in many years." He sighed heavily. "Such a waste."

"We shall see where the waste lies once this is over," Akiri retorted, grateful for this brief interlude in which to regain a measure of control over his breathing. He leveled his sword, muscles ready to erupt into action again.

This time when Orn came at him, he did so with more caution, feigning left and then right in an attempt to throw Akiri off balance. Akiri responded with a series of controlled thrusts, three of which found Orn's flesh but failed to penetrate. Orn countered with a flurry of punches. Though Akiri avoided most of them, the final one found its target. A particularly vicious strike carrying enough power to instantly render most men unconscious landed solidly on the side of his head. Even Akiri could not absorb a blow of such ferocity entirely unaffected. Badly dazed for a few seconds, he was forced to give ground in order to defend himself.

He circled around to his right, remembering what Lowd had told him. But Orn anticipated his move and matched his steps in order to keep him to the front.

After several minutes of this deadly but unproductive dance, Akiri a let out a snort of impatience, and raised his sword high for an extravagant downward sweep. Against an opponent of Orn's blinding speed, this seemed like a serious error of judgment. The pishaac leapt forward, wrapping his arms around Akiri's lower chest and lifting him completely up from the ground.

The crushing strength of Orn's grip was unbelievable, preventing Akiri from taking even the smallest breath. Although he was now in the position he'd intended, his sword was far too long to strike effectively, and in this python-like hold, he had only precious moments to act before succumbing to unconsciousness. Already his eyes were watering and the blood was starting to pound loudly in his ears.

Allowing the sword to slip from his hand, he reached down to free the dagger tucked inside his belt. While his fingers searched blindly for the dagger handle, the ever-increasing pressure on his ribs made it feel as though they would cave in completely at any moment. He had gambled, and knew that he might have lost.

At last his fingers made contact and he was able to draw the weapon, but his strength was rushing away like water draining over a mighty waterfall. With his vision badly distorted and hearing nothing but a roaring in his ears, he struck with the dagger at what he hoped was the most vulnerable part of Orn's back.

The pishaac became aware of what was happening at the very last second. His grip slacked and he threw Akiri to the ground. Crying out in a mixture of pain and fury, he shuffled around while groping behind him. The blade had not sunk more than halfway, but it was positioned in the most awkward part of the back to reach.

Much as Akiri's body ached for a brief respite, he knew there was no time for such indulgence. Scrambling to his feet, he ran straight at Orn, burying his shoulder into the center of the pishaac's chest, sending both of them crashing down hard onto the stone floor.

Orn shrieked in agony as the protruding dagger was forced in all the way down to the hilt. Akiri rolled away and raced to retrieve his sword. By the time he had it, Orn was already rising, a look of pure fury burning in his eyes. He took an unsteady step forward, then halted.

"I am not beaten yet, human," he growled.

"Yes, you are."

Akiri raised his sword and moved in cautiously. He would not be careless with such a dangerous enemy, even though he was injured. The pishaac crouched and readied himself for the coming onslaught.

His body re-energized by his success, Akiri swung his sword with astounding force at Orn's head. As before, the pishaac raised his arm to shield himself. But this time Akiri's blade penetrated nearly an inch deep. He wondered if the injury to Orn's back had somehow weakened his defenses on the front. The pishaac winced and backed away, but Akiri was determined to press his advantage. Again and again his sword struck, inflicting ever more serious wounds. Orn tried to counter, but no longer had the speed or strength to be effective. Akiri continued to rain deadly steel down upon him until all his limbs were covered in deep gashes and drenched in blood.

At last, Orn's arms fell limply at his side. He looked at Akiri, this time not with hatred or anger, but in acceptance of his fate. Akiri halted his assault and stepped away.

"If it is in your mind to allow me to leave, know that I cannot," Orn told him. "The magic that binds me to this place prevents it."

"That was not my intention," Akiri replied. "You will die this day. I pause only to offer you a swift death, if you so wish it."

It was plain to see that the pishaac was struggling to stay on his feet. The amount of blood he had lost was enormous. He was helpless, and Akiri had no desire to prolong the suffering of an opponent who could not defend himself.

Orn regarded him for several moments before slowly nodding. "Thank you. I accept your offer." He turned and presented his back. "You only just missed my heart the first time. Just a touch below that mark will serve the purpose well."

The dagger was still buried deep into his flesh. Raising his sword, Akiri thrust the point firmly into the spot suggested. The pishaac gasped just once and then dropped to his knees. After Akiri wrenched the blade free, he planted a boot in the creature's back and toppled it.

It did not move again.

His death produced a small feeling of regret in Akiri. To slay a being who might be the last of his kind was not something that sat well with him. He creased his brow as he removed his dagger from the body and set about cleaning both of his blades on the pishaac's corpse. Regret was not a feeling with which he was familiar. All creatures had their time. Should it be now or in a thousand years, it was all the same in the end.

Kyra let out a triumphant roar from outside the courtyard. She, at least, was pleased by the outcome. It was enough to banish ill thoughts and urge him to complete his task.

"We will return home soon," he told her.

Then, a mere instant after speaking, the memory that King Zemel might not permit Kyra to live struck him mind like a hammer.

"No," he whispered. "My king would not deny me. Not once I've safely returned the Scepter to him."

But no matter how many times he said this to himself, the doubt plagued him.

Chapter Nineteen

The gates to the temple shrieked with ear-splitting shrillness as Akiri pulled them open.

Ahead of him lay a dank corridor that exuded death and decay.

His keen eyes penetrated the darkness, but he noticed the subtle differences between the powers granted to him as a Dul'Buhar and those he now possessed. Although his strength and endurance seemed much the same as before, there was no doubt that his hearing and sight were less acute than they had been. Colors were less bright and distant sounds more difficult to define.

The passage sloped gently upward for a few hundred feet, with walls that were bare, apart from the disused iron sconces set into them. At the end stood a double door, its wood rotted away and the handles hanging precariously. Above this, ancient letters had been chiseled into the wall.

With open eyes you seek the light,
The sun and sky will banish night,
But only darkness shows the way,
Where winged bat can find its prey.

Akiri read the words several times before reaching for the door. On making contact, the wood crumbled away at his touch. Tossing the ruined pieces aside, he looked beyond into a short passage that ended in a narrow archway bathed in light, banishing all trace of the previous gloom. He couldn't see the source of the illumination, which only served to make it all the more unnerving.

Drawing his blade, Akiri moved on. On the other side of the archway, the walls were lined with lit torches. He examined them closely – no smoke. Kept alight by magic, he decided.

The corridor soon split left and right, but each direction appeared to be identical. Allowing his instincts to guide him, he headed down the right hand passage, but after a hundred feet or so, this also split two ways. This time he turned left.

Things rapidly became complicated as every few feet the way forward would split yet again. Right – left – left – right – left – Akiri did his best to recall the rapidly increasing number of turns he had made. But after a time even his sharp mind was being taxed to its limit. Eventually he turned back while he was still able to remember the way, but after rounding the corner that should have taken him back to the entrance, he found to his dismay only another hallway. He went over the turns he had taken in his head, certain that he had not made a mistake.

With no other option, he continued to thread his way through the maze, but only found more identical looking turns and passages. Several times he marked the walls with his dagger, but when he attempted to return to the same spot, the marks were always gone.

A cry of frustration slipped out. He would not die this way – lost like a child in the forest. He sat on the floor with his back up against the wall. There had to be a way through. There *had* to be. For more than an hour, he remained absolutely still while thinking on this, his mind going around in circles. Eventually, he found the final two lines of the poem at the entrance repeating themselves over and over in his mind.

But only darkness shows the way,

To where winged bat can find its prey.

It couldn't be that simple, he thought. Surely not?

But perhaps it was? Maybe he had been looking for something too complicated?

Standing up, he took a deep cleansing breath, closed his eyes, and simply began to walk. The echoes of his footfalls sounded loud in the confined space.

In less than a minute, the substance of the dark shifted, and he sensed that he had reached the next passage split. Pausing, he listened hard. For a moment, there was nothing. Then it came to him: he could definitely hear the high-pitched chirping of a bat. It was pulling him to the right.

A smile formed as he followed the sound. Filled with confidence, he walked blindly on. Eight more times he turned, following the guiding call. Then, all at once, a rush of hot air washed over him. He could both hear and feel that the space had opened up in front of him, but the chirping had now stopped. He had reached his next destination. Wherever and whatever that was.

He cracked open his eyes and found that he was in a circular chamber roughly a hundred feet in diameter. The maze had gone. Only the ruined door remained.

Deep recesses had been cut into the wall every few feet. Inside each stood a life-sized statue of a chain mail-clad warrior holding a longsword in one hand and a small round shield in the other. There were no other doors that Akiri could see. But on the floor was another etching of ancient letters.

When battles rage and blood is spilled,
The warrior's heart is truly filled,
But rage and lust will help you naught,
When comes the fight that must be fought.

He had no time to consider these words. A loud crack had his hand flying to his sword. One of the stone warriors had stepped down onto the floor, longsword leveled. Its movements were slow and labored as it lumbered toward him.

Taking the initiative, he struck the warrior just above its hip, but rather than a loud ringing of steel on stone, the statue simply crumbled to dust the moment his sword made contact.

Akiri stepped away, concerned that it was too easy.

A moment later, his concern was justified.

Another statue in the wall came to life, and the empty place where the first one had stood was now occupied by two identical stone figures. Akiri dispatched these just as easily, but the moment they fell, another came to life. Again the empty spaces were filled. How many of these could he fight, he wondered? More than most men. But even he had limits.

There were soon well over a dozen stone warriors for him to keep at bay, though the situation was not yet critical. Their movements were so slow; it would take a lot more than this to overwhelm him. Only one of them had been able to get close enough to start swinging his sword at Akiri before being turned to dust. But it was obvious that against an enemy that was both tireless and perpetually multiplying, there could only be one eventual outcome.

Positioning himself between two of the recesses to avoid being flanked, Akiri fought on. His sword was a blur of silver light as he mowed down his opponents like a farmer harvesting wheat. But the faster he mowed, the faster the chamber filled with yet more warriors.

Dust from the fallen statues covered the floor; more of it clung to Akiri's sweat-soaked skin. He could feel his strength beginning to falter, and much as the thought of retreat disgusted him, he knew the only sensible course was to flee the chamber and live to fight another day. His eyes shot over to the entrance, but where the broken door had once been there was now nothing but a solid wall. There was no longer any way out. Unless he could discover how to defeat these cursed things, he would most surely die.

While continuing to swing his sword, he thought again about the riddle etched on the floor that was now completely obscured by at least two inches of stone dust. The answer to this felt just as much out of sight. No matter how hard he considered the problem, only one solution came to mind. But it was one that went against his every normal instinct. If he was wrong, he would unquestionably die; but that was looking certain anyway, so what did he have to lose?

Gathering his remaining strength, he let loose a flurry of blows to clear away a small space at his feet. He then dropped to his knees and cast aside his sword. The mass of stone enemies converged on him, their swords held aloft ready to deal a killing stroke. Akiri lowered his head as if in submission and waited.

Even allowing for the slow movements of his foes, it still felt like an eternity before anything happened. In an instant, the air became still and the statues froze into place. The one standing closest to him had his sword hovering only inches above Akiri's head. He was still moving away when there was a sharp clicking sound, like a giant snapping his fingers.

One by one, the statues crumbled to dust, filling the room with a choking gray cloud.

Akiri covered his eyes and nose until the dust gradually settled. All he could concentrate on was the single line of verse repeating in his head:

When comes the fight that must be fought.

He laughed aloud. The poem was referring to the inner battle. Rage and lust would be of no help at all in that fight. Quite the opposite, in fact. For a true warrior, to fight against his natural instinct to do battle when attacked was an almost impossible task. More so for a Dul'Buhar.

As he picked up his sword, a narrow door appeared in the wall to his left. Pushing it open, he stepped cautiously through into a cavernous space which had no rights being inside a temple. The place made his skin crawl. The jagged walls and uneven floor told him that this was a natural formation, though the six-foot-tall white marble obelisk standing close to the far wall was obviously not. Torches set on either side clearly illuminated the words of yet another riddle written on the front.

Your strength and mind should be commended,
And now your journey is nearly ended,
There are no more puzzles for you to solve,
Just a simple stroll to test your resolve.

Almost at the moment he finished reading, there was a loud rumble and the ground trembled so violently that he was forced to cling to the obelisk in order to keep on his feet. A few yards away, the floor began to crumble and split. The gap became wider and wider until finally a chasm of more than thirty feet across and spanning the entire breadth of the cavern had opened up. Steam spewed from its depths, striking the ceiling and then raining down searingly hot tiny droplets upon him.

The noise eventually faded and the ground became still. Akiri saw that the chasm had filled to the brim with wildly boiling water. As he approached, the heat from this rose up to blast his face and arms. On the other side of the gap, tantalizingly inviting him to enter, was a silver door set into the wall.

Akiri knew that even he was not capable of leaping such a great distance, and to immerse himself in the water could only mean instant death. He then caught sight of a row of objects just below the surface of the water. Columns of stone just large enough to stand upon were rising up from the depths, though not reaching all the way to the surface. He should be able to hop from one to the next and so reach the other side. But it would be at a terrible cost. His feet would be boiled in the process.

As the poem stated, this would indeed test his resolve. Closing his eyes, he settled his mind. The pain would be intense, but he *would* endure. He would accept it as being a part of himself. He was Akiri. His will was iron.

The first step sent great waves of pain shooting through him, yet he merely sucked his teeth for the briefest of moments and looked to the next column. He focused all his thoughts on getting to the far side. But not even his mental discipline could prevent the physical damage that was being done to his feet and ankles, testing his endurance to its extreme limits. Each column he came to was set slightly deeper than the last, and by the time he was halfway across, the water was up to his shins. A series of low grunts slipped out as he continued to fight back the agony.

When there were only two steps remaining the water was up to his thighs and the pain was virtually unbearable, but the end was near. After stepping onto the final column, he let out a savage cry of both triumph and agony and leapt the remaining distance.

Gasping and croaking, he dragged himself away from the chasm edge, no longer able to stand. This was as far as he would go. He knew this. Although he had managed to endure the pain, the injuries he'd suffered had left him unable to walk. He had seen before what boiling water could do to a man's flesh. It did not simply damage the skin; it cooked all the way through to the bone, leaving a limb useless… permanently.

He hesitated before daring to look at his ruined legs. As he moved, it was like a switch had been flicked. From burning agony, suddenly there was no pain at all. His legs were completely dry and showed no sign of any blisters or redness. What was more, the water in the chasm had now ceased to boil, and ice was slowly forming on its surface.

Still hardly able to believe what he was seeing, Akiri reached down to touch his lower legs. It was true; they were healed. That, or they had never been injured, he realized. The rapidly cooling air drew forth a huge and heartfelt sigh of relief.

Standing up, he regarded the silver door. There were no riddles carved anywhere he could see, but he wasn't yet ready to declare victory. Nothing could be certain until he had the Scepter in his hands and he was away from this place.

The door opened when he drew near, as if in polite invitation. Akiri paused to cast a glance behind before entering, hoping that the ice would remain in place long enough for him to be able to cross back again should that route be necessary. Beyond the threshold, he saw a room thirty feet long and twice that across. At the rear lay an altar of onyx and gold, upon which stood a jade statue depicting a howling wolf. There, resting at the feet of this creature, lay the object he had fought so long and hard to find – the Scepter of Xarbaal. It was unmistakable. The old man's drawing didn't do it justice. Diamonds, rubies, and emeralds crusted the shaft, glittering around the arcane scrawl of symbols etched into the gold. But it was the claw at the top and the black stone it secured that offered a glimpse of its true nature.

This was a thing of *power.*

Akiri could not prevent a deep sigh of satisfaction from slipping out. This was the object that would give him his old life back. Every corner of the room was piled high with gold, silver, and precious jewels – enough to make a man a king should he so desire – but Akiri had eyes for none of it. He was driven by duty, not treasures. The Dul'Buhar would provide all he ever needed.

He approached the altar and stripped off his shirt before picking up the Scepter. He had no desire to handle an item steeped in such legend with his bare hands. Even though the thin cloth of his garment was unlikely to offer any real protection, it still felt better than nothing at all.

The wolf's head medallion was hanging on the front of the altar exactly as Lord Marshio Lowd had described. Akiri considered leaving it where it was, but he had made a promise to retrieve this trinket should the opportunity arise. The jewel he had been offered in exchange was of particular magnificence and would make a fitting gift for his king.

After shoving the medallion in his pocket, he strapped the Scepter across his back and headed out. Thankfully, the ice had remained in place, and there were no other obstacles to hinder him. Apparently, getting into this place was the challenge. Once that was achieved, one could move about freely.

During the ride back to Plenty, he found it difficult to contain his excitement. Thoughts of home, of battle, and of being back with his men swirled around in his mind, driving him almost to distraction. His exile was nearly over, and his honor would soon be restored. He decided not to tarry in Plenty a moment longer than was necessary. It was growing dark, but that was of little matter. He would ride on through the night.

A tiny smile crept upon his lips. Kyra called out from high above, but he was barely aware of this. For the very first time in his life, Akiri allowed his mind to become lost in the world of pleasant daydreams.

Chapter Twenty

On entering the town, Akiri noticed almost immediately that many of the people were regarding him with far more curiosity than he'd experienced when first arriving in Plenty. That he had returned from the temple alive seemed to be the most likely reason for their added interest. Even so, their dingy and unhealthy appearance, along with clothing that was little more than rags, served to give him a chill. It was like being watched by the dead. More unnerving still was the fact that many of them were starting to follow him, though they remained at a wary distance.

By the time he reached Lowd's home, there were more than two dozen men and women following in his wake. He had barely dismounted when the door flew open and the lord came hurrying out, his face alight with glee.

"You're back!" he exclaimed, throwing his hands in the air. "By the gods. You actually made it back."

Akiri secured his mount. "Yes. But I cannot linger. Let us conclude our business quickly."

"Yes, of course." He ushered Akiri inside and led him into a small den.

Lowd poured them both a glass of wine, his hands trembling with excitement. Akiri set aside the glass and retrieved the medallion. The man's eyes were immediately captivated by it.

"I have no desire to stay and celebrate," Akiri said. "So if you would just give me the diamond, I will be on my way."

But Lowd was transfixed. Moving forward slowly, he reached for the chain holding the object of his desire. Akiri made no effort to keep it from him.

Lowd held it up at eye level, his face aglow. "Do you have any idea of how long I've hoped for this day?"

"And now it has come," Akiri told him sharply, already beginning to feel impatient.

Lowd did not seem to hear him. "Do you know what this is?" he asked. "It was made by Kyzeech herself. She used it to punish the priests and priestesses at the temple for disobeying her laws."

"I have no interest in your trinket's history," said Akiri. He thrust out a hand. "Just give me what I came for."

"Perhaps you don't care… but you should." There was an ominous tone to Lowd's voice as he put the chain around his neck.

No sooner was the medallion in place than Akiri began to receive urgent messages of warning from Kyra. A moment later the howling call of a wolf carried inside the house. This was quickly followed by another, and then another. In almost no time at all, dozens of them were blending together into a single wild song.

Akiri jumped to his feet. "What devilry is this?"

"There is nothing to fear," Lowd assured him. Reaching into his pocket, he retrieved the cloth-covered diamond. After unwrapping it, he casually tossed it over to Akiri. "Here. Take it. You have certainly earned your reward."

Akiri shoved the jewel into his pocket as Kyra's warnings

became ever more urgent. *Danger! Danger! Danger!* came through in a frenzy. It was impossible to ignore. Unsheathing his blade, he stepped aggressively toward Lowd. "You will tell me what is happening. And you will tell me now."

Lowd smiled. "Nothing that I didn't make happen." He gave a sigh. "I'm afraid I was slightly less than honest with you, my friend. The truth is, *I* was the one who wanted the medallion. Owning it has been my central preoccupation for the past ten years."

"I will ask you only one more time. What is happening outside?"

"Why don't you go to the window and see for yourself?"

"No. *We* will go."

Grabbing Lowd roughly by the arm, Akiri forced him to walk ahead. They had only taken a few steps out of the room before he heard dozens of feral snarls, together with the sound of a horse whinnying in terror. He peered through the window looking out onto the front yard.

Where the townsfolk had previously been, there were now dozens of human-sized creatures, but they were clearly no longer human any longer. With heads resembling that of a wolf, fingers tipped by long black claws, dark fur covering every inch of their bodies, and great globules of saliva dripping from evil looking fangs, they swayed to and fro exuding menacing intent. Three had already attacked Akiri's horse, ripping it to shreds, and had begun to greedily consume large mouthfuls of its bloody flesh.

"Lycan," said Akiri in a half-whisper. "The whole town?"

"Naturally," Lowd replied.

Akiri snatched him up by the collar. "Explain yourself."

Lowd simply smiled. "There is no reason to get rough. They won't come inside. There is something about silver that repels them. That is why I have it surrounding the entire house."

"How did this happen to these people?" he asked.

Lowd shrugged. "All I know is that they were cursed by the goddess Kyzeech long ago. How long ago, I couldn't say. She cursed them and then drove them from her temple."

"So why are *you* here?"

"I first came here many years ago with my father. We had heard the evil rumors about this place, but my father dismissed them all as nonsense. He knew there were rich silver deposits nearby and hoped to stake claims on them. He even brought a small group of mercenaries along to intimidate the locals, just in case they had already staked their own claims."

Lowd shook his head and chuckled. "What a fool. He marched in here thinking he would frighten the people into submission. Even as a young boy, I could see the great danger in that. Of everyone who came here, I was the only one who made it out alive."

Akiri tore his attention from the macabre scene outside and looked incredulously at Lowd. "And yet you willingly chose to return?"

"Not for a long time," he replied. "I was only eleven years old when all this happened. After my escape, my mother sent me to live with an uncle to be instructed in the art of magic. She felt it would help to protect me; but sadly, I was never very good at casting spells. But I *was* good at accumulating knowledge. I learned everything I possibly could about the lycan and about this town. I tracked down the origin of the legend, and in time came upon the story of the cursed followers of Kyzeech and the Temple of the Blood Moon. By the time I was old enough to return home, my mother had remarried. It wasn't long before her worthless husband had gambled away the entire family fortune and left us destitute." His eyes grew distant and sad. "I remember the day we were forced to leave our home. My poor mother couldn't stop weeping." His lips tightened. "She took her own life that very night."

Akiri glanced back outside. The lycan were slowly moving closer to the house.

"I wandered for a time," Lowd continued, "living off the charity of relatives. But none would have me for very long. It was only when I was reduced to staying in the servants' quarters at the manor of a distant cousin that everything changed. I learned that she was in possession of a rare jewel that was said to have been crafted by Cleofila, the goddess of healing and long life. I knew such an item would fetch a handsome price – enough to restore my fortune many times over."

"So you robbed your own kin?" asked Akiri, not trying to hide his contempt.

"Not my proudest moment, to be sure. But I was desperate. So yes, I robbed her."

Akiri sniffed. He had seen Lowd sneaking glances at the pocket in which he had placed the diamond. "And now you intend to go back on your word and rob me as well."

"I'm afraid so," he admitted. "You see, I discovered that the jewel was able to suppress even the most terrible of curses. It took some time before I was able to learn how to use it properly, but once I did, I knew I had to return here. So now, as long as the jewel is in my keeping, I am able to keep the people of Plenty in human form whenever that suits me. Which up until now has been most of the time. But as you can see, now that you possess the stone, the spell is broken. So obviously, I cannot allow you to take it with you."

Akiri's anger was boiling. His desire to run the man through was almost more than he could resist. "And what purpose does the medallion serve?" he asked.

A sinister smile crept up from the corners of Lowd's mouth. "Ah, that is the final piece I required. It gives me absolute control over the lycan. With this in my possession, there is nothing I cannot accomplish. I will have a weapon far deadlier than any army. I can even make myself a king if I so desire."

Akiri removed the diamond from his pocket. He cared nothing for the petty schemes and desire of this wretch. All he cared about was returning home. How best to make that journey continue, though? It would be impossible for him to overcome so many of the unearthly creatures gathered outside. He would be safe so long as he remained in the house, but he had no intention of doing that for much longer.

"Take your jewel then," he said. "Make it safe for me to be on my way."

Lowd heaved a sigh. "I'm sorry, my friend. I cannot allow you to leave now. You have seen too much."

Akiri regarded him for a long moment. He then began to chuckle softly. "You are indeed a fool."

Lowd furled his brow. "What are you talking about?"

"One of the first lessons I learned during my training is that battles are not always fought with steel and muscle. Should I leave your house, I will certainly die. We both know this. I cannot possibly prevail against so many creatures. And if you had a brain in your head, you would have simply allowed me to leave and then waited until the lycan had finished their work before retrieving your diamond. After all, you now have the medallion to control them. But you chose not to do this. And that was a fatal mistake."

He paused, aware that Lowd was still not fully grasping what he was saying. "You see, I do not have any need to fight the lycan. As you stupidly revealed to me, they will not enter this house. Placing silver around it was a wise precaution to take before gaining possession of the medallion. Should the magic of the jewel ever fail, you would still have been safe in here. But now that same protection is working against you, as the lycan cannot come to your aid. You are trapped in here… with me."

Like a giant wave, realization washed over Lowd. He made a wild dash for the front door. Akiri smiled coldly. To him, the man's movements were as slow and clumsy as a wild beast with a badly broken leg. In a blindingly swift motion, his sword swept clean through Lowd's exposed neck.

The lord's decapitated body halted in its tracks for an instant, then crumbled to the floor. His head rolled a few feet before coming to a halt, his terrified expression still frozen on his face.

Akiri shook his head. If only all his enemies were as stupid.

Outside, the lycan were becoming increasingly restless. Some had begun to attack one another in brief but savage skirmishes. Akiri could hear Kyra in his mind. She was in a state of complete panic. He picked up the medallion that was now lying in a rapidly spreading pool of blood.

"It's all right," he said. "They will not hurt me."

But this did nothing to calm the dragon. Akiri opened the front door and took a step just beyond the threshold.

His appearance sent the lycan into a wild frenzy. Several charged, sliding to a halt just short of the silver embedded walkway. They remained on the fringe, flailing their clawed hands and snapping their jaws.

Akiri placed the medallion on the ground and calmly looked out upon the cursed assembly of creatures for a moment. Then, raising his blade vertically, he slammed the tip hard down directly between the glittering ruby eyes. In a flash of green fire, the medallion exploded into myriad tiny shards, the sheer force of it sending Akiri flying back

As his sight returned, the cries faded away and a dead silence replaced it. Before him were the people of Plenty returned to their human form. They lay scattered about the street like fallen leaves, each of them naked and unconscious.

A roar from Kyra overhead broke the silence, followed quickly by massive waves of relief.

Akiri regarded his ravaged horse with a heavy sigh. This would slow him down considerably. The saddle and bags had been ripped free and thrown several yards away. As he set about retrieving these, several people began to stir. He hastened his movements, having no desire to be around when what would surely be a highly confused and frightened group started to ask questions.

His haste was in vain. A young man with matted blond hair stumbled toward him, his arms outstretched. He was clearly trying to form words, but no sound came out at first.

"Go to your home," Akiri told him. "There is nothing to be done here."

"The… the curse," he finally managed to croak. "It's gone."

"Yes," Akiri affirmed. "It's gone."

The man dropped to his knees, his eyes darting about for a moment. Then tears began to run down his cheeks. "Was it you?"

Four more townsfolk had awakened and were staggering over to Akiri. Grumbling, he slung his gear over his shoulder.

"Please wait," begged the young man. "I need to know… was it you who freed us?"

"It was," Akiri replied. "Lowd is dead and the medallion is destroyed."

This brought him to uncontrollable sobs. "Th-thank you."

Akiri simply nodded and started toward the street. An older woman with a bent posture and a weather worn face caught his arm. She looked at him pleadingly.

"Are you sure?" she asked. "Is the curse really lifted?"

Akiri brushed her aside. "I am sure."

The weeping man struggled to his feet. He tried to catch up with Akiri, but he was walking at too swift a pace.

"Tell us your name," the man called after him. "Please, I beg you."

Akiri turned his head without breaking stride. "I am Akiri."

Kyra trumpeted a roar as if to punctuate his words. He could feel that she approved greatly of what he had done. But the fact was, he hadn't destroyed the medallion and lifted the curse in order to help the people of Plenty. He had merely been attempting to save his own life. He was not a hero. Enough years steeped in blood and war had taught him that, in reality, heroes did not exist. They were stories – nothing more. Kyra was making it abundantly clear to him that she did not share that view.

It occurred to him that perhaps young dragons were not so different from young humans – both tended to be idealistic and naive. The real world did not suffer fools. And only a fool risked his life needlessly.

"A lesson you had better learn quickly," he told her.

As he reached the edge of town, Kyra descended to walk beside him. He reached over to her, and this time she did not shy away. Instead, she leaned in and pressed her snout into his thigh. Smiling, Akiri patted her fondly on the neck.

"Come," he said. "We have a long way yet to travel."

Kyra shook her head and continued at his side. Akiri felt as if this was where she truly belonged. It was easy to see why the Tul'Zahar had been so attached to their dragons.

These comfortable and pleasing thoughts continued most of the time, but sneaking its way into them every now and then was the nagging doubt of how King Zemel would react on learning of Kyra's presence in Acharia. The prospect of her death caused almost uncontrollable feelings of rage and desperation to rise within him.

I must have faith in my king, he kept reminding himself.

But no matter how much he tried to ignore it, the fact remained that his faith was being called into question. Words that his uncle had spoken continued to plague him. And the face of his mother would not leave his dreams.

Chapter Twenty-One

Akiri purchased a horse and provisions in a small hamlet three days' walk east of Plenty. Though a horse was vital for getting home as soon as possible, he almost regretted buying it when Kyra took to the sky and remained in flight for most of the time thereafter. He had enjoyed having her walking beside him. Time passed quickly with her inside his thoughts. It was not an invasive or disturbing thing. Far more like being with an understanding companion – something he had never had before, not even among the Dul'Buhar.

The journey home would take several weeks, and in spite of his overwhelming desire to complete his task by delivering the Scepter of Xarbaal to his sovereign, he resolved to use the time to explore his connection with Kyra.

Though he could still identify only a few thoughts from her clearly in his head, he found that he could know her precise location in the sky if he concentrated hard enough. He tried to call her to him on several occasions, but Kyra was stubborn and did not seem to like being summoned. Even so, he was quite sure that she would come quickly enough if he ever truly needed her.

It was when they were only a week away from the

Acharian border that Kyra confided her belief that they were being watched. He believed her, despite the fact that his enhanced senses could detect no one lurking nearby.

They had just crossed the border into Vrundavia when these suspicions were confirmed. He had lit a fire a few yards away from the road and was preparing a meal when he heard the rustle of footsteps approaching from the nearby trees. The undergrowth was dense and populated by all manner of forest creatures, a situation Kyra was currently taking advantage of by circling low and searching for prey. Akiri gave no indication that he had heard anything untoward. Better to let whoever it was think their clumsy attempts at stealth had been successful.

"Bloody damn thorns," muttered a child's voice from the darkness.

Akiri recognized it at once as belonging to Vazhta. He groaned and sat back on his elbows. "Come out, demon."

A moment later Vazhta appeared at the edge of the firelight. His face was scratched and his clothes torn. "How you mortals live in such a horrible world is beyond my understanding," he grumbled. "Everywhere you step there is something to snag your clothes and cut your flesh."

"Your complaints well fit your appearance," remarked Akiri. "What do you want?"

"I see that you now have the Scepter," he said. "So why do you think I have come?"

"I told you already. I am returning it to my king."

Vazhta sniffed. "Then you are the greatest fool I have ever known. It will drive him mad and cause the death of countless people."

"And why would you care about that?"

"I don't," he admitted. He dropped down on the other

side of the fire from Akiri. "But the one I serve does."

"Do not believe him," came another voice.

Vazhta scrambled to his feet. "Hagrik!"

"Yes, my old friend. I am here." Hagrik walked casually up to Vazhta with a bright smile on his face. "You didn't actually believe I would sit back and allow you to acquire the Scepter, did you?" His eyes fell on Akiri. "Not that I imagine for a moment this mortal will hand it over. In fact, I'm quite surprised he hasn't already destroyed that ridiculous form you've taken."

"You seek only to confuse Akiri with your lies," Vazhta responded, hotly. He shoved Hagrik forcibly away from him. "Now go! Leave me alone."

Hagrik pushed him equally hard in return. "I will not. And you can't make me."

Had he not known that the two beings before him were far removed from what they appeared, Akiri could easily have been amused by this spectacle. Demon spirits they might be, but at this moment they looked and sounded just like quarreling children.

"Mishna will not allow the Scepter to be returned to Xarbaal," growled Vazhta. "You can tell that to your master. He will not succeed."

Hagrik turned to Akiri. "You do know that it is Vazhta who serves Xarbaal, not me. I hope you are intelligent enough to see that."

"I am intelligent enough not to trust either of you," replied Akiri. "And neither of you will lay your hands on the Scepter."

"I do not want it," claimed Hagrik. "All I seek is for you to destroy it. That proves I am the one to be trusted. Vazhta would take it to his master, whereas I have no desire even to touch it."

Vazhta spun to face Akiri. "He plots your death. Should you try to destroy the Scepter, it would kill you. Hagrik wants you dead so that he can take it without risk."

Hagrik flicked a dismissive hand. "Your lies will not avail you." A sinister smirk formed. "But as you speak of plotting a death…"

The blade appeared in his hand in a flash. Akiri barely had time to blink before it was plunged into Vazhta's heart. Vazhta reached out and clutched at his killer's shirt, gasping for breath.

Hagrik smiled. "Until next time, old friend."

After slumping to his knees, Vazhta looked to Akiri a final time. "Don't… trust… him."

A golden aura slowly emanated from the dying demon. Akiri watched in wonder as tiny flakes of light broke away from its flesh and floated up into the night sky. Soon it was as if a million fireflies were swarming all around him. Then, in one enormous flash, the body vanished.

Akiri jumped to his feet, sword in hand.

With a sigh, Hagrik tossed his blade to the ground. "He was right about one thing. I have absolutely no intention of fighting you. You have no idea how difficult it is for our kind to take on human form. It will be weeks, if not months, before Vazhta can return."

He took a seat by the fire, completely ignoring Akiri's wary stance.

"So he is not dead?" Akiri asked.

Hagrik chuckled. "Certainly not. Much as I wish he were so easily dispatched, it would take far more than mortal steel to end his life. But at least we can now speak in peace."

"I will not destroy the Scepter. And do not think I have forgotten that it was Vazhta, not you, who wanted it destroyed. You are both liars. I will fulfill my duty and return it to my king."

Hagrik eyed him closely. "I know you will. You are far too single-minded to do what is wise. But that is of no consequence. The Scepter of Xarbaal will not remain with your king for long. Its power is too great. It will consume him. And when it does, it will then return to the hands of the gods."

"If you know I will not be swayed, why take the trouble to come here?"

"Because I was commanded to do so," he replied flatly. "We are all answerable to someone, are we not? And Mishna is not the sort of mistress that one questions."

"So Vazhta was lying? You serve Mishna, and not Xarbaal?"

"Does it really matter whom I serve? The fact is that the gods have taken notice of you. I overheard the conversations you had with your uncle, and he was right when he said this is not a good thing. More often than not it ends in tragedy. King Zemel has attracted their attention, to be certain. He covets what he should not possess. But you…" He shook his head and laughed. "You are far more interesting."

"And why is that?" Akiri asked, and silently called for Kyra.

"For a start, the manner in which you spurn things that could so easily provide you with untold wealth and power. You have acquired the Scepter of Xarbaal, yet have not entertained even a single thought of keeping it for yourself. You also took the medallion made by Kyzeech and chose to destroy it… I must warn you, she will *not* be pleased about that. Now you have a priceless jewel crafted by Cleofila in your possession. Might I ask your plans for this?"

"You may not."

Hagrik shrugged. "As you wish. I'm guessing that you plan to give it to your king too, or some other such foolishness. Three divine treasures, all of them cast aside. That alone is enough to attract the attention of the gods. But there is more. And it is my hope that you will listen to what I say."

Kyra circled directly above, her powerful wings silent, her sharp eyes focused intensely on Hagrik.

"Mishna foresees a great destiny for you," he continued. "But I do not need to be a god myself to see that too. This world is one of death and chaos. It was born from such things. However, should you pass safely through the turbulent days ahead, she knows that you will help remake what the gods created."

"And just how will I accomplish this?"

"That is unclear. But I have witnessed the rise and fall of many empires. I have watched what happens when mortals try to make themselves gods. King Zemel is doomed; that is a certainty. You, on the other hand, are not… at least, not yet. Should you survive his folly, you will one day find yourself wielding tremendous power. And many lives will depend on how you use it."

Akiri regarded him closely. "I find it difficult to believe that the gods would care about any of this. You know more than you have so far revealed. If you wish to continue speaking with me, you will get to the point quickly."

Hagrik locked eyes with Akiri, a scowl on his face. "You are an arrogant one." After a lengthy pause, his shoulders slumped. "Very well. There is a war coming. One that will rip the world asunder. The gods have looked into the future and have been unable to see its outcome. All they know for sure is that you are somehow the key."

"There is always a war," Akiri pointed out.

"But this one will not be fought here, on this brutal world," he said. "This war will take place in the heavens. The old gods are returning; Mishna can feel the ripples in the universe. Xarbaal is summoning his kin, all of whom have extended their cruel hands into the mortal realm. Alone he can be defeated. But when his brothers and sisters arrive, both heaven and earth will be set ablaze like never before."

Akiri knew the stories well enough: how the old gods once ruled mortals with cruelty and spite. How they were eventually driven away by their own children, banished for all eternity.

"I will ask you one final time," Hagrik concluded. "Will you destroy the Scepter?" There was a long silence.

"My answer is this."

Hagrik looked up just as Kyra's talons dug into his shoulders. He let out a muted cry before being lifted into the air. Akiri smiled, impressed by how quietly Kyra could approach from the air. As she rapidly ascended to a great height with the boy still gripped securely in her claws, Akiri sent her thoughts of appreciation. Though the boy was a demon spirit, Akiri did not like the idea of dispatching Hagrik's child form himself. Kyra, on the other hand, did not see the creature as anything other than what it really was.

A solid thump on the ground a short distance to his right told him that it was done. Only a few seconds later, rising lights from the body lit up the night sky. As before, it was followed by a spectacular flash.

Akiri smiled. No more meddling from the gods. No more lies. Even if everything Hagrik had said was true, there was nothing to be done. If the old gods were returning, then so be it. And if there was a part for him to play upon their arrival, he would play it.

None of this changed his mind. Whatever was coming, he would be among his men and serving his king when it came.

Chapter Twenty-Two

Akiri had never before felt such elation as when finally crossing the border back into Acharia. To pass unseen for the time being, he was forced to rid himself of his horse. As far as the Acharian army was aware, he had been exiled. Should his presence within their borders be discovered too soon, it could seriously complicate matters. They would certainly attempt to strip him of his possessions, and he was not about to surrender the Scepter to anyone but his king. If killing some of his own people became necessary in order to avoid capture, he would do so, but he wished to avoid such measures if at all possible.

Kyra was becoming increasingly tense, staying out of sight during the day and not sleeping at night. He wondered how often dragons needed to rest and resolved to study a bit more about the creatures once back among his men. The worry still lingered: what if King Zemel rejected his connection to Kyra? What then?

He needed to believe all would be well.

Along the way, he heard news of a fierce battle that had taken place in the Houndfang Pass. It seemed that Acharian forces had taken massive losses before eventually driving the enemy back. Worse still, because of these losses, they had been unable to pursue King Nehala's retreating army to wipe them out completely. As a result, the enemy had regrouped on the southern border and were preparing to launch another attack.

Akiri thought back to the time he had been arrested. If only he had remained in the camp for a few hours longer, he would have been able to pass on details of his plan to General Laronso. There was an area he had detected where a small force could have moved in unseen behind the enemy, forcing them to fight on two fronts and cutting off any possibility of retreat. Thanks to the narrow and rocky terrain in this part of the pass, no more than a thousand swords would have been needed for this tactic to work successfully, saving countless Acharian lives in the process. Akiri's anger rose at the way things had unfolded instead. He promised himself to see the end of King Nehala as soon as possible.

Each day it became more difficult to move about without being noticed. There had always been tight security this close to the capital city, but nothing comparable to what he was now seeing. Patrols and checks had more than doubled during his absence. He wondered what might have prompted such measures.

It was mid-morning when he arrived at the last garrison before reaching Gol'Naruth – where King Zemel had instructed him to report upon his return. Its granite walls and iron gates were indeed a welcome sight. This was the home of the Dul'Buhar, and where he had spent so much of his youth. Borlon had been a brutal task master who had not tolerated sloth. To show him anything less than supreme effort was certain to earn you a savage beating. Most candidates for the order didn't even make it through the first month. This period was specifically designed to test a child to his very limits and weed out the weak – both physically and mentally. Those who made it through this opening onslaught usually went on to become fully fledged Dul'Buhar. Those who did not, returned home in disgrace.

Akiri noticed straight away that the ramparts were not guarded by any members of the order, which told him they must be in the south with the main army. It also suggested that, whatever damage had been done at Houndfang Pass, it had not halted the campaign completely. This was good. Akiri longed for battle. He could already picture himself fighting alongside his men once again, this time wielding his father's sword and seeing the blood of King Nehala's men pouring to the ground like crimson rain.

He approached the garrison in full view along the main road and walked straight up to the entrance, fully aware that a long line of crossbows from above was tracking his every move. At ground level, six soldiers lined up in front of the raised portcullis with swords already drawn. They recognized him immediately.

A soldier bearing a captain's sash stepped forward and held out his hand. "Do not come any closer, Akiri. You are exiled and have no business coming here."

"I will speak with whoever is in command… *Captain*," he responded, steel in his tone. "I will reveal my business to him alone."

The fear in the man's eyes was plain to see. Exiled or not, Akiri's mere presence was still sufficient to intimidate even the strongest will. "You will leave now or you will die where you stand," he shot back. These would have been firm words were it not for the tremor in his voice, further betraying his insecurity.

Akiri glanced up. At least ten bows were trained on him.

"Give that order and you will join me in death. Now go fetch your commander before I lose patience."

The captain shifted awkwardly on his feet, his indecisiveness almost comical to Akiri. Enforcing the king's orders in the face of Akiri's threat was suicide. The men at his back knew that truth, too.

A lone figure ducked through the portcullis to save the situation. He headed straight for the pair with long, deliberate strides.

Akiri recognized the gray eyes and grim demeanor instantly. "It is good to see you, Borlon. But I expected you to be with the army. Not playing nursemaid to this lot."

Shoving the captain aside, Borlon drew his sword and pointed it at Akiri's throat. "You are the biggest fool I have ever met, boy. Why not simply slit your own throat and be done with it?"

"It would seem you intend to save me the trouble, old friend," he responded, trying to suppress a smile.

Borlon's blade continued to hover less than an inch from Akiri's flesh for several more seconds. Finally, with a laugh, he withdrew it. "I'm glad to see you haven't changed *too* much," he grinned, sheathing the sword. "Still as fearless as ever, even without your gifts from the king."

"A testament to the excellence of my training," Akiri told him.

If Borlon was in the slightest bit flattered by this comment, he did not show it. He merely jerked his head toward the portcullis. "Come with me."

Akiri followed his former teacher into the main parade ground. Normally this would have been filled with men training and honing their skills, but it was now relatively empty. Common soldiers did not have the same dedication as the Dul'Buhar, and those now guarding the stronghold were unlikely to be the best King Zemel possessed, or they would not have been left behind from the front line.

"Are any of the order still here?" Akiri asked.

"No," Borlon replied. "Not even the young ones still in training. All have been sent south."

This was disturbing news indeed. Those yet to have earned their place in the Dul'Buhar were never sent into battle before their training was complete. It took too many years to develop a young man into a suitable member of the order to risk his life prematurely. As commander, Akiri would never have allowed such a thing to happen.

Borlon could sense his disapproval. "They are not being sent into the fray just yet," he explained. "But if things continue as they have been…" His words trailed off.

The man might be a harsh and brutal teacher, but it was well known that he cared deeply for his students. The situation obviously troubled him as much as it now did Akiri.

The interior of the garrison was stark and functional. Beyond the main entrance stood an onyx tablet, upon which the names of every Dul'Buhar member to fall in battle had been etched in gold. Students were required to memorize all of these, and to know exactly the circumstances of how each one had died. The tablet had been Akiri's idea. A sense of history and belonging were essential, he considered. A man cannot truly be a part of something unless he fully understands its past.

He paused to gaze down at the names. Fifty-seven in all. Every one of them had died a good death, and each had earned a place of honor in the hearts of those who survived. With head bowed, he ran his fingers slowly over the tablet.

"Come on," Borlon called, opening a door to his right.

"Leave the dead be for now."

Akiri pulled his attention back to the moment and followed his former instructor along a series of corridors until they reached a room near the west guard tower.

Borlon glanced over his shoulder as he opened the door. "What's suddenly put you in such a good mood?" he asked.

Akiri hadn't realized it until then, but there was a broad grin splashed across his face. "I suppose it's just good to be home," he replied.

This was his old room. At least, it was the one he had used when at the garrison. Everything was still the same as when he'd last been there. In the far corner was the bed he had made for himself the same week as being named commander. The desk had been Borlon's previously, as had the small table and chairs where Akiri would meet with his captains to discuss training schedules and strategy. A wardrobe on the other side of the room was the only item with any elegance and decoration. This had been a gift from the king's personal attendant – a show of appreciation for once saving his life.

Akiri let out a soft sigh. "It is odd what one finds beautiful."

Borlon plopped down at the table. "What do you mean?"

"I never gave much thought to this place," he explained. "But seeing it now… it is beautiful."

Borlon coughed a laugh. "It's just a room with barely anything in it."

He sat across from his mentor. "To me it is finer than a palace apartment."

"And how would *you* know what a palace apartment looks like?"

Akiri hesitated, unsure how much of his story to divulge.

Until the king actually held the Scepter of Xarbaal in his hands, his mission was not over. He had hoped that at least a few members of the order with whom he could share his thoughts would be here. But could he do the same with Borlon? His old instructor had never sworn on the oath stone and so was not an official member of the Dul'Buhar. On the other hand, he *had* served the king for decades. Apart from the monarch himself, Akiri respected no one more.

Borlon chuckled. "You can speak freely. I was sent here to watch for the possibility of your return. King Zemel didn't want there to be an unfortunate incident. He gave me no details, only that you might be arriving soon and that I should send word if you did. I attended to that detail the moment I was told you were approaching the gates."

It was a relief to hear this. Akiri did not enjoy the idea of keeping secrets from Borlon. His counsel had been invaluable to him over the years, and his insight was uncanny. Even without the oath stone, he had never known the man to speak falsely.

"Who leads the order in my absence?" he asked.

"General Laronso has taken responsibility for logistics, but the king has not chosen anyone to lead. I assume this is because he intends to restore your command." Borlon's face darkened. "Though I doubt you will be pleased with what you find."

Akiri frowned. "Why is that?"

"The battle with King Nehala saw a third of your men die."

His words hit Akiri like a hammer to the chest. "How did this happen?"

Borlon's fists clenched. "It was decided to send them into battle without support, so as to test the enemy's strength. The official reason given was that if Nehala's men were faced with the might of the Dul'Buhar, it would instill fear in their hearts and increase the chance of retreat."

"What idiot devised that plan?" Akiri demanded. He slammed his hands on the table. "They were being sent to face many thousands of men. Even the Dul'Buhar could not hope to overcome such mighty odds."

"I cannot say whose plan it was, but it's clear they were hoping for the order to be destroyed. Most generals and commanders have always been resentful of the authority King Zemel has handed to the Dul'Buhar. Without your presence, they have become far bolder in their opposition."

"Then they are all fools indeed. Any one of my men could lead the order equally well. If the generals think they have less to fear, they are wrong."

Borlon shook his head. "I'm afraid you both underestimate your own influence and overestimate the men you lead. It's true they are all great warriors, but none have your leadership skills. They are now excluded from all battle strategy decisions. Little by little, they are being marginalized completely."

"I smell the foul stench of the House Galliani behind this," Akiri muttered.

"Normally I would agree," Borlon told him. "But they are not alone. Most of the noble houses are set against you. They do not like the idea of a slave holding power over them."

Akiri's blood was boiling. More than ever, he wanted to complete his task and return to his men. He would show the nobles precisely what a slave could do. Dul'Buhar sacrificed their freedom to serve the king, but there was no higher honor. In their minds, being a *slave* was far better than living a life of selfish pursuits and mindless frivolity.

"We will see what happens when I am back in my rightful place," he growled.

Borlon chuckled and leaned back in his chair. "I cannot wait to see it. But for now, tell me of your adventure. What wonders have you seen since leaving Acharia? When I heard you were seeking out Tuvarius, I feared you would not return."

"You knew him?"

Borlon nodded. "Quite well. A difficult man, to say the least. I couldn't believe it when the king told me whom you were planning to meet. I wanted to ask why. But I was ordered long ago never to speak of any man who had served with the Tul'Zahar."

Akiri briefly considered asking Borlon about his father, but on reflection decided it was best to stay away from the subject. "The Tul'Zahar betrayed the king and the people of Acharia," he remarked instead. "They do not deserve to be remembered."

A rueful expressed came over Borlon's face. "I'm afraid I can't help but remember them, lad. I was there when they marched on Gol'Naruth. In fact, I was damn near torn to shreds by one of their bloody dragons." He lifted his shirt for a moment to reveal a jagged scar that ran across his chest. "I got this in the very first hour of battle. Almost bled to death." He waved a hand. "But that's a story for another time. Surely you had some adventures worth recalling."

Akiri smiled. "A few, perhaps."

He went on to give a reasonably full account of events following his exile, though taking care never to identify exactly which treasured item he had returned with. Nor did he say anything of his time with Kyra beyond their fight in the arena. When he came to the death of Tuvarius, he noticed Borlon's countenance darken.

"There was no other choice," he explained. "I could not risk the knowledge he possessed being passed on."

"I understand why you did it," said Borlon. "And had Tuvarius known you as I do, he would have expected it. It's just the idea of killing a member of your own family… no man should have to do that."

"I hardly knew him," said Akiri. "And it served my king."

Borlon nodded. "Of course. You're absolutely right."

Once Akiri's tale was finished, they talked for a time about the battle in Houndfang Pass. Although Borlon had not actually been there, he had received detailed accounts. Akiri shifted continuously in his seat with barely contained anger as he heard of blunder after blunder committed by the commanders. Sending the Dul'Buhar in alone at the onset was just the first of many terrible mistakes.

"It's a wonder there is an army left at all," he growled.

"There is real danger of an invasion," Borlon told him. "Our forces are reeling. And I have heard that King Nehala's perceived victory has been a rallying cry for all our enemies. Those who have been too fearful to stand against us in the past are now finding courage." He locked eyes with Akiri. "You are desperately needed, my friend."

Rising from his chair, Akiri retrieved a map of Acharia from his desk and spread it out on the table. For the next few hours, he and Borlon went over the situation while piecing together a course of action. It was late into the evening when they finally stopped long enough to eat. When they had finished their meal, Borlon leaned back in his chair and stretched his arms. His joints cracked loudly in protest.

"I'm getting old," he yawned. "Too old for war and

blood. Soon they'll retire me."

"Nonsense," Akiri objected. "You can still best most men half your age."

He smiled. "Perhaps. But the price I pay these days is high. Afterward, it feels as if I've been stretched on the rack and whipped with a thousand canes." He shook his head. "Soon these old eyes will close forever. And to be honest, I am almost looking forward to it."

The thought of his mentor and former instructor no longer at his side deeply disturbed Akiri. The man's teaching had been the sole reason he had survived many deadly encounters. His wisdom had guided him as a commander right from the beginning.

Borlon registered the concern on Akiri's face. "I'm not there yet, lad," he said. "But soon."

"Not too soon. You still have duties to perform."

Borlon laughed. "That I do." He pushed himself to his feet. "And if I'm to be capable of performing them, I must rest now."

He looked unusually weary and the creases on his scarred face deeper than Akiri had noticed before. Even his posture appeared ever so slightly bent.

Borlon opened the door to leave, but then paused. "When you told me about your fight with the dragon, I couldn't help but wonder. Did you by chance… feel anything?"

Akiri cocked his head, feigning ignorance. "Feel anything? Like what?"

"Never mind." Borlon shook his head and chuckled. "It was a stupid question. Take no notice of it."

After he had gone, Akiri stretched out on his bed and allowed his mind to drift. Kyra was somewhere far to the north, just close enough to maintain their connection. *Stay where you are,* he told her. *Let me sort this out.* Her response was a wave of deep concern and anxiety. It was unsurprising.

"Trust in the king's wisdom," Akiri whispered to himself. "It's almost over now."

Chapter Twenty-Three

It was five days before Akiri received a reply from the king. *Come at once* was all it said. Borlon insisted on accompanying him on the long ride into Gol'Naruth.

"I've been confined here long enough," Borlon said. "And I would very much like to be there when you are rewarded…" He eyed the bundle strapped across Akiri's back. "For whatever that thing you carry is."

Akiri was pleased to have his former mentor with him. He promised himself he would request that Borlon be allowed to return with him to the Dul'Buhar so that training of the prospects could continue properly. He was certain that it was only the absence of students that had driven the man to his current melancholy. Borlon might be old and battered, but he was far from useless. All he needed was a purpose. Akiri would see that he was given one.

These thoughts were driven away as he watched the black spires of Gol'Naruth draw ever closer. It had been several years since he had passed through its massive gates, and that was always a moment that inspired awe in him. How could it not? Looking upon the sheer strength of its walls, the soaring heights of its towers, and the magnificent splendor of its halls was an experience like no other. It had stood for hundreds of years as a testament to the power of Acharia.

He remembered how, as a youth, he would climb to the top of the walls of the training garrison after lessons and stare out at the city for hour after hour until forced to go to bed.

"You're thinking about living in that place one day, aren't you?" Borlon had asked him one evening.

He was about fourteen at the time, and already able to best most of the adult soldiers in the stronghold.

"No, sir," he replied, not once taking his eyes away. "I could never live there."

"Why not?"

"I am neither a king nor a noble," he said. "I am a warrior, so my place is here. But I would defend Gol'Naruth to the last." He looked at Borlon with fierce determination. "No one will breach her walls while I live."

Borlon gave his shoulder a fond squeeze. This was the first time Akiri had ever seen his teacher show any emotion other than anger or frustration. But it was a fleeting moment of relaxation, followed by a sharp slap on the back on his head.

"Now get your ass off to bed," he was told sharply.

The trainer's word was law. He had hurried away.

His mind shifted back to the present. The city streets surrounding the palace were bustling with activity. Shipments from the north had apparently arrived only days before, which meant the shops were packed with people hoping to get their hands on sorely needed supplies before they were all sold out.

He recalled Geridia's criticism. The architecture here *was* vastly different to that of Vurna. The merchant had not been wrong about Acharians preferring function to form. But that could be splendid in its own way too. Even the humblest of shops and houses were built to withstand the harshest weather, keeping its occupants safe and comfortable. A few bore some minor decoration – a mural here or a frieze there – though in Akiri's opinion this made little difference. The deep red of the local stone was all that was needed to make them pleasing to the eye.

Word of Akiri's exile had been shocking news for many people, prompting a good number of citizens to stop and stare as he and Borlon rode their way through to the palace. Though several soldiers eyed him as well, the sight of the grizzled trainer at his side was enough to prevent them from doing anything more.

Leaving their mounts at the main gate, they approached a row of twelve soldiers standing guard. These men had obviously been told to expect them, and with military precision they saluted and formed an opening for the new arrivals to pass through. The ironclad gates moaned balefully as they swung open.

Akiri's nerves were on edge. Never before had he felt this way when entering the palace, but since being separated from the king's power, he had experienced many disturbing feelings. All that was about to be over and this prospect induced a slight grin.

"Calm yourself, lad," Borlon said, chuckling. "No need to be nervous."

"I am just eager to get back to my men," Akiri responded.

"As am I."

Beyond the gates, the parade ground was empty, aside from the statues of past monarchs set at regular intervals around the perimeter. The towers standing on all four corners of the palace's primary entrance climbed impossibly high, each with the tiny speck of a crimson flag flying proudly from its distant peak. Directly ahead, the building's doors were flung wide with a pair of guards dressed in brilliant silver ceremonial armor standing to attention on either side.

On the ramparts, sentries pointed crossbows down, their expressions inquiring and confused. The sight of Akiri had always inspired awe and fear, but for an exile to walk fearlessly through the gates of Gol'Naruth was something unheard of. Again, though, Borlon's presence was enough to keep them from doing anything more.

As they reached the entrance, an older man came out to greet them. Akiri immediately recognized him as Lord Jerimea Kortain. Both he and Borlon bowed.

Kortain smiled and returned the gesture. "It is so good to see you again, Akiri. You have no idea how happy the king was when news of your return arrived."

"I am pleased to be back, My Lord," he replied.

"Come," Kortain told him. "It is time for you to receive your reward."

He led the way through a multitude of spacious chambers and broad hallways. The palace in Vurna might have been considered large, but it was really of no size at all when compared to Gol'Naruth's royal residence. Here, one could wander for days in the halls and never enter the same room twice. It took a full twenty minutes before they reached their destination. Akiri smiled as he approached the granite archway. This was the place where he had taken his oath long ago.

Kortain paused and turned to Borlon. "You are to wait outside."

Borlon frowned at Akiri. "You'll have to tell me about it later, I suppose."

Akiri slapped him on the shoulder. "Once this is done, we can talk all you want on our way south."

He caught sight of a tiny change in Kortain's expression, but it was gone in an instant. Nevertheless, his senses instinctively sharpened. All at once, he could hear that there were more than twenty men and women awaiting them inside. Their hushed tones and shuffling feet sounded tense. This was typical, though. The king had an unsettling effect on all of his nobles. Kortain gestured for him to proceed, but did not follow.

The archway led into a large circular chamber. The outer wall was of polished white marble, with the names of all the gods inlaid in gold lettering. An inner circle of white columns surrounded a black floor, over which stood a vast domed ceiling. At the apex of this dome was a ten-foot-diameter opening that allowed sunlight to illuminate the entire enclosure.

King Zemel was standing in the very middle of the room, a crimson cape draped over his shoulders. He was wearing the same crown that had been placed upon his brow during his coronation, a much heavier and infinitely more ornate arrangement than the usual thin gold circlet he wore on a daily basis. It gave him a look of authority and power that Akiri imagined only he could ever exude.

The nobles and high-ranking officers who stood on either side of the king were dressed in their finest attire, as befitting the magnitude of the occasion. The moment their eyes fell on Akiri, the room went completely silent.

The king took a step forward and regarded him. Though his face was expressionless, his eyes were alight with anticipation.

“I knew you would not fail me,” he said quietly.

Akiri dropped to one knee and cast his gaze downward.

“You see?” The king’s voice suddenly boomed from the walls. “The very best among us has returned. And he has brought with him our salvation.” He crossed over to Akiri and placed a hand on his shoulder. “You may rise.”

As contact was made, Akiri felt the king’s hand trembling. He stood, but kept his eyes averted.

“You have it, then?” Zemel asked.

“I do, Your Highness.” He removed the Scepter from his back and passed it over still in its wrapping. “As you commanded, I have brought you the Scepter of Xarbaal. What was stolen is now returned.”

Akiri could see his sovereign’s fingers fumbling as he sought to reveal his prize. After a few failed attempts, he simply tore the cloth away, finally exposing the object of his obsession for all to see.

“At long last,” the king whispered.

He stood gazing at the Scepter in silence for more than a minute. Finally, he turned to Akiri. “Do you understand the enormity of what you have done? With this, there will be nothing that can stand in my way. No army will ever dare to challenge me again.”

Before Akiri could respond, Zemel began to cackle with laughter. It was a harsh, grating sound, constantly rising in volume and intensity. In no time at all his eyes had grown unnaturally wide and his features contorted into a mask of sheer malignancy. When words again came from his lips, they were dripping with vindictiveness. “I will make them pay. All those who once thought me weak will now be forced to watch as their world burns around them.”

A razor sharp chill shot all the way down Akiri’s spine.

He had never seen his king behave like this before. "Your Highness?"

Zemel turned to face him. "Yes. Of course."

In an instant, all trace of his frenzy vanished. So complete and rapid was the transformation it was hard to believe that it had shown itself at all. "Tell me, Akiri," he said with perfect rationality. "What did you think when you heard details of the battle at Houndfang Pass?"

"I was angered, Your Highness," he replied.

"As was I. In fact, I am still angry. And as luck would have it, some of those who were to blame for that fiasco are standing here today."

Akiri saw three of the generals he recognized shifting nervously.

"What do you think should happen to such fools?" Zemel asked, a wicked grin on his lips.

"They should be stripped of their command and sent home," he replied.

The king frowned. "Are you sure? I would have expected a harsher sentence than that from you. Their incompetence caused the death of many of your fellow Dul'Buhar. Do you not wish to seek vengeance?"

Akiri thought on this for a moment. "I was not present at the battle, Your Highness. So it should fall on those who were."

The king threw back his head in what this time sounded like perfectly normal laughter. "The absence of my power has softened your heart, Akiri. But soon we will remedy that. In the meantime, you can bear witness to their punishment."

Spinning to face the others, he thrust the Scepter forward. Three streams of black smoke issued from the black egg clutched within the eagle's claw. The generals scurried back, but it was a pointless exercise; the smoke merely followed and enveloped them anyway. All three men dropped to the floor writhing and screaming as – with cruel slowness, section by section – the flesh was melted away from their bones. The rest of the nobles gasped in horror at what they were seeing. It took more than five minutes before the generals finally fell silent. At the finish, there was nothing left of them but three badly charred and completely unidentifiable masses.

Akiri could not help but feel a small measure of pity for the men. Their crimes might have deserved execution, but he had always believed that a soldier's death should be swift and clean. What he had just witnessed was something he would reserve only for the most heinous of offenses.

"You do not approve?" asked the king.

"It is not for me to pass judgment, Your Highness," he replied.

"Of course not. You are indeed a loyal servant." Zemel cast his eyes over the rest of the group. "Which is more than I can say for any of you."

He glanced back to Akiri. "Do you know the difference between a noble-born and a commoner?"

Akiri shook his head.

"A noble has wealth. But a commoner has worth."

A smile of satisfaction at his own wit formed on the king's face. The Scepter began to emit a red glow that crept up his arm and within seconds had encompassed his entire body. At the same time, the floor of the chamber began to tremble, sending the nobles scattering in every direction. Zemel let out a thunderous laugh that seemed to carry the power of a hundred voices combined into one.

Large chunks of the wall and ceiling began to break

loose, shattering on the marble floor and sending millions of tiny shards flying through the air like swarms of angry insects. The terrified assembly raced for the archway, most of them screaming in blind panic, but the king would not allow them to leave. A wall of flame sprang up, blocking their escape.

Akiri could only watch as his king delighted in the fear he was causing. Unable to leave, the lords and ladies huddled together pathetically, wailing and begging for the king to spare them. It was in that moment Akiri finally saw the madness. It was etched into every inch of King Zemel's aspect and burned unmistakably in his eyes. Tuvarius had been right. It was hard to believe he had not seen it for himself before now. How could he ever save his monarch from such overwhelming insanity?

Was this the same dilemma his father had faced?

"Now, my fine nobles," roared the king. "I will end your suffering. No more will you be forced to wear your masks of deceit. No more will petty schemes encompass your every waking moment."

Their cries for mercy mingled with prayers to any number of differing gods as King Zemel spread his arms wide. A flash of brilliant red light shot forth, blanketing the entire chamber. Every noble suddenly became motionless. To Akiri's eyes, it was as if they had all been turned to stone. A moment later, with a rush, he realized that this was exactly the fate befalling them. Gradually, all trace of natural color was drained from their flesh, transforming them into a group of gray and lifeless statues. Once this was complete, piece by piece they cracked and dissolved until nothing but a pile of dust on the floor marked where each noble had been standing.

The red light faded, and all became still. Only the sound of birds drifting in from the open ceiling disturbed the peace.

Zemel took stock of his handiwork for several minutes, pushing the remains around with the tip of his boot and giggling like a small boy.

"Are you not pleased?" he asked.

Akiri was unsure how to respond. His eyes drifted to the Scepter. He had not come even close to fathoming the incredible power it possessed. Unleashed on an enemy army, it would be devastating beyond imagination. With such a mighty thing in his hands, he knew the king could easily put down the uprising. But one look at Zemel told him that he intended to go much further than that. It was easy to see that his ambition for conquest knew no limits.

"You know I live only to serve you, Your Highness," he said finally. "So what I say is said out of complete loyalty." He hesitated, but the king motioned for him to continue. "I think you should set the Scepter of Xarbaal aside. What I have been told is correct. It is far too dangerous to be wielded by mortal man."

King Zemel laughed softly. "You really are so much like your father, aren't you? You have the same lack of vision. The same ignorance when it comes to the nature of power, the demands of it. You have no understanding of what it means for me to hold the Scepter. You think I am insane, don't you? You think my mind is too weak to control this thing. You think I am a fool easily corrupted, forever broken by the forces crushing down on me. But you have no idea who I am, what I am capable of."

"No, Your Highness. I only want to–"

"Protect me," he said, cutting him short. "I have heard

all this before; from both your father and your uncle. I remember the day clearly when your father came to me and begged me to destroy the Scepter. He had the same look in his eyes that I see in yours now. I remember how angry it made me." He smiled broadly. "But I am not angry with you, Akiri. Not in the slightest. You have provided me with the means to complete what I know in my heart must be done."

"And what is that, Your Highness?"

"Don't you know? Have the years spent in never ending battle not given you at least a small measure of wisdom?" He ran his palm lovingly up and down the Scepter's length. "The mortal world is the same everywhere. Wars upon wars. Rivers of blood flowing in an eternal stream of death. And all because there are too many kings and emperors with conflicting ambitions. I will be the one to bring an end to that. I will do away with them all. Under my rule, the world will know peace at last." His eyes flashed even brighter. "Only I can accomplish such greatness. Surely you of all people understand this, Akiri. It *must* end."

"I understand, Your Highness. I understand all too well."

In a rush of action, Akiri reached for his dagger. But fast as he was, Zemel was ready for him. Akiri's hand had barely touched the weapon's handle when an invisible force held him in place with unrelenting power.

King Zemel clicked his tongue. "A pity you could not see reason. But it is of no real consequence. I do not require your approval. And unlike your father, I *will* have your obedience."

"This is madness, Your Highness," Akiri grunted, straining to break free from the ever-increasing pressure around his arms and torso.

"No. Not madness… fate. I promised you a reward for

your service. And you shall have it. In spite of your defiance, I owe you a great deal." He moved closer. "Your former self will be restored. And thanks to the Scepter, this time your strength and abilities will be twice that as before. I will transform you, Akiri, though I'm afraid your skull from now on will be little more than an empty shell. There will be nothing left of your mind… of you. It will be the same for every member of the Dul'Buhar. You shall go forth as instruments of my will to slay my enemies. None will be able to stand in your way."

The horror of what King Zemel was saying stabbed repeatedly into Akiri's heart. He was destined to become nothing more than a mindless killer, with no bond to his men or any concept of honor. Everything that had made him into the man he was would be lost forever. It was an unthinkable fate. He strained even harder against the force holding him, but it was hopeless.

Raising the Scepter, Zemel touched him lightly on the forehead. A wave of heat shot through Akiri's skull and down his spine, but then the king's eyes popped wide and he stumbled back.

"What have you done?" he demanded. "Where did you… how… a dragon?" His face turned bright crimson, veins bulging from his neck. "Traitor!"

The pressure around Akiri intensified to an unbearable level as Zemel vented his fury. He could hear his heart pounding in his ears. In seconds it would all be over, but even that would be better than the existence the king had described.

With the darkness of death closing in, a piercing screech tore at his ears. King Zemel glanced up just as a set of razor sharp talons slammed into his chest, tearing into his flesh.

He stumbled back before eventually crashing into the marble wall.

Akiri was at once released from the force holding him. Falling to his knees, he saw Kyra standing a short distance away. At her feet was the Scepter. He then looked over to Zemel slumped against the wall, grasping at the wound in his chest and moaning.

"Take the Scepter!" Akiri shouted. "Go now. Fly!"

For a moment he thought Kyra was going to be stubborn and try to stay with him. But then she grasped the Scepter in her claws and her wings pounded furiously. She rose almost vertically back up through the oculus and into the clear blue sky before disappearing out of sight.

Breathing a sigh of relief, Akiri struggled to his feet and staggered toward the exit. Just a few yards clear of this he saw five guards racing toward him, swords drawn.

"The king is hurt," he called out. "Protect the king."

The guards sped by without so much as a pause, pushing Akiri aside as they ran.

Knowing that this deception would last only a short time, the thick sinews of his legs burst into a run. He was familiar with some of the palace layout in this wing and knew of two secret passages that would take him outside and clear of the grounds, but both of these were barred by solid iron doors with locks too stout and complex to be overcome without a key. The main palace gates would almost certainly be shut and heavily guarded after such an upheaval. There would also be the crossbows looking down on him from the ramparts, so any attempt to fight his way out that way would be close to pointless. Eventually, he would be overcome by sheer numbers.

There simply was no other route he knew of that would

get him back onto the city streets and away. Barely had this decision been made when he spotted a lone figure standing in the corridor ahead, sword in hand and with a dire look in his eyes. Akiri stopped ten feet in front of him.

"I know what happened," said Borlon. "I know what you did to the king."

"I only did what I know is right," Akiri replied. "Stand aside. I do not wish to fight you, old friend."

Borlon sniffed. "You don't? So you would rather escape. Is that it? The mighty Akiri would rather run and hide?" He paused to lock eyes for a moment. The severity then left his face and he sheathed his weapon. "In that case, you are more intelligent than I gave you credit for."

Akiri creased his brow. "What are you doing?"

"Repaying an old debt," he replied.

No sooner had he spoken than there came the sound of heavy boots coming toward them.

Borlon pointed to a door just a few yards further down. "In there."

Akiri followed him into an empty parlor. From behind the closed door they listened carefully until the guards had all passed by. Borlon then crossed to a large bookshelf. Reaching behind it, he fumbled until there was a sharp click. With a smile, he pulled the unit aside, revealing a dark and narrow passage.

"The palace is filled with these," Borlon told him. "Especially useful if you happen to be running from a mad king."

They walked at a brisk pace along ground that sloped steadily downwards for the first hundred yards before leveling out. Akiri could see well enough in the pitch dark, but was amazed at how easily Borlon was able to navigate his way without the benefits of being a Dul'Buhar.

After what seemed like more than an hour, they reached a flight of steps that led up to a foliage-covered iron grate, through which narrow rays of sunlight were filtering through. Akiri guessed that they were now at least a mile west of the city.

"Here is where I leave you," Borlon said.

"Come with me," Akiri offered. "Surely the king will kill you for helping me."

"I cannot. My place is here. Besides, there is no way for the king to know what I have done. I will simply say that I failed to find you when scouring the palace."

"Then I thank you for your help. And for everything else you have done."

With no more than a brisk nod, Borlon started back the way they had come.

"One more thing," Akiri called after him. "To whom did you owe the debt?"

Borlon glanced over his shoulder with a sideways smile. "Your mother."

For a moment Akiri was taken aback. "Is she still alive?" he asked.

There was no reply. Borlon had already vanished into the darkness.

The call of Kyra echoed in his mind, telling him he needed to move quickly before the search for him was spread far wider. After running up the stairs, he pushed at the grate. It was rusted shut and didn't budge. He took a deep breath and marshaled all of his strength. This time there was a loud snap followed by an ear-rending screech as the metal gave way.

Cautiously, Akiri climbed out, relieved to find that they

were roughly where he had imagined they would be. For a few seconds he gazed back at the palace. This would be the last time he would see it. In spite of everything, he could not help but feel regret. In the end, he had failed both himself and his king.

Kyra's call snapped him back into the moment. *Run. Now.*

Akiri cast his eyes west. He would not look back again… ever.

Chapter Twenty-Four

Two weeks had passed since Akiri's flight from everything he had ever known. After purchasing a horse from a nearby trader, it had been a simple matter of staying ahead of any pursuit. No one the king might choose to send after him had his endurance, or could come close to matching his precise knowledge of Acharia's terrain.

After traveling west for a time, he had turned north until reaching the coast. From there he had used his remaining gold to gain passage on a fishing vessel to the shores of Mothmonia. Upon landing, he continued west into the foothills of the Black Mountains. These stretched for hundreds of miles, providing a natural barrier to the lands of the Xilial tribes – a group of barbarian raiders that had plagued the nations on the northern coast of the Almari Sea for generations. Many efforts had been made to wipe them out, but the mountains were difficult to pass and the land beyond them brutal and unforgiving. The Xilial would simply melt away until their enemy was forced to leave or face starvation. Those who didn't turn back were slaughtered. Too weak from hunger to fight, they were easy prey.

Kyra was not comfortable here. The air had grown bitterly

cold, and there was a constant wind pressing down from the north, making flight a struggle for her. Not that Akiri had any idea where they should be going. He was beyond King Zemel's reach, but for the first time in his life, he was truly lost. His life felt utterly without purpose or meaning.

As he sat staring into a small fire, with a rabbit Kyra had caught for him roasting on a spit, he went over events in his mind. Kyra was curled up beside him, jerking and grunting, eyes closed. He wondered what a dragon's dream might be like. His own at present were troubled and confusing. For his entire life, he had been at peace with his place in the world, perfectly able to leave behind any of the fear and self-doubt that afflicted most men. But now…

"Pathetic."

The voice was hollow and distant. Akiri was on his feet in an instant, sword at the ready. Kyra was at his side just as quickly, hissing and growling while darting her head from side to side.

"Show yourself," he demanded.

"Because of you, I cannot."

A soft yellow glow appeared in the gloom a few yards away. It had the vague outline of a human, but possessed no features or other characteristics that he could make out. The glow hovered a few inches above the ground, and though without face or eyes, Akiri could sense that it was looking directly at him.

"You *and* that cursed beast of yours. Do you know how much it hurt when he dropped me?"

"Hagrik?"

"Of course," he replied. "And I say again, you are pathetic."

Akiri sniffed and sat back down. "And how exactly am I pathetic, demon?"

Kyra was still on her guard, placing her body protectively between Akiri and the specter that was Hagrik.

"You survived King Zemel's madness. You have your freedom. And what do you do with it? You just sit there and brood."

"I am not brooding," he retorted hotly, even though he knew full well that he had been. "Why are you here? Have you come to gloat?"

"I was hoping that you might now have seen the error of your choice."

Akiri smirked. "Indeed I have, demon. Though not in the way you might think."

There was a brief pause while Hagrik considered this. "I do not see the Scepter with you," he remarked, his voice suddenly thin and rasping. "What have you done with it?"

"Nothing. I honestly have no idea what has become of it."

"What?" The glow began to pulse rapidly. "You mean you threw it away?"

"Not at all." He reached over to pat Kyra affectionately on the haunches. "My good friend here has taken care of it for me."

"You gave the Scepter of Xarbaal to the dragon? For what purpose?"

"You were right that it cannot be wielded by mortals. And yet I still will not hand it over to the gods. So I told Kyra to hide it away where only she could find it."

"You fool! You cannot give such a thing to a mindless beast. Have her retrieve it at once."

Akiri's tone turned hard and his eyes cold. "She is not mindless. She has hidden it away, and that is the end of the matter."

"No. You're right. It is *you* who are mindless."

After a few moments, the glow dimmed and ceased pulsing. The rasping edge to Hagrik's voice was also now gone. "I spoke in haste. Forgive my harsh words. Give me the Scepter, Akiri. I know you are lost. You need direction – a reason to go on. I can give you this. You have spent your life in service to something greater than yourself. Now you have nothing. I can fill the void in your heart."

"If you think I would serve the gods, you are mistaken," he said, his contempt clear. "You have nothing I desire."

"Do not be so certain. My master is powerful beyond anything you can understand. All the things you could ever want are yours for the asking. Wealth. Power. A kingdom of your own, if you so wish it."

Akiri regarded the spirit for a time. A purpose. That was the only thing he desired. Could this demon really provide him with one? He looked over to Kyra. As she met his gaze, three simple but compelling words from her echoed in his mind.

You are Akiri.

In that moment, he understood clearly what he must do.

"The only thing I want from you is your absence," he told Hagrik.

Decision made, he nodded to Kyra. The young dragon needed no second bidding. With fangs bared and talons outstretched, she leapt straight at the shimmering specter. A pained cry of terror emitted from somewhere within its light. A second later, it vanished completely.

Akiri smiled at his only companion. "Well done."

Kyra shook her head and gave a deep, catlike purr.

Later, after finishing his meal, Akiri lay down to rest. He would sleep untroubled tonight; it would be the first time in many weeks. He *did* need a purpose. But it would not come as a gift from the gods, or kings, or demon spirits. He would need to seek it out on his own. The world was vast and filled with mysteries waiting to be solved. He would carve out a place for himself. Let the world tremble at his coming. And let the heavens burn if they must.

He was no longer the commander of the Dul'Buhar. But that didn't matter. Kyra was right.

He was Akiri. And that was enough.

THE END

Lightning Source UK Ltd.
Milton Keynes UK
UKHW011858270921
391272UK00004B/1083

9 780692 79572